THE RUSSIAN'S SLOTH

ALSO BY CAP DANIELS

BOOKS IN THIS SERIES
Book One: *The Russian's Pride*
Book Two: *The Russian's Greed*
Book Three: *The Russian's Gluttony*
Book Four: *The Russian's Lust*
Book Five: *The Russian's Sloth*
Book Six: *The Russian's Envy* (2024)
Book Seven: *The Russian's Wrath* (2024)

BOOKS IN THE CHASE FULTON NOVELS
Book One: *The Opening Chase*
Book Two: *The Broken Chase*
Book Three: *The Stronger Chase*
Book Four: *The Unending Chase*
Book Five: *The Distant Chase*
Book Six: *The Entangled Chase*
Book Seven: *The Devil's Chase*
Book Eight: *The Angel's Chase*
Book Nine: *The Forgotten Chase*
Book Ten: *The Emerald Chase*
Book Eleven: *The Polar Chase*
Book Twelve: *The Burning Chase*
Book Thirteen: *The Poison Chase*
Book Fourteen: *The Bitter Chase*
Book Fifteen: *The Blind Chase*
Book Sixteen: *The Smuggler's Chase*
Book Seventeen: *The Hollow Chase*
Book Eighteen: *The Sunken Chase*
Book Nineteen: *The Darker Chase*

Book Twenty: *The Abandoned Chase*
Book Twenty-One: *The Gambler's Chase*
Book Twenty-Two: *The Arctic Chase*
Book Twenty-Three: *The Diamond Chase*

OTHER BOOKS BY CAP DANIELS
Stand-alone Novels
We Were Brave

Singer – Memoir of a Christian Sniper

Novellas
The Chase Is On

I Am Gypsy

THE RUSSIAN'S SLOTH

AVENGING ANGEL
SEVEN DEADLY SINS SERIES
BOOK #5

CAP DANIELS

ANCHOR WATCH
PUBLISHING
** USA **

The Russian's Sloth
Avenging Angel
Seven Deadly Sins Book #5
Cap Daniels

This is a work of fiction. Names, characters, places, historical events, and incidents are the product of the author's imagination or have been used fictitiously. Although many locations such as marinas, airports, hotels, restaurants, etc. used in this work actually exist, they are used fictitiously and may have been relocated, exaggerated, or otherwise modified by creative license for the purpose of this work. Although many characters are based on personalities, physical attributes, skills, or intellect of actual individuals, all of the characters in this work are products of the author's imagination.

Published by:
⚓
ANCHOR WATCH
PUBLISHING
** USA **

All rights reserved. No part of this book may be reproduced or transmitted in any form or by any means, electronic or mechanical, including information storage and retrieval systems without written permission from the publisher, except by a reviewer who may quote brief passages in a review.

13-Digit ISBN: 978-1-951021-48-1
Library of Congress Control Number: 2023945996
Copyright © 2023 Cap Daniels – All Rights Reserved

Cover Design: German Creative

Printed in the United States of America

THE RUSSIAN'S SLOTH

Russkiy Lenivets

CAP DANIELS

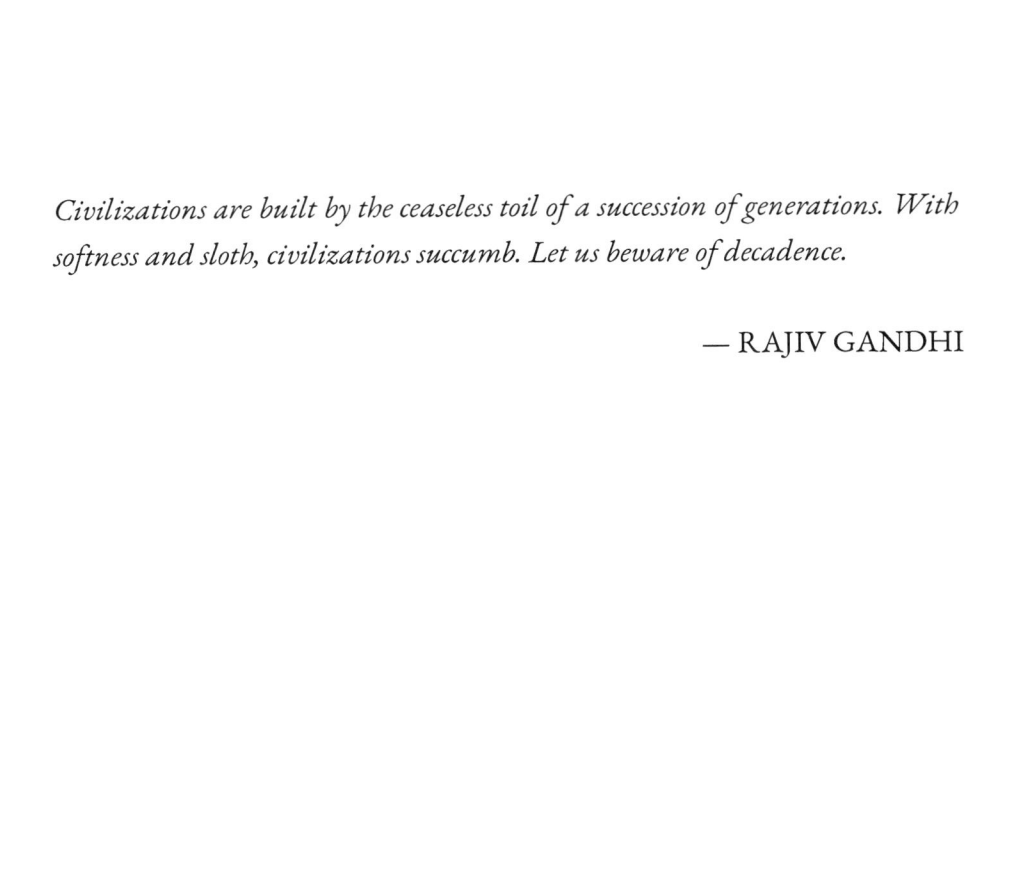

Civilizations are built by the ceaseless toil of a succession of generations. With softness and sloth, civilizations succumb. Let us beware of decadence.

— RAJIV GANDHI

1

Amerikanskaya Devushka
(American Girl)

Kralendijk, Bonaire, Netherlands Antilles

Anya Burinkova, former Russian SVR assassin, sat against the multi-colored wall of the crowded Caribbean bar and watched intently as a couple stepped onto the stage and lifted microphones to their lips. The lyrics to Tom Petty's "American Girl" scrolled by on the screen behind the obviously amateur performers.

The man sitting beside her, with his fourth or fifth Bonaire Herfst Bok cradled in his hand, was far more taken by Anya than by the off-key karaoke singers butchering the classic rock song. His attention wasn't misdirected. Anya drew far more than her fair share of adoration from men all over the world. Her Eastern European features beneath long blonde hair tied up in a hurried ponytail gave her an advantage the rest of the women on Earth envied and sometimes despised.

The man, Department of Justice Supervisory Special Agent Ray White, was sucking the life out of the final few days of the first real vacation he'd enjoyed in over a decade. The last time he'd strolled on a Caribbean beach, he'd confidently pulled off his shirt without a thought of the twenty extra pounds the coming years would pad his midsection with. Back then, his life and career had been simpler—long before the Russian had arrived with her inability to follow protocol, regulations, or even laws. She was a wildcard, and perhaps his personal game of Russian roulette with a fully loaded revolver, but the one thing she would never be is boring.

He felt her hand slip into his and tug. "Come dance with me, Ray. This is song about me, yes? I am American girl."

He pulled his hand away. "I don't dance."

She stuck out her bottom lip. "Look into room and point to man who will say to me no if I ask to dance."

"Then go dance with one of them. I'm too old, and I know way too much about you."

"What do you know about me that makes you not want to dance with me? I am pretty girl, no?"

"Pretty? Yes. A pain in my ass? Also, yes. Leave me alone and go play with somebody who doesn't know what you can do with a knife."

Special Agent Gwynn Davis slurped the last remaining ounce from her daiquiri and leapt to her feet. "Come on, Anya. I'll dance with you."

Ray White leaned back in his chair and turned to his protégé. "What's the over-under on how many guys hit on those two before the end of the song?"

Special Agent Johnathon "Johnny Mac" McIntyre raised a finger and motioned for two more beers. "Set the number wherever you want, boss, and I'll take the over."

The beers arrived, and the duo on stage made a clumsy transition to Shania Twain's "I Feel Like a Woman," and that's when it happened. A pair of frat boys whose alcohol-fueled self-confidence outweighed their common sense, stepped behind Anya and Gwynn and placed their hands on the swaying hips of the two most beautiful women in the hemisphere. Anya took a step back, pressing herself against her handsy suitor who clearly thought he'd just won the Moscow lottery. Before the young man could turn Anya's bump into his grind, the Russian twisted his right hand until the soft tissue holding his wrist together strained almost to the point of failure and he found himself on his back at her feet.

Gwynn's reaction to the unwelcome grope was far less subtle. Her heel landed solidly on top of the man's bare foot at the same instant her elbow collided with his chin. Anya *helped* her assailant to the floor, but Gwynn *sent* hers to the ground.

A round of applause rose from the celebrating bar crowd, and the singers took a bow. They were the only ones oblivious to the true recipients of the crowd's approval.

Gwynn grabbed Anya's hand and led her to the stage. On the way past the DJ booth, she whispered to the karaoke master, and in seconds, the two deadliest women on the island broke into a roaring rendition of Georgia Satellites' "Keep Your Hands to Yourself."

After three more beers, Ray conceded and danced with the woman who could be his undoing. The song was something in Dutch that sounded a lot like "I Will Always Love You"—Dolly's version.

"You are wonderful dancer, Ray White. Why would you not do this with me before?"

Self-conscious of his beer breath, he turned his head away. "There are a lot of things I'm good at that I'll never do with you."

She leaned back with her arms around his neck. "This is curious thing for me. You are smart, handsome man, and I am pretty woman who is also smart. I give to you many chances to kiss me, but you do not. What is wrong with me inside your mind?"

He forgot all about the beer on his breath and stared down into the smoky blue eyes that could tear a man's soul from his chest. "I'm not good at being number two."

She cocked her head, and her long ponytail swept across her shoulder. "I am no good for you because you are not first man for me?"

He stepped back and let her hands fall from around his neck. He caught her left with his right and led her from the dance floor. "You're smarter than that, Anya. You know what I'm talking about. There's one love of your life, and you're never going to give up on him for me or anyone else."

She jerked her hand from his. "This is not true, and that is terrible thing to say."

They reclaimed their seats, and he lifted his empty glass with disappointment. "It is true, and the truth is never a terrible thing to say."

"If is true, who is person who is love of my life?"

He cocked his head and waggled a finger toward his useless bottle. "You're in denial, Red Sonja. Everybody knows you'll always carry a torch for your little sailor boy Chase Fulton."

She put on the terrifying scowl that Russian women invented. "Chase is married to other person, and not to me. This is foolish thing you say, and do not say this again."

He threw up both hands. "Hey, take it easy. I was just pointing out the obvious. The truth is, I can't believe you haven't already killed this 'other person' Chase is married to."

Anya huffed. "This is terrible idea. I am first person to be suspect if Chase's wife, Penny, is murdered, but if you will be for me alibi . . ."

Ray stuck a finger in each ear. "I can't hear you!"

The Russian traced a line on the table with the tip of her finger, and Gwynn leaned in. "What's wrong, Anya?"

"Nothing. I was having nice memory of day watching baseball match at college where Chase was best player."

"You watched him play baseball? Why haven't you ever told me that story?"

"No, I did not watch him play in baseball match. He took me there to watch others on team, and I had chili dog for first time."

Ray slammed his hand onto the table. "Game! It's a baseball *game*, not a *match*. Some American girl you are."

"I know this," Anya said. "But is for me fun to say *match*."

Ray said, "Speaking of matches, this little escape to Fantasy Island has to come to an end. We've got another assignment for the three of you. This time, you'll be matching wits with a guy named Nikiti Morozov in Seattle. Ever heard of him?"

2

Poznakom'tes's Lenivtsem
(Meet the Sloth)

Washington, DC

Supervisory Special Agent Ray White dropped a pair of file folders onto his desk. Each was overflowing and bound by a thick rubber band. "Okay, boys and girls. Meet Nikiti Morozov. For the purposes of this mission, we'll call him the Sloth."

Anya reached for the thicker of the two files, but White playfully slapped her hand away. "Not yet. You have to listen to my spiel first."

Anya frowned and turned to Gwynn. "There are laws inside America for not hitting employees, yes?"

Before Gwynn could get involved, White said, "I didn't *hit* you. I *encouraged* you to keep your hands off a file. Now, quit wasting my time."

Anya reacted by snatching the file before Ray could stop her a second time, and she fired the rubber band at his hand as *encouragement* not to *encourage* her further.

White spoke as Anya thumbed through the file. "Nikiti Morozov is a former member of the Communist Party in the glory days of the Soviet Union. It's rumored that he made his fortune auctioning off nuclear weapons technology to the highest bidder after the Wall came down."

Johnny Mac perked up. "So, we're going after an international nuclear arms dealer?"

White rolled his eyes. "Sorry to disappoint you, Johnny, but you won't be able to add that one to your résumé. It's just your run-of-the-mill art theft case."

"Art?" Anya asked. "What kind of art?"

White motioned toward the file she held. "Keep flipping. You'll see. It's serious paintings by the Old Masters, and . . ."

Anya burst out, "I know this painting! Is *Devochka s Persikami* by Walentin Alexandrowitsch Serow, and is inside Tretyakov Gallery in Moscow. I saw this when I was little girl."

White recoiled, and Gwynn leaned closer. "I like it. I minored in art history, but I've never heard of Alexandrowitsch."

Anya pulled the photograph of the painting from the file and handed it to Gwynn. "You have probably never heard of any Russian painters besides maybe icon painters like Andrei Rublev."

Gwynn shook her head. "Sorry, never heard of him either."

"Is okay. Russian painters are not given same respect by rest of world like Italians and Western Europeans. Is very sad because they are quite good."

Ray waved both hands. "Come on back, girls. We're having a mission briefing, not a Russian art history class."

Anya lifted the picture from Gwynn's hands. "Is not possible for Nikiti Morozov to have this painting. I am certain it is inside Tretyakov Gallery."

White shrugged. "I'm just telling you what's in the file. That's all we know about Morozov. He's a recluse. The last time he was spotted in public was just over two years ago when he had to be taken to the University of Washington Medical Center for an emergency surgery."

"What was surgery?" Anya asked.

"We're not sure, but he was taken by a private ambulance and returned after three days by the same ambulance."

"Why does that matter?" Johnny Mac asked.

Anya shrugged. "Maybe it does not, but if we know this, maybe we can use type of surgery to get close to him. Perhaps he needs private Russian nurse like me."

White chuckled and leaned back in his chair. "I think you're better suited for taking lives than saving them."

Anya put on a devilish smile. "Is sad for you. This is something you will never know because you are too proud to play second fiddling."

"It's second fiddle. And it's not a matter of pride. It's a matter of, well, it's just . . . No, I'm not doing this with you. You always do this to me, and I'm not letting it happen this time. This is my briefing, and you're my agent. Now, shut up and listen."

She lost her smile. "I am doing only to you what you allow. This is all."

White held up a finger, and Anya stopped pushing . . . temporarily.

"We believe Morozov has a team of observers who constantly keep their ears to the ground in the art world for rumors about one of these Old Masters' paintings possibly being for sale before they go to auction. Apparently, the artsy types like handling their business on the down-low."

Anya's eyes darted between White and the two younger agents. "What is keeping ear to ground? This does not make sense."

White peered across his glasses. "You're doing it again."

"Doing what again?"

"Interrupting me just because you can."

"I am sorry. I will sit here with ears to floor for you, and I will not interrupt anymore."

Gwynn tried and failed to hide her chuckle. "It's an Old West term. They say Native Americans could press an ear to the ground and hear horses coming."

Anya scowled. "I promised to not interrupt, but that is stupid. No one can do this."

White whispered, "Excuse me. May I please continue my"—and then in an unmistakably commanding voice—"briefing!"

Johnny Mac and Gwynn cowered, but Anya never flinched. "Is okay for me if you continue, but yelling is not good communication technique."

White raised a finger and cocked his head, but before he let himself explode, he took a long, deep breath and shuffled the stack of papers in his hand. "So, anyway. We think this guy buys paintings on the silent market." He locked eyes with the Russian. "Don't do it!"

Inside his skull, White yelled, *Why is it impossible to stay mad at her?*

Anya gave him a soft, innocent smile.

White said, "So, he buys these paintings, and then they show up on the auction circuit within a couple of years. We have no idea what he does with them between the time he purchases them and when he sells them. We don't know why he's a recluse. We don't even know for sure if he's done anything illegal except for one accusation of selling a forgery as an original."

Johnny Mac perked up. "Now it's getting interesting. Is he some kind of modern-day master who can copy the work of these Old Masters?"

White shrugged. "Maybe, but whatever's going on in Jabba the Hutt's lair, I want you three to figure it out, and if it's criminal, you're going to build a case." He turned his attention directly to Anya. "Your track record on building cases that go to trial is pretty shaky, so I want you to listen closely. Do not kill this guy! Do you understand?"

She feigned innocence. "I am special agent of Justice Department, not assassin. And besides, I have never heard of this Jabba Hutt person."

White pulled off his glasses. "Forget about Jabba. Davis will explain that one to you later. But you know what they say . . . You can take the girl out of Russia, but you can't take the assassin out of the girl."

Anya huffed. "Who says this? This is stupid American saying from stupid person who knows nothing about Russia and less than nothing about assassins."

White motioned toward the files with the stem of his glasses. "Study those. Memorize them. Formulate some theories. Then, bring me a plan for how you three are going to get inside and figure out what's going on in Seattle. Any questions?"

Johnny Mac said, "I thought you said this was a run-of-the-mill art theft case. It doesn't sound like this guy Morozov is stealing anything. From what you said, he's buying paintings straight from their owners. What am I missing?"

White said, "I'm glad one of you was paying attention. Read the files, and we'll reconvene this afternoon. Anything else?"

Anya looked up. "Can I kill him if he is making counterfeit paintings?"

White closed one eye and leaned back. "Maybe."

The junior agents and Anya left Ray White alone in his bigger-than-necessary office and piled into their shared space across the hall. Nothing above the sounds of rustling papers and growling stomachs rose from the three of them as they studied every page of the files.

A knock came at their office door, and Anya hopped to her feet. "Yes?"

A woman in a green apron stood in the doorway with three long, thin bags in her hands. "Here's your sandwiches."

Anya stared at the woman and then back at Gwynn. "Did you order sandwiches?"

Gwynn shook her head, and the woman in the apron studied a receipt stapled to the first bag. "It says here somebody named Raymond White ordered them for Davis, McIntyre, and a name I can't pronounce."

Anya claimed the bags. "Yes, this is us. Thank you."

Anya closed the door just as quickly as she'd opened it, and Gwynn looked up with disbelief in her eyes. "This is weird. Agent White has never bought us lunch before. I'm not turning it down, though. What's in the bags?"

The Russian handed out three identical Italian subs, and the stomach growling ceased.

With the sandwiches reduced to crumbs and wadded paper wrappers, the three dived back into the files.

Anya dropped a file onto her lap, leaned back, and stared at the ceiling. "Something is missing from story. FBI has stolen-art division. If this is truly crime about only paintings, why is FBI not handling case?"

Johnny closed his file. "You know, you're right. That's an excellent question."

Gwynn jumped in. "I agree with Johnny, but I don't think it's a good idea for *you* to bring up the question to Agent White. You should let one of us do it."

Anya cocked her head. "Why is this? I love asking questions to Ray. I like when his face is red and he takes off necktie with great force."

Gwynn giggled. "Yeah, that's exactly why I don't think you should bring it up. You tend to get under his skin, and as much fun as that is to watch, I think he might be more receptive if Johnny asked the question."

"Whatever makes cookie crumble," Anya said.

Both agents stared at her in utter confusion.

She threw up her hands. "What? Is American phrase, no?"

"Not exactly," Gwynn said. "But maybe it should be."

The Russian sighed. "It is good this is not real phrase because nobody wants crumbled cookie or drinking of spilled milk while crying."

Gwynn rolled her eyes. "Yeah, just stick with basic English for now, and we'll work on your common phrases later. Deal?"

Anya seemed to ignore Gwynn's suggestion and said, "I need computer with internet connection, please."

Johnny pointed toward his desktop. "You can use mine. Just make sure you don't download anything that will get me fired, and remember to log out when you're done."

Anya rose, kissed Johnny Mac on the forehead, and slipped into his chair. "Thank you. But maybe I will order lingerie from Victoria's Secret."

"Don't you dare," he said.

Anya laughed. "You will make very good supervisory special agent, I think. You sound just like Ray when you scold me."

Johnny dropped himself back into his chair. "I'll take that as a compliment."

"Perhaps it was compliment, or perhaps you are getting only old and grouchy like Ray."

He ignored the quip and stuck his head back into the file.

Ten minutes of silence later, Gwynn stood and walked behind Anya. "What are you looking for?"

She rolled her chair to the side and motioned toward the screen. "I was looking for major theft of fine art in past decade. We have only few pictures of Morozov's collection. If he is big deal in world of stolen art, he will have maybe one or maybe more of these."

Gwynn scanned the website and gasped. "That's the Bührle Collection in Zurich. That was one of the biggest private art thefts in history, and there's still some question about whether the men who were arrested, tried, and convicted of the crime were the real perpetrators.

"That is correct, friend Gwynn. You are very smart."

Gwynn shook her head. "No, it's not smarts. It's one whole semester in college. We studied the Bührle Collection exclusively."

"Tell to me story of painting stolen from this collection," Anya said.

Gwynn cleared her throat. "Well, the robbery was one of the most brazen in history. In February of oh-eight, three guys—we assume they were guys—strolled into the private E. G. Bührle museum in Zurich wearing ski masks, and one of them pulled a handgun. After everyone was face-down on the floor, the other two guys yanked four paintings off the wall. The museum didn't have any metal detectors because the entry hall was too narrow, and they didn't have a history of checking visitors' bags when they came in."

Johnny squinted and shook his head. "What? They had millions of dollars' worth of art hanging on the walls, and they didn't think to check for guns?"

Gwynn raised her eyebrows. "That's Switzerland for you. They don't think about guns. That museum is in a quiet and extremely safe part of Zurich."

Anya made a guttural sound. "It doesn't sound very safe to me if three robbers in masks came inside with gun and steal paintings."

Gwynn said, "According to everything I've read, that was the only major crime reported in that neighborhood for over ten years."

"Then is perfect place for robbery," Anya said. "Why were there questions? Is there some reasonable explanation for thinking they were not real robbers?"

Gwynn shrugged. "Beats me, but maybe it's because they were well connected with the Russian mafia."

Anya frowned. "Maybe this is true, and maybe we will catch real men in ski masks and FBI will be purple with jealous."

Gwynn palmed her forehead. "Again, let's work on the American metaphors privately before you work them into conversation. It's green with envy, not purple with jealousy."

"Almost same," Anya said. "Neither color makes sense for emotions. Tell to me about paintings that were stolen."

Gwynn continued. "They grabbed four paintings and got away in an unmarked van. One report said the paintings were hanging out of the back door of the van as they drove away. I don't know if that's true, but it sounds like something the Bratva would do. They're not known for their subtlety."

"This is true," Anya said. "Russian men are very brave, but the Brotherhood is not organization for brilliant minds. Is more gang of thugs than intellectuals."

Gwynn said, "Whoever they were, they got away with a Monet, a van Gogh, a Cézanne, and a Degas. The Degas is actually one of my favorite paintings. It's called *Count Lepic and His Daughters*, and he painted it around eighteen seventy. It's a portrait of Count Ludovic-Napoléon Lepic and his two daughters. The girls look like china dolls. It's not Degas's finest work, but I love the two little girls. Anyway, it was the least valuable of the four paintings."

"How much?" Johnny asked.

Gwynn said, "All in, the four paintings were worth at least a hundred sixty million. It's hard to put a price on such rare pieces. They hardly ever show up at auction, so there's very little sales history on them. That's not really what makes the Zurich robbery interesting though."

Johnny let out a low whistle. "I'd say a hundred sixty million is pretty interesting."

Gwynn said, "Just wait 'til you hear this. Less than a week before that robbery, there was another heist, although it was a little different. The thieves broke into a gallery at night in the town of Pfäffikon, which isn't far from Zurich, and they stole a pair of Picassos worth over four million bucks."

Anya said, "You know so much about art. Why are you not on FBI team instead of Department of Justice?"

Gwynn wrapped her arms around the Russian's shoulders. "Because you and I were meant to be, baby."

3

Golyye Spagetti
(Naked Spaghetti)

Anya logged out of Johnny Mac's computer. "Do we have plan to get inside organization of Nikiti Morozov?"

Gwynn and Johnny exchanged empty glances, and Gwynn said, "I've got nothing. Do you have any ideas?"

"I have only one idea," Anya said. "And Johnny is going to love idea."

He slid forward in his seat. "Oh? Let's hear it."

"You are still in love with beautiful woman in Technical Services Division, yes?"

He slid back in his chair. "I wouldn't say we're in love. I mean, we're still ... you know."

"Yes, this is love. I can see it inside eyes." Anya slid the desk phone toward Johnny. "Make call to her and put on speaker."

Johnny reached for the phone, but Gwynn caught his arm. "Wait a minute. We can't just pull other people into an op. We have to get Agent White's approval."

Anya scowled. "This is not true. We are not bringing her in yet. We are only asking question if she can do—or cannot do—what we need. This is all. I will talk with Ray when time comes for bringing her in. Make call, Johnny."

Johnny Mac turned back to Gwynn, and she removed her hand. "Okay, but don't say I didn't warn you. Agent White is going to kill us over this."

Anya rolled her eyes. "I will not let this happen. Besides, he cannot really kill us. This is against law. Maybe he will be a little mad, but not so much if plan works."

Johnny pushed the speaker button and dialed the Technical Services Division in the basement of the DOJ building. After three rings, the woman who'd occupied Johnny's attention for weeks answered her phone. "Tech Services, this is Doctor Mankiller."

"Hey, Celeste. It's Johnny. How's it going down there?"

"Oh, hey, Johnny. It was just a regular boring morning, but now that I've got you on the phone, it's looking up. You're not calling to cancel naked spaghetti night, are you?"

Anya blurted out, "I love spaghetti. We can come too, yes?"

Celeste said, "Sure, the more the merrier, but it's strictly no clothes and no utensils."

Johnny turned a shade of red Anya had never seen, and she giggled. "I believe we are embarrassing your boyfriend. He is turning colors underneath skin of face."

Celeste said, "He does that a lot. What's going on up there where the action is?"

"I have maybe plan, and we cannot do without you. What do you know about two-hundred-year-old paint?"

The technical genius groaned. "Uh, you'll need to be a little more specific. What kind of paint?"

Anya said, "Not so much paint, but paintings by Old Masters. This kind of paint."

"What do you want to know?"

"If we bring to you painting, can you make exact duplicate?"

Celeste said, "That depends on how exact you mean."

"Is necessary to be perfect match with also perfect chemistry of paint, and canvas must be also correct age. You can do this, yes?"

The line was silent for a moment before Celeste said, "Are we talking about forging priceless paintings in the DOJ Tech Services lab?"

Any said, "No, this is not what we are talking about. Forging, yes, but not priceless paintings. They have prices."

Celeste sighed. "I almost forgot how frustrating it can be to talk to you,

Anya. The answer is, I don't know. I've never tried it, but I can get to work and see what I can come up with. I'll need a sample painting I can destroy while I'm learning. Can you get one approximately the same age as the one you want me to copy?"

"Yes, we can do this, but first we must talk with Agent White about this."

Celest gasped. "You mean you're calling me about tech services on an op and Agent White doesn't know?"

"Yes, this is correct. He does not know, but also you do not know about operation yet. We only asked question if yes, you can do, or no, you cannot do."

Celeste said, "Go talk to Agent White, get his approval, then bring me a sample painting. I think I can do it. Oh, and Johnny, don't be late. Your spaghetti will be on your favorite plate at seven thirty."

Without a word, Johnny punched the button to disconnect the call. "Well, thank you. That was humiliating."

"What are you talking about?" Anya asked. "We are all very jealous now because we have no one to have night of naked spaghetti with. You are lucky man."

Gwynn stood. "There's a warped little part of my brain that really wants to know what she meant by 'your favorite plate.'"

The shade of red Johnny turned in that moment was even more intense than any he'd worn during the call, and Gwynn and Anya giggled like schoolgirls.

Ray White neither knocked nor slowed down when he burst through the door. "What's so funny, and why are you briefing Johnny's girlfriend on our op?"

Anya caught her breath. "Johnny Mac and Celeste are eating spaghetti with fingers and being also naked."

White stared down at Johnny as Anya continued. "We did not brief Dr.

Mankiller on operation. We simply asked if she could forge painting. This is plan for getting inside to meet your sloth, Nikiti Morozov."

White paused and continued staring at his golden boy. "My God, man. Naked spaghetti? Really? And you let these two know about it?"

Johnny held up his hands in innocence. "Boss, it wasn't me. It was . . . I mean, it wasn't my idea to call her."

White shook his head. "Okay, I don't hate the idea. Did she say she could do it?"

Gwynn spoke up. "She said she could try, but she'll need a painting from the same period as the one we want to fake so she can practice without destroying an original masterpiece."

White raised his eyebrows. "So why aren't you looking for a painting for her?"

Gwynn checked her watch. "Maybe we could borrow one from the FBI stolen art division."

Almost before she finished the statement, White roared, "No! We're not bringing the Feebs in on this one. It's none of their business, and if they get a whiff of it, they'll take over before they exhale. Absolutely not. Leave them out of this and find another source. You're the art history major."

"It was a minor, boss, and I didn't really learn that much."

"Then you better start learning," White said.

He turned to Anya and hooked a finger. "You, in my office, now."

"You are in grouchy mood today. I will have spaghetti with you if this will make you in better mood."

He pointed out the door and across the hall. "Now."

Once inside his office, White closed the door and softened his tone. "Have a seat. Whose idea was it to bring Mankiller in on this one?"

"It was my idea, but I am sure both Johnny and Gwynn would have thought of this in time."

"It's good work, Anya. I like it. Next time, though, just run it by me before you start shopping around for help on an assignment. Can you do that, please?"

"Yes, I will do this, but you should know both of them wanted to ask you first. I forced them to have call with Dr. Mankiller."

He fell into his chair and loosened his tie. "You shouldn't have the ability to force my agents to do anything. Let's just play ball inside the park a little more, okay?"

She squinted. "I am sorry, but I do not know what this means. Play ball inside field?"

White puffed out his cheeks and blew out a long breath. When his lungs were empty, he slumped in his seat and pulled out a bottle of Weller Single Barrel and two tumblers.

Anya studied the orange label. "This is very expensive bourbon, and you are being too nice. Tell to me what is happening."

He slid one of the tumblers across the desk, and Anya lifted it between her fingertips. As the aroma of the thousand-dollar whiskey reached her nose, she cooed. "This is very nice bourbon, Ray. Talk to me."

He stood from his leather chair and rounded the island-sized desk. Turning on a heel, he deposited himself into the wingback beside Anya's. Raising his glass to hers, he said, "Here's to doing whatever has to be done to get the bad guys."

Anya touched her glass to his, and they both enjoyed their first sip.

White stared into his glass and swirled it slightly while the Russian watched his every move. Finally, he said, "You don't have to do this anymore."

"What are you talking about?"

He ran a finger around the rim of his glass. "You've already done more than any of us thought possible. You nearly died on the last assignment, and you've got a whole new life in the islands with your tourist business. If you want to leave, I can't keep you here any longer."

"But what about case of Nikiti Morozov? You need me for this case, no?"

He never took his eyes off the bourbon. "Yeah, we need you for this one, and if you survive, we'll need you for the next one, and the one after that, and so on. I don't see it ever ending."

Anya let her tumbler rest on her thigh. "You are saying I can just walk away and be free, yes?"

Ray took another swallow. "Yep, that's what I'm saying. It's over, Anya. All the chaos you bring with you everywhere you go, all the training you put Davis through, and all the craziness you put up with from Johnny Mac . . . It's all over, and you're free to go."

She slid forward in her seat and leaned toward White. "There has to be more to story. This is not enough. It cannot simply be over. Tell to me what is really happening."

"Damnit, Anya, stop looking a gift horse in the mouth. You're free. We're done. I'm done . . . I'm done." His voice trailed off, and he couldn't bring himself to look at her.

"Ray, I am sorry. This is my fault. I have done something outside of park, and you are in trouble for something I have done. This is truth, yes?"

He rested his head on the back of his chair and stared into the ceiling. "I wish that was it, Anya, but this isn't your doing. Just sit here beside me and drink whiskey with me for a few minutes in silence. Can we do that, please?"

She laid a hand on his forearm and raised the tumbler to her silent lips.

After a long moment, Ray placed his hand atop hers and stared into the most beautiful and mysterious eyes he would ever see. With his whiskey glass empty, he said, "I have cancer, and they say I've got less than a year to live. It's inoperable and completely fatal."

Instead of the typical "if there's anything I can do" response, Anya said, "What is name of cancer?"

Ray refilled his tumbler. "It's notochordal sarcoma, a tumor called a clival tumor where my spine meets my skull."

"Is cancer only inside spine or also in other bones?"

Ray said, "You're the first person I've told, and this isn't exactly the response I expected."

Anya said, "I will give to you sympathy after we know options."

He took a swallow. "You're obviously not listening. It's inoperable. If they take the tumor, I'd be paralyzed from the neck down."

Anya wasn't fazed. "You were told this by best surgeon in all of world?"

White shook his head. "How is it possible for you to be so frustrating every time I talk to you?"

"Is one of my talents. Give to me few minutes."

She pulled her cell phone from her pocket and dialed a long series of numbers. When someone answered, Anya spoke in a language Ray didn't immediately recognize. The call lasted two minutes before she held out the phone and pressed the speaker button. She said, "Is now Anya and also Ray White on speaker of phone."

A disembodied voice spoke in what sounded like German-accented English with a hint of French. "Hello, Mr. White. My name is Dr. Stefan Müller. I am the director of neurosurgery at the Clinique de Genolier in Switzerland. I am also a board-certified oncologist and Olympic silver medalist in super-G and downhill. I tell you this because training for the Olympics is more difficult than training for neurosurgery, and I am very proud of the medals. Our mutual friend, Ms. Burinkova, tells me you have been diagnosed as having an inoperable clival chondrosarcoma."

Ray eyed Anya. "Yeah, that's what the doctors here at Georgetown in DC tell me. It's one point nine centimeters and encroaching on my spine."

Dr. Müller said, "I see. How about day after tomorrow in the early afternoon?"

Ray frowned. "What about it?"

Before the doctor could reply, Anya said, "*Er wird dort sein. Danke und merci, doctor. Verabschiedung.*"

She ended the call and pocketed the phone.

Ray asked, "What just happened?"

"I made for you appointment with best neurosurgeon in all of world in two days. I told to him you would be there."

Ray sighed. "Anya, I told you it's inoperable. What are you doing?"

"Yes, but this is only opinion of doctors here inside United States. Dr. Müller is best of all neurosurgeons. If he says to you tumor is inoperable, then is okay for you to die, but until then, you are alive and maybe is possible to take out tumor."

He downed his bourbon. "No, Anya. I'm flattered and all, but I can't go to Switzerland. I've got Blue Cross Blue Shield. They're not going to pay for me to see a Swiss doctor."

"This is not problem," Anya said. "Money does not matter when life is at stake. You will go, and I will pay. This is friend thing to do, and this is reason we have money. Is no argument. I will make for you reservation on flight and hotel. You will leave tomorrow. This is not negotiable. Johnny Mac can pretend to be in charge of operation while you are gone. This will please him, and the others do not need to know where you are going or why. For now, this is our secret, and I am spy, so I am very good at keeping secret."

White stared through the bottom of his tumbler at the distorted world beyond the crystal. "Would you tell Johnny Mac to come in when you go?"

Anya squeezed his arm and stood, but before she reached the door, White said, "Ana Fulton . . ." When she turned and they locked eyes, he said, "Thank you."

4
Povysheniye
(Promotion)

"What was that all about?" Johnny Mac asked when Anya stepped through the door and into their shared office.

"It was something only for me," she said.

Johnny frowned. "Only for you? Was it work related?"

Before she could answer, Agent White appeared. "All right, listen up. We've got an operational change, and I need to speak with each of you individually. Davis, come with me."

White and Davis left the room, and Johnny slid his chair close to Anya's. "What's going on?"

She said, "I am not certain, but perhaps mission is on hold for few days. Something has come up."

"What's come up?" he demanded.

"He will tell to you when is your turn to speak privately. I think there are maybe private things he needs to tell each of us, but not all of us together. This makes sense, yes?"

"Is he breaking up the team?"

Anya sighed. "This I do not know."

"Just tell me what he told you."

"I cannot. He told to me in confidence, but I think he will tell also to you privately."

Johnny leaned back in his chair and let the possibilities run through his head. "Am I being promoted?" Anya pretended she didn't hear the question, and Johnny said, "That's it, isn't it? I'm being promoted. I knew it!"

Anya examined her hands for a long moment. "Wait, Johnny. This is not what is happening. Agent White will tell to you what is happening, but please do not expect promotion today."

He deflated. "What is it, then?"

Gwynn returned to the office wearing a painful expression and slumped into her chair. Without looking up, she said, "He wants to see you, Johnny."

The instant Johnny closed the door behind him, Anya reached for Gwynn's hand. "Is okay, Gwynn. I have for him best doctor in all of world. Do not be so sad. Is not time for this yet."

Gwynn leaned forward and bit her bottom lip. "It's over."

"What is over?"

Gwynn looked up. "This. All of this. Us. It's over. You're leaving, Agent White is leaving. I don't . . ."

Anya slipped a finger beneath her partner's chin and raised her face. "Look to me, friend Gwynn. I am not leaving, and Ray has only appointment with doctor. Nothing is over."

Gwynn cleared her throat. "But Agent White said he released you."

"Yes, he said also this to me, but why would I go away? We have still work to do, and I made commitment to finish job and also commitment to you. I made promise to teach you to fight, and this is not finished."

Gwynn blinked, and the beginning of a smile came to her lips. "So, you're not leaving?"

Anya frowned. "No, this would be ridiculous."

"I'm not sure I understand," Gwynn said. "If I was being forced to do a job against my will, I'd bolt at the first opportunity."

Anya brushed her partner's hair behind her ear. "This is difference between your American mind and my Soviet Union mind. We learn this when we are children. Freedom is not possible inside mind of child in Soviet Union. Is not even concept we could understand."

"But the Soviet Union hasn't existed since nineteen ninety-one."

Anya tilted her head. "I was sparrow, and assassin, and adult woman of nineteen years when Berlin Wall came down. Soviet Union is not on map of world today, but for child like me who knew nothing of world outside—world on other side—of Iron Curtain, Soviet Union is forever burned into our flesh and onto our souls. I love you, my friend, and I am forever glad you never had to know the sting of this red-hot branding iron of hammer and sickle."

The two sat, staring silently into each other's eyes and hearts until Gwynn said, "You're the best friend anyone could have . . . ever."

Anya leaned forward and wrapped her arms around her partner. "This is true also of you, friend Gwynn."

Before the embrace ended, Johnny Mac burst through the door. "I knew it. I told you!"

Gwynn and Anya looked from their embrace.

"What is screaming about, Johnny Mac? What did you know?"

"They're making me a temporary supervisory special agent while Agent White is away on family medical leave. I'm in charge of the Seattle operation."

"That's not exactly true," Agent White said from the doorway. "You're *responsible* for the Seattle op, Johnny Mac. That's not the same as being in charge." He raised a finger and pointed at Gwynn and Anya. "Those two are in your hands. If they get hurt or killed, it's your fault. If they blow the op and Morozov gets away, it's your fault. If they bust this guy and put him away for life . . ."

Johnny grinned. "It's my win."

White laughed. "Not hardly. If they bust Morozov and get a conviction, it's their win. Welcome to the supervisory ranks, Johnny—even if it's only temporary."

Johnny looked like a balloon with a slow leak.

White said, "I'll be back in a few days, kiddies. Play nice with each other. Johnny, don't be an ass, and you two, don't be a pain in his ass. Don't kill anybody, and don't surrender to the Chinese or the Canadians. I better find this ship still floating without any cannonballs through her hull when I get back. Got it?"

Gwynn rose and stepped in front of Agent White. She whispered, "Everything will be fine here, boss. Just take care of you, and we'll take care of Seattle."

Anya hugged White. "I will miss you. Is so much fun to make you furious. I think now I must do this to Johnny Mac, yes?"

"Don't hurt the man. He's young and fragile."

Anya put on the mischievous smile that opened far too many doors. "Maybe I should make for him tea and give him opportunity to kiss."

White gave her a playful shove. "You'll have to take that up with his little girlfriend down in Tech Services, and I don't think you want to tangle with anybody named Mankiller."

"Maybe you are right," Anya said. "Is obvious that Johnny prefers dark hair and eyes. I am ugly gosling to him."

Gwynn giggled. "It's ugly *duckling*, but there's not a man alive who'd call you that. You know I'll drink tea with you anytime. No kissing required, right?"

White said, "That's enough. Speaking of Dr. Mankiller, you should run your butts down to her underground lair. She's got some toys for you. Johnny and I have some things to discuss."

Once inside the Technical Services Division in the basement, Gwynn said, "Hey, Celeste. How's it going?"

"Hey, yourself," she said. "Look at you two looking all hot and official. You better be keeping your hands off my man up there."

Anya said, "Do not worry. All of world knows he is off market and has only eyes for you."

Celeste pulled off her glasses. "That's sweet, but you two are wearing two-thousand-dollar suits and looking like supermodels in them while I'm down here in jeans and a ratty T-shirt, packing C-4 explosives into a Rolex."

"Why would you do this?" Anya asked.

Celeste screwed up her face. "In case I want to blow somebody's hand off. Why else?"

Gwynn said, "Okay, that's weird, but Agent White said you had some things for us."

"Oh, yeah, I do. Come with me."

Gwynn said, "Just promise me one of them isn't a Rolex."

Celeste froze and turned on a heel. "Want one?"

Anya immediately said, "Yes!"

Celeste grabbed the Russian's hand. "I knew you would. You're my girl."

She led them through two sets of double doors that each required an ID card and a thumbprint. "Pretty cool, huh?"

Anya shrugged. "Is only perceived security. I can defeat in four minutes if I want no one to know, and maybe ten seconds if I do not care who knows."

Celeste giggled. "I like you a little bit more every time I see you, and I fear you a lot more every time you open your mouth."

"I take this as compliment."

Celeste motioned toward a table with two pairs of glasses resting on a cloth. "The ones on the left are for Gwynn. They match your prescription. The others are for Anya."

The Russian said, "But I do not need glasses."

Celeste said, "Trust me. You need *these* glasses. Go ahead. Try them on."

They lifted the glasses from the cloth and placed them on their faces.

Gwynn said, "Oh, wow. These are great. But what's so special about them?"

Anya squinted through hers. "Is only clear glass. I see nothing differently."

Celeste said, "It's not about what you see. It's about what the glasses see."

She pulled a covering from a small painting on the wall of her lab. "Does that look familiar?"

Gwynn said, "Sure, that's the *Mona Lisa*. But isn't the real one bigger?"

"Nope, that's the actual size. Thirty by twenty-one inches. Everybody assumes it's bigger because most people have never seen it. Anyway, with your right thumb and index finger, touch the top and bottom of the frame around the right lens of your glasses while facing the painting, as if you're adjusting the position of your glasses to get a better look."

Anya did as she was instructed and took a step forward.

Celeste touched her arm. "No, once you initiate the process, you have to stand still. You can't move for three seconds, at the least. Five to seven seconds is even better."

"Even better for what?" Anya asked.

Celeste grinned. "I thought you'd never ask. Turn around."

They turned to see a laptop computer with three images on the screen. All three images were the *Mona Lisa* painting, and a progress bar populated at the bottom of the screen. When the bar was full, Celeste stroked a few keys, and a report popped up on the screen. The first line of the report read FORGERY in bold lettering, followed by four columns of ratios.

"Isn't that cool?" Celeste asked.

Anya said, "Anyone can see the painting is not real. This does not take magic glasses and computer."

Celeste said, "That's what I hoped you'd say, but what about this one?"

She unveiled a second painting that was significantly larger than the *Mona Lisa* fake. It showed a woman in a flowing dress and carrying an umbrella in a field of green vegetation with a child in the background."

"Oh, I know that one," Gwynn said. "It's a Claude Monet. Give me a second, and I'll pull the name from way back in my memory. Is it *Lady with Parasol*?"

"Close," Celeste said. "It's *Woman with a Parasol*, and it was created by

Claude Monet in eighteen seventy-five. Art historians believe it's Monet's wife and child."

"Is that a fake, too?" Gwynn asked.

"Put your glasses back on and have a look."

They did, and each of them fingered their frames just as Celeste had instructed. A few seconds later, the computer came to life and brought three pictures of the painting onto the screen.

Celeste said, "The ones on the left and right are yours, and the one in the middle is a high-definition image taken by Lloyd's of London for insurance identification."

"Why's the progress bar moving so slowly?" Gwynn asked.

"That's because this one is either the real thing or an excellent forgery. The *Mona Lisa* was blatantly fake, so the computer didn't struggle with it. This one is different."

When the progress bar finally filled, Celeste hit a few keys, and a report popped up. Instead of the bold declaration of it being a forgery, the top line read: "Possibly Authentic. Rescan."

Gwynn covered her mouth. "Oh, my God. Is it real?"

Celeste squirmed. "Yeah, it's real. It's on loan from the National Gallery, but it's going home tonight. For some reason, they don't move paintings during the day."

"Can I look at it more closely?" Gwynn asked.

"Sure, but don't touch it. It's rigged with more alarms than you could imagine."

Gwynn spent several minutes examining every inch of the painting. "It's magnificent."

Celeste checked her watch. "I hate to cut this short, but I need to show you why you're really here."

Anya held up her glasses. "Do you mean these are not reason?"

"Those are part of the reason, but here's the bigger part." Celeste unveiled a small oil on canvas without a frame. "This is called *Butterfly*, and it was painted by an unknown artist in the mid-twentieth century. It has no real value except as a training aid."

Gwynn narrowed her gaze. "Training aid?"

"Check this out." Celeste uncovered a second painting that looked identical to the first, then she motioned toward the paintings. "Find the forgery, ladies."

They donned their glasses and stood motionless in front of the art. Two minutes later, the computer declared both paintings to be the authentic original.

"How can this be?" Anya asked.

Celeste dusted off imaginary debris from her shoulders. "Ask, and you shall receive. You challenged me to create a forgery that could pass for the original, and I've done it . . . sort of."

"What do you mean, sort of?"

Celeste pulled a handheld device from a drawer. This gizmo measures paint thickness. Watch."

She aimed the tool at one of the paintings, and a tiny laser dot appeared on the canvas. She then moved to the second painting and made the same measurement. Holding up the tool, she pointed to the screen. "See the difference? The copy is thicker. Well, not really thicker. Actually, the oil paint hasn't fully cured yet, so it still contains quite a bit of liquid and is technically denser than the original since that paint has been drying for over half a century."

Gwynn pointed to the paintings. "You painted one of those?"

"Not exactly. My robot painted it, but I wrote the code to make it do it, so that counts, right?"

"Sure, why not?" Gwynn said.

Celeste placed the device back into the drawer and pulled out a thin, pencil-shaped object. "This is what's going to make it possible to create almost-perfect copies. With this device, I can determine the chemical composition of the paint without scraping it off the canvas and running through a gas chromatograph. I designed and built this device ten years ago to help detect if cars had recently been repainted. Who knew it would one day find a purpose in the world of black-market art?"

"What else do you have to show us?" Anya asked. "You are obviously in hurry for something."

Celeste blushed. "I've got a date with Johnny tonight. He says he's got some exciting news. I'm keeping my fingers crossed that he was able to talk to the Tech Services guys over at Langley about my application."

Anya said, "This is not what he has to tell you. He is excited because—"

Gwynn grabbed her arm. "Hush, Anya. Don't steal Johnny's thunder. Let him tell her."

The Russian rolled her eyes. "Whatever."

5

Parametry
(Options)

Special Agent Johnny McIntyre sat across the table from the astonishing raven-haired beauty with a brain the size of Manhattan and studied his steaming cup of after-dinner coffee. "I've got some pretty exciting news."

Dr. Celeste Mankiller gave him a smile every man in the restaurant would love to receive. "I know you do, and I can't wait to hear it. I was beginning to wonder if you were going to tell me. So, spill it, G-Man."

"Well," he began, "you're looking at the Department of Justice's newest supervisory special agent."

Celeste said, "Oh."

"Oh? Really? That's your reaction to the best news I could possibly get?"

Celeste shook her head in short staccato motions. "No . . . that didn't come out right. I'm sorry, Johnny. Of course that's fabulous news. Congratulations! Seriously, I mean it."

Johnny's frown endured. "Where were you just now? What was on your mind?"

She ducked her head. "I'm embarrassed and ashamed to tell you. It's too selfish."

He reached across the table and took her hand. "Don't worry. For now, the promotion is just a temporary assignment while Agent White is taking some time off to attend to a family medical thing. This doesn't mean we have to stop seeing each other. It's okay to be a little selfish about that. I don't want our jobs to keep us apart, either."

She said, "Yeah, I get it."

Johnny studied her expression with the discerning eye of a professional investigator. "Wait. That's not what you were thinking, was it? You weren't worried about my promotion keeping us apart."

She wouldn't let her eyes meet his. "Yeah, that was it. I'm fine. I'm sorry. I didn't mean to rain on your parade. I'm super happy for you, and I know you want that more than anything. Dinner was amazing. Thank you. Now, why don't we go somewhere and celebrate? We could go dancing, or . . . we could go back to my place."

He pulled his hand from hers. "I'm a cop, Celeste. I can tell when someone isn't telling the truth."

She scowled. "Wait a minute. Are you calling me a liar?"

He pushed his coffee cup away. "I'm just saying you're not telling me everything. What am I missing."

She folded her napkin and threw it onto her plate. "Forget it, Johnny. It's obviously not that important."

"Forget what? What just happened?"

She stood. "You're the super cop. Figure it out. I'm taking a cab. Oh, and good luck with Charlie's Angels. You're out of your league, and they're going to walk all over you."

He watched her go, but only seconds after she'd stepped through the front door of the elegant DC restaurant, she was back and plowing through her purse. She withdrew a one-hundred-dollar bill and threw it on the table. "I don't want to be a burden, so there's my half of dutch."

He stood and reached for her hand. "What's going on, Celeste? What did I do?"

She closed her eyes, took a long breath, and spoke in a calm, measured tone. "You didn't do anything, Johnny. That's the problem."

With that, she was gone, and Johnny was left standing beside the table with every eye in the dining room staring directly at him.

He tossed a second hundred onto the table and stomped his way to the bar. "Bourbon, neat. And make it something good."

The bartender wiped the mahogany landing strip in front of Johnny and leaned in. "How good?"

He looked up at the wall of bourbon behind the woman and pointed at the top shelf. "Something from up there."

"Ouch," she said. "There are only two things that make a man order from up there—the best day of his life, and the worst day. Which is it for you?"

He settled onto the barstool and slumped. "Both."

She slid the heavy tumbler across the bar with a generous pour. "That's Pappy ten year. Let me know what you think."

He lifted the glass and inhaled the smoky aroma before touching the rim to his lips. After the burn of the initial taste subsided, he took his first tasting sip and sighed. "Oh, that's nice. Excellent choice."

She tucked her towel into her apron. "Thanks. Enjoy."

Johnny studied the ripples in his whiskey when he tapped the rim with his fingernail, and time seemed to melt around him.

"Is everything okay, man?"

The bartender tapped on the bar in front of him. "Hey, man. Are you okay?"

Johnny shook himself back to reality. "What does it mean when a woman says, 'You didn't do anything, and that's the problem.'?"

The bartender threw a hand onto her hip. "Oh, boy. Is that what happened in the dining room earlier?"

Johnny nodded and took another small sip. "Yeah. Everything was going fine until I told her I got a promotion. For some reason, that made her mad, and I have no idea why."

"It wasn't the promotion. It was something else. When a woman says that, either somebody hit on us and you didn't stop him, or you promised her you'd do something, and you forgot."

Johnny popped to his feet, slammed the fifty-dollar glass of whiskey as if it were water, and threw some cash on the bar.

* * *

Celeste drove her thumb into the illuminated, round button beside the door of the brownstone and immediately knocked almost before the bell rang inside.

Anya pulled a fighting knife from a hidden sheath beneath the entry table as she stepped toward the door. "Who is there?"

"It's Celeste, and I really need to come inside."

Anya pulled the door inward and tucked the knife behind her wrist. "What is wrong?"

The tech wizard slipped by her and into the kitchen. "What do you have to drink?"

Anya sheathed the knife and stepped through the opening and into the kitchen. "I have everything. What do you want?"

Celeste huffed. "I want tequila—a lot of tequila—but that's a bad idea. How about wine?"

Anya motioned toward the cabinet. "Red is inside there, and white is in cooler."

Celeste pulled open the door and snatched a bottle from the front of the shelf while Anya placed a trio of glasses on the counter.

Celeste pulled the cork and eyed the third glass. "Who else is here?"

"Is friend Gwynn. This is okay for you, yes?"

After emptying the bottle into the three glasses, Celeste headed for the living room.

Anya held a glass toward Gwynn. "Look who is here, and she is not happy."

Gwynn took the glass from Anya and curled her feet beneath her. "What's up, Celeste?"

"Johnny!"

Anya poked Gwynn. "I told you I should tell to her about Johnny's promotion."

Celeste poured a healthy mouthful from her glass. "Oh, I know all about his supposed temporary"—she raised a hand to form air quotes—"promotion. He's so proud of himself. I asked him to do one thing for me. One! I guess it was too much to ask. I should've known. Men!"

Anya said, "What is this thing you asked from him? Maybe is too much."

Celeste lowered her chin and raised her eyebrows. "Too much? Really? This is girl time. You get that, right?"

Gwynn screwed up her face. "Yeah, about that. Anya isn't really the girl-time kinda girl, but I'm listening. So, what didn't Johnny do?"

Celeste eyed Anya. "Are all Russian women like you?"

"No. Most are very beautiful and also smart. I am exception to both of these things."

"Yeah, right," Celeste said. "Anyway, I'm sure you know, but I applied for a job at the CIA in the Office of Technical Services, and I asked Johnny to put in a good word for me over there and tell them what kind of work I do over here at Justice. That's all I asked. I really want to get into the clandestine services game. It's seriously important to me, but apparently, I'm not important enough for him to remember."

Anya set her glass on a side table. "This is not true. He cares for you very much, but it has been busy week for us, and Johnny is excited—"

Gwynn laid a hand on Anya's leg. "I've got this. You just sit there, drink your wine, and look . . . well, the way you look."

"But I was not finished with explaining to Celeste—"

"Oh, yeah, you were finished. Watch, listen, and learn, comrade."

Gwynn turned to Celeste. "Anya's right. We've been insanely busy ramping up for the new mission, but that's no excuse. Are you sure he didn't call them? Did he say he forgot?"

Celeste emptied her wineglass. "No, he didn't say it, but I know he didn't call. When I accused him of not doing it, he didn't deny it."

"I have idea," Anya said, but Gwynn cut her off.

"Let's not have ideas right now, okay?"

Celeste's cell phone rang, and she yanked it from her purse. "I don't recognize that number, so I'm not answering it. What's your idea, Anya?"

Before the Russian could spit it out, the phone chirped, and Celeste eyed the screen.

Dr. Mankiller, I'm sorry for the late call, but this is Marcus Parker at the Office of Technical Services at Langley. Please call me back.

Celeste covered her mouth with her free hand. "Oh, my God! It's somebody from CIA Tech Services."

"If this is so important to you, you should have answered call," Anya said.

Celeste thumbed the phone, and the line rang twice. "Hello, Dr. Mankiller. This is Marcus Parker, and I'm the assistant director of the Office of Technical Services out here at Langley. I noticed your résumé on my desk, and I spoke with an SSA McIntyre with the Organized Crime Task Force over at Justice. He says you're the real deal."

She cleared her throat. "Uh, hello, Mr. Parker. I'm sorry I didn't answer earlier. I was—"

"It's okay, doctor. I understand. According to SSA McIntyre, I'd be a fool to pass up the chance to get you on my staff."

"I don't know what to say, sir. I'm flattered."

"Why don't you stop by my office tomorrow morning around ten, and we can have an informal chat."

"Ten . . . tomorrow. Yeah, sure, that'd be great. I, uh, don't know where your office is, though, sir."

"In that case, Dr. Mankiller, I'll come to your office, and you can show me around the DOJ's techno hobby shop while we talk about your future with the Agency."

The line went dead, and Celeste sat staring at the cell phone in her hand. "That was the CIA."

Gwynn's grin widened. "What did they say?"

"He said he's coming to the lab tomorrow for a tour and to talk about my future with the CIA."

"So, Johnny came through?" Gwynn asked.

Celeste bowed her head. "It looks like it, and I'm an ass for storming out on him. He's going to hate me."

Anya said, "This is silly thing to believe. It was only small disagreement and maybe little anger, but he is in love with you. Everyone knows this . . . except maybe you."

The tech shook her head. "I'm such an idiot. I'm calling him."

Anya threw up her hand. "Wait. Before you do this, you must hear also my idea."

"Can't it wait long enough for me to call and apologize?"

Anya checked her watch. "Okay, yes. Five minutes only, though. Is getting late, and we must make telephone call to Georgia."

Celeste placed the phone to her ear and waited. She furrowed her brow. "Johnny, it's me, Celeste. I so badly wanted you to pick up. I'm an idiot, and I'm really sorry. I promise to make it up to you. It won't happen again, I promise. Please call me. It doesn't matter what time. Just call, okay? I'm sorry." She laid the phone on her thigh "He sent me to voicemail. He's got to be furious with me. I was such an ass to him."

Anya said, "He is man, and you are beautiful, exciting, and brilliant woman. He will not be mad for too long with you. Now, are you ready for my idea?"

"Sure, let's hear it."

Anya resituated herself on the couch. "Is money a problem for you?"

Celeste scowled. "What? What do you mean?"

"I mean, if you go to work with CIA, will you have more money than here with us?"

She shrugged. "I guess that depends on how well I negotiate my deal with them, but in general, the techs over there are GS-twelves and thirteens, so yeah, it would be a nice raise. Plus, they get a special salary rate of twenty-five percent above scale."

Anya said, "What if you worked in private company for maybe two or three times payment at CIA?"

"There aren't many jobs in my field outside the government."

"What if I told to you I know people who would pay very high salary for what you can do?"

Celeste perked up. "Are they legal?"

"Yes, they are legitimate team of operators. Mostly, they were Special Forces, but the leader of team was never inside military."

Gwynn slapped her leg. "Anya, no! No! You're not calling Chase. Nothing good can come of that."

"Everything good can come of this," Anya said. "Maybe Celeste has better job with laboratory of her own and much better salary. Is okay." She paused and turned to Celeste. "I will call and make to Chase recommendation that he should hire you for team."

"Wait a minute," Celeste said. "Is that the same Chase who used to be your boyfriend or whatever?"

"Chase is not boy. He is big, strong man, and he is very good at covert operations. They have person named Marvin who is very smart. They call him also Mongo because he is very big—over two meters and maybe one hundred forty kilos."

"Oh, my," Celeste said. "He *is* a big boy."

Gwynn cocked her head as the metric to English conversion danced with the wine in her brain. "Wait. Isn't that like three hundred pounds?"

Anya said, "Yes, he is very big, but inside, he is kind and gentle like kitten, and he is person who builds for them what they need. But he cannot do things you can do. You would very much like working with this team."

Celeste let her finger glide across the rim of her wineglass. "I don't know. Let's see what the CIA offers before you screw up my government pension."

Anya smiled. "You will not need government pension after only few years with Chase. He is most generous and kind person I have ever known, and for question, yes, he was my only real boyfriend of whole life."

Celeste looked down at her vibrating phone. "Speaking of boyfriends..."

6

Zhutkiy (Spooky)

Anya settled to the floor beside her bed. She stretched her back and long legs, just as she'd done every morning since she'd begun training as a gymnast for the Soviet Union so many years before. The slow, deliberate stretch until her fingers were interlaced beneath her foot felt familiar and warm as the muscles surrendered and relaxed. The doorbell interrupted the second phase of her routine, and she hopped to her feet.

"Good morning, Anya. I hope I'm not disturbing you."

She pulled the door open and smiled. "Good morning, Ray. Is nice to see you. I did not know you knew where I live."

He stepped through the doorway. "I know a lot of things about you, but that doesn't stop you from constantly surprising me."

"Come, come. I will make tea, or perhaps you would like coffee with me."

"Tea sounds nice. Thank you."

Anya closed the door and twisted the deadbolt. "Come with me to kitchen. We will talk while water is warming."

He followed her through the foyer and into the tiled kitchen, where her copper teapot rested on the eye of the stove. She filled the pot and twisted the control, igniting blue flames and beginning the water on its journey to becoming tea.

"You are not here on matter of business, are you?"

Ray pulled a chair from beneath the small table and settled onto it. "This is what you might call a dual-purpose visit. First, I want to thank you for getting me in to see Dr. Müller. I didn't sleep much last night, as you might imagine, but I did some research on him, and the general consensus seems to be that he's one of the best in the world."

"This is not true," Anya said. "He is not *one* of best. He is *the* best neurosurgeon in all of world."

Ray played with a small salt shaker molded to look like a tiny bird. "I checked into the clinic, as well, and there's over a year waiting list to get an appointment. How is it that you can call up the doctor and get me an appointment in two days?"

"Is good to have friends."

He slid the shaker back in place beside its twin. "You're being modest. Come on . . . how'd you do it?"

She shrugged and leaned against the counter. "Dr. Müller saved life of someone who is very dear to me, so I did for him favor, and he believes favor is big enough to always 'owe me one,' as they say. You know this saying?"

"Yeah, I know the saying. You scratch my back, and I'll scratch yours."

"Is back itching? I will look for maybe rash or bug bite if you want. You do not have to also scratch my back. I am—"

Ray chuckled. "No, that's not what I meant. My back is fine. It's just a saying that means I'll do you a favor if you'll do one for me."

"Ah, this is confusing saying, but is okay. So, I never call to Dr. Müller and ask for favor until yesterday, and of course he says yes."

Ray said, "Well, whatever you did for him, it must've been a big one. I really want you to know how much I appreciate you calling him."

"You have said already thank you for this favor. Is not necessary again. You are my friend, and you have problem I can help to solve. This is friend thing to do."

The teakettle whistled, and Anya pulled it from the flaming eye. She poured two cups over teabags with tabs written in Cyrillic and slid one toward Ray. "Honey?"

"Yes, please."

She dribbled honey into his mug until he waved her off, and then she added a few drops to her mug. "What is other reason for coming to my house this morning?"

Ray blew across the dark surface of the tea. "It's about Johnny."

"Oh, is okay. Celeste was here last night, and they are not fighting anymore."

"Fighting? What are you talking about?"

Anya frowned. "You did not know this?"

"Know what?"

"Celeste wants to work in other place for maybe CIA, and she thought Johnny did not make request of CIA to offer her position in Technical Services."

Ray lifted his mug, but he stopped before touching his lips. "Celeste is leaving?"

"Maybe. She has maybe interview today and maybe offer from CIA soon, but I told to her also I would make call to Chase and ask if he needs someone like her. He will make better salary and more interesting work for her."

Ray leaned back in his chair. "I'm not so sure that's a great idea."

"Is wonderful idea. She would like very much working with Chase's team."

"No, that's not what I meant. I don't think it's such a great idea that *you* call Chase. That would put him in a tough position. Trust me, I know how hard it is to tell you no, and I'm sure it's no different for Chase."

"You are worrying for nothing. He his strong man with strong will. He will tell to me no if this is what he means. He is very good at telling to me no." She let her gaze fall to the floor.

Ray said, "Let's get back to the subject of Johnny Mac. You know I put him in charge while I'm gone, but that doesn't mean he can make any real decisions. I just need you and your sidekick to go easy on him. Do you think you can do that?"

"For Gwynn, this will be easy. For me, not so easy. I am sometimes not very obedient. When I have idea, I do it instead of asking if is okay. I think this will not change, no matter who is in charge."

White grinned. "Oh, I know, but don't do anything outrageous while I'm gone. Can you promise me that?"

"I can make promise to try, but may not be possible. Mission is dangerous and may require adapting and changing plan many times. Gwynn and I will do this, but is not always time to ask for permission."

"I get it," he said, "but at least make Johnny feel like he's in charge when you can."

"Yes, I can do this. I do it all of time with you."

He shook his head and enjoyed his tea.

"When is flight?" Anya asked.

Ray checked his watch. "Three hours. I plan to be back by the weekend if everything goes well so you won't have to put up with Johnny too long."

"If tumor is real, Dr. Müller will do surgery immediately. He is very aggressive doctor. You will be there until he says is okay to fly back to America."

Ray placed his mug back on the table. "Oh, I thought this was just a consultation. I didn't know he would do the surgery right away."

"Is silly to fly so far for only consultation. He is not man of procrastination. He is man of action. You will see."

Ray examined his mug and downed the final sip. They rose from the table in unison and laced their arms around each other.

He whispered, "You're a pain my butt, Anastasia Burinkova, but I've got a feeling you may have just saved my life."

She held him a moment longer. "You have very cute butt, so being pain in it is fun for me. You will call on telephone to tell me what Dr. Müller says to you, yes?"

"Yeah, I'll call." He stepped back. "Listen, there's one more thing.

Johnny doesn't know about my cancer. I told him it was a family medical thing I had to take care of. That's not really a lie, but it's not exactly the truth, either. I'd appreciate if you and Gwynn could keep this on the down-low until . . . well, until you can't."

"Yes, of course. We will tell no one, but we are worried for you."

"Don't worry. We all have to go sometime. Maybe this is my time."

She gave him a shove. "This is not your time, Ray White. I have to be pain in butt for you for many more years."

"Does that mean you're not leaving?"

"I am not leaving," she said. "I made promise to you and to friend Gwynn. I am woman who keeps promises. Now, go. You have plane to catch and doctor to meet. I have art thief to catch."

"About that," White said. "You make sure Celeste Mankiller doesn't leave the DOJ until we finish this job. We need her and her copycat painting robot."

Without another word, she opened the door and watched Ray White's cute butt walk down the stairs to the waiting black Suburban at the curb.

* * *

An hour later, Anya joined Gwynn, Celeste, and Johnny Mac in their small office, and the new boss called the meeting to order.

"Okay, here's what I have in mind. You two are going to steal a painting that Morozov can't live without."

Anya's eyes lit up. "I like this plan. Maybe you should be always in charge."

Johnny raised his hand. "Don't get too excited. You're not actually going to steal the painting. We're just going to borrow it. But first, you're going to try to buy it."

Gwynn leaned in, but Anya said, "I liked plan better when we were going to steal painting. Anyone can buy painting. This is boring."

Johnny said, "Oh, I think you'll change your mind when you hear who's going to be there. Next Saturday evening, Sotheby's auction in Chicago is offering eleven pieces of art, four of which have never been sold at auction. One of those four is a painting called *The Tsarina's Monk* that supposedly came by way of a private commission around nineteen oh seven. It depicts Rasputin in his monk's habit."

Anya said, "I know also this painting. Is called *Monakh Tsaritsy* in Russian. Is very controversial. I have never seen it, but I have seen photograph. Is shocking and dark."

Johnny slid a pair of pictures across the desk. "I'd say that describes it quite well."

Gwynn and Anya lifted the pictures, and Gwynn gasped. "That's spooky."

Anya studied the picture. "Rasputin was strange person, and I think also spooky."

"Do we know who painted it?" Gwynn asked.

Johnny pulled out a blown-up image of the lower right corner of the painting. "It's signed, but no one can make out the signature. Apparently, the signature doesn't appear on any other works of art from the period. Legend has it that Rasputin claimed the image was painted by Ugly Neba, whatever that means."

Anya said, "This means Angels of Heaven. After Rasputin had religious conversion, he believed he interacted with angels almost constantly. He even said he could not always tell difference between people and angels because they were so common to him. Like I said, he was very strange person."

Johnny did his best to sound like Agent White when he slapped the desk. "Children, we don't have time to go down any rabbit holes. Try to stay with me. You three are going to the viewing and reception on Friday night in Chicago. Anya and Gwynn will pose as representatives of an anonymous buyer, and Celeste, you'll be there to run the tech. Is everyone good with that?"

Celeste made a face, and Johnny asked, "What?"

She said, "It's just that it would be cleaner if I were in the gallery with Gwynn and Anya in case the glasses fail and need to be reset. Also, somebody has to carry a signal repeater so we can pipe the images and data out to the van. Having a tech team in a van outside makes crunching the data a lot faster and safer. I just want you to have all the facts before making the decision."

Johnny contorted his nose. "Of course I thought about that, but now that you mention it, I think you're right. My original idea was a good one. We'll put the three of you inside the gallery and a tech-ops van on the street. Got it?"

Heads nodded, and he continued. "Good. We don't believe Morozov himself will be there, but there's no question that he'll have his people at the reception and the auction. I need the two of you to identify them and make sure they notice you."

Anya slid a hand around Gwynn's arm. "We are impossible to forget, so this will be for us very easy."

7

VETRENYY GOROD (THE WINDY CITY)

Anya stared into the darkening evening between skyscrapers as Celeste, Gwynn, and she stepped from the chauffeured car and onto Superior Street in Chicago. "This is beautiful city. Why have you not brought me here before today?"

"I've never *brought* you anywhere," Gwynn said. "But Chicago wouldn't be high on the list if I were your travel planner."

"What is wrong with city of Chicago?"

Celeste said, "I'll take this one. The violent crime rate is out of control. Homelessness is a huge problem. It's bitter cold in the winter, and the wind never stops blowing. A few really great restaurants are Chicago's only endearing quality, in my opinion."

A bellman dressed in a uniform that would make him right at home with the queen's guard grabbed his chest as if suffering a stab wound. "That hurts, ladies. Our fair city may be everything you said, but now, you've got me and the Peninsula, the best bellman, and the finest luxury hotel in the city."

Celeste slid a folded bill into the bellman's palm. "Forgive me. I may have been a little hasty to judgment. We're thankful to have you and such luxurious accommodations."

"What brings you ladies to town?"

Grasping the opportunity to lay the first bit of groundwork in the city, Anya said, "I am here to purchase painting, and my associates are here to make sure no one stops me."

"Ah, really?" the bellman asked with what could've been authentic interest. "Would I know the painting?"

"Probably not. Is Russian and is called *Monakh Tsaritsy*. This means—"

The bellman said, "Tsarina's Monk."

The three women stared at him, and Anya said, "How do you know this?"

The man shrugged. "I married a girl from Sochi on the Black Sea. I listened to a million conversations in Russian with her mother—God rest her soul. Even an uneducated schmuck like me picks up a few words in thirty years' time."

He loaded their bags onto his cart, and Anya gave him a sparkling smile. "*Spasibo*."

He shot her a wink. "*Pozhaluysta*."

To their surprise, the bellman managed to beat them to their suite.

"You're quick," Gwynn said.

He tipped his cap. "Just efficient, ma'am."

After offloading their bags, he asked, "Shall I have someone come unpack for you?"

"That is not necessary," Anya said. "But we may need to have some things pressed. You can do this for us, yes?"

He offered a nod. "*Da*. My name is Phillip, and I'm at your service."

The three unpacked, and Anya poured champagne. "To visiting city of Chicago for first time!"

The three clinked glasses, drank, and nestled into the luxurious sofa.

Celeste examined the tiny bubbles rising in her flute. "This isn't bad for complimentary champagne."

Anya laughed. "Nothing is complimentary. We pay for everything, even if Phillip says is complimentary."

"Touché."

"I have for you question," Anya said. "What would three women do inside city of Chicago if traveling only for fun?"

Gwynn said, "We're not traveling for fun. We're on assignment. Don't forget that."

"Yes, of course, but I am saying if maybe we were not police officers. Maybe we were accountants or maybe teachers on holiday. What would we do?"

Gwynn lowered her chin. "Don't do it, Anya. Work comes first. We can play when the work is done."

Celeste drained her flute and placed it on the table. "Oh, come on, Gwynn. Live a little. Let's play Anya's game. The first thing that I'd do is go shopping. There are some amazing shops here."

"Like New York?" Anya asked.

The tech rolled her eyes. "Well, no, not like New York, but pretty close. Hey! Maybe we can do both shopping and working. We do need something unforgettable to wear to the gala and the auction, right?"

Anya and Celeste turned to Gwynn, who was still shaking her head. "Well . . . maybe it wouldn't hurt to do a little shopping. You know, just to make sure Morozov notices us."

Anya frowned. "He will not be here. He is recluse, remember? He will send person, but this person will be easy to find."

"What makes you say that?" Celeste asked.

"He will be alone, only interested in one painting, and will probably be Russian. But there is one more way we will know for sure. I will spend much time with painting and make it obvious that I want to purchase it. This will get his attention, and he will be obviously concerned."

"I love how your brain works," Gwynn said. "I wish mine could do that."

"Your mind is beautiful," Anya said. "You think inside of law, and this is important for job. Everything that happens around you is either legal or is not, and you know all of this. For me, law is fuzzy line and sometimes not line at all."

Gwynn poured more champagne. "Trust me, I know this about you. I've never seen anyone with less regard for rules than you."

"Rules are limits, and for me, I do not accept limits. When I was little girl, my mother said to me, 'You can do everything, Anastasia. Never forget this.'" She bowed her head as the few memories she had of her mother poured over her.

Gwynn laid a hand on her leg. "I'm sorry, Anya. I'll never understand what you went through as a little girl, but I do care, and I want to help."

Anya laid her hand on top of Gwynn's. "This is why you are my dear friend. I will forever have you inside my heart in place right beside my mother."

Gwynn squeezed. "I don't know what to say. I'm honored."

A moment of silence passed, and Anya said, "I am sorry for having memory like this. Is okay now. Phillip will get for us car and driver so we can go shopping, yes?"

Celeste grabbed the phone. "I'm on it."

Thirty seconds later, she placed the phone back in its cradle with a flourish. "Our car will be ready in thirty minutes."

Phillip held the doors and installed them in the back of a Town Car, and the driver took in the sight of the three most beautiful tourists in the city. "Good evening, ladies. Where are we going, and am I overdressed?"

Giggles arose, and Anya said, "We will go first to Versace. You know this store, yes?"

The driver checked the traffic, pulled the car into drive, and accelerated away from the curb. "I'll have you there in no time."

Less than five minutes later, he pulled to a stop and stepped from the car. He opened the rear door and was rewarded with his first up-close look at the blonde Russian goddess, the girl-next-door brunette, and the raven-haired PhD.

He produced a card. "Call this number when you're ready to go, and I'll appear as if by magic."

Anya plucked the card from his fingers and gave him a smile. "And I can keep card for anytime I might want you to appear like magic?"

He almost blushed. "For that, there's a different number, but I'll be glad to give you that one, too."

The shopping adventure turned into an excursion, and Anya's credit card, drawn on a bank in the Cayman Islands, suffered a few painful blows. The driver and his Town Car proved unnecessary with so many shops so close together, just off the world-famous Magnificent Mile. With the shopping complete and an unforgettable dinner at a French restaurant even Anya couldn't pronounce, they stepped back onto the sidewalk of Rush Avenue.

Anya's eyes explored the street in search of threats, but she saw none. "I have idea. I think we should go for walk."

Celeste locked eyes with Gwynn and said, "Uh, I'm not so sure that's a great plan. This is Chicago, and we should probably let the driver take us back to the hotel."

Anya scoffed. "This is ridiculous. Is only few-minute walk back to hotel, but I want to see river."

"It's not exactly safe for the three of us to be walking around at this hour."

Anya eyed Celeste as if she'd spoken Greek. "Safe? We have with us Special Agent Gwynn Davis, who is very dangerous woman. We have no reason to be afraid."

Gwynn said, "Easy, there. I'm not exactly Wonder Woman, but I'm pretty sure you can get us out of any situation that comes to us."

Anya shrugged and held up her thumb and index finger about an inch apart. "Maybe I have tiny bit of skill on street to keep us safe. Is okay, Celeste. Come, come. We will walk to river and then back to hotel. If you do not feel safe, we will call for car, okay?"

The tech said, "Okay, but we've got a few thousand dollars' worth of clothes, shoes, and jewelry being delivered tomorrow, and I intend to be alive to wear every bit of it."

Anya hooked her arm. "I promise to you I will not let anything happen to you, and you can wear everything all at once if this is what you wish."

The southbound stroll deposited them at the edge of the Chicago River, and Anya seemed captivated.

Gwynn gave her a hip bump. "Pretty cool, huh?"

"Is very small river. I expected much bigger."

"If it's big water you want to see, just turn around and follow the river to the east. You'll fall right into Lake Michigan."

"Maybe I will do this so I can say I have been in water of Lake Michigan. I think I would like to see all of Great Lakes. You have seen them, yes?"

Gwynn studied her friend, who wore the look of a fascinated child. "Not yet, but let's add the other four to our list, and we'll make it happen."

Celeste said, "Hey, how do I get in on this girls' trip."

"You are invited, too," Anya said. "This reminds me. You thought about my offer to call my friend Chase for you, yes?"

Celeste sighed. "Yeah, I thought about it, but I have to hear what the CIA offers before I'm willing to look elsewhere."

"Offer is good when you decide. Come on. Let's cross bridge and explore more of city."

Celeste stepped back. "I'm afraid I'm going to take a pass."

Anya said, "Have you never heard saying about life beginning at edge of zone of comfort? This means—"

Celeste chuckled. "Yeah, I know what it means, and this bridge across this river definitely represents the edge of my comfort zone."

Anya said, "You have gun, yes?"

"No, I don't have a gun. I'm not an agent. I'm a Tech Services geek. I don't even have a badge."

"This is why you want to work for CIA? Because you can have badge and gun?"

Celeste said, "I'm not sure you know what the CIA is. They don't carry badges or guns in this country. When they're overseas, sometimes they're armed, but not always."

Before the tech knew what had happened, she realized they'd crossed the bridge and ventured farther south into the city. "You're good."

Ten minutes into their exploration, Anya turned down a darkened street, and Gwynn and Celeste hesitantly followed.

"Well, look what we've got here, boys."

Four young men stepped from the shadows, two in front of the women and two behind.

Gwynn pulled her credentials from her pocket and held up her badge. "You're making a mistake, boys."

The men laughed. "Oh, look. A badge. Isn't that cute? I'll take that *and* your purse, bitch!"

The man moved toward Gwynn, but Anya stepped between them. "My friend said you are making mistake. This means you can walk away and not be hurt. This is what you should do."

"Oh, is that right? Now some Australian or German chick's gonna tell us what to do, huh?" The man reached into his back pocket and produced a switchblade.

Anya smiled. "This is cute little knife. Your small mistake is now great big terrible decision. I will take from you little knife and shove it down your throat if you do not turn and walk away."

The two men from behind drew knives of their own and stepped forward.

Anya hissed. "Is last chance to walk away."

The man lunged toward her, and she sidestepped the attack, sending a crushing elbow strike to his chin. He wilted to the street, and Anya spun on a heel.

Gwynn drew her Glock with her right hand and pushed Celeste behind her with her left. "Put down the knives, and get on your knees!"

The first of the two men from behind lunged toward Gwynn and reached for her gun. She yanked it from his reach, planted a foot in front of his, and pivoted, sending the man face-first onto the sidewalk.

Anya dodged a slicing blow from the second man and caught his arm. The sound that followed when the bones and soft tissue of his elbow separated was almost as sickening as the bellowing cry he made when his face collided with the storefront. A stream of blood followed him down the wall until he came to rest in a heap with a broken arm, a destroyed nose, and several missing teeth.

The single man remaining on his feet scanned between Anya and Gwynn before making the best decision of his life. He turned and ran, leaving his three defeated friends lying in the street.

Celeste pulled out her cell phone, but Anya grabbed it. "What are you doing?"

"I'm calling nine-one-one," Celeste said.

"No, you cannot do this. Is terrible idea. We cannot give statement to police. No one can know we are also police."

Celeste studied the carnage. "How did you two . . . ? I mean, that was amazing."

Anya laced a hand through Celeste's arm. "Chicago may be dangerous city for *other* people, but for Gwynn and me, is just another day at office."

8

ODNA IZ DEVUSHEK (ONE OF THE GIRLS)

Celeste lay alone in her bed, reliving the events of the evening. The question that wouldn't leave her mind was about the man she was falling in love with. *Could Johnny Mac put down would-be attackers on the street the way Anya and Gwynn had done?*

Not all special agents were created equal, of course, but the brutality and blinding speed of the two agents who were quickly becoming superheroes in her mind left Celeste believing the skill Gwynn and Anya displayed on the street was not something they learned in the Federal Law Enforcement Training Center, and maybe, if they could learn to do it, so could she.

Breakfast was scrambled eggs, toasted English muffins, bacon, orange juice, and a pair of enormous, looming questions.

Celeste wiped her mouth. "Can you two teach me to do that?"

Gwynn looked up from her eggs. "Do what?"

Celeste waved her fork through the air. "That thing you did last night when those guys tried to mug us. Can you teach me that?"

Gwynn turned to Anya. "This one is all yours, comrade."

The Russian didn't hesitate. "Yes, of course we can teach to you skills, but skill is not what makes us dangerous. We have also willingness to put skills into action. This is thing that cannot be taught. You must have this inside you if you will be what Gwynn and I are."

Celeste recoiled. "Who wouldn't have the willingness to do that in a life-and-death situation?"

Anya shrugged. "You have heard of fight-or-flight reactions, yes?"

"Yeah, sure. Everybody knows about that."

"Is incomplete."

"Incomplete?" Celeste asked. "What do you mean?"

Anya laid down her fork. "There is third option, and is most often reaction people have when faced with possible death. Fight-or-flight is option you can choose, but third is freeze. We do not choose to freeze when faced with danger, but often it happens. This is what we train to prevent."

Celeste let the profoundness of Anya's lesson sink in. "I guess this is my real question. Would I learn stuff like that if I went to work for your old boyfriend?"

Gwynn almost choked on her latest mouthful. "Boyfriend? Oh, that's good, but you're not seriously thinking about leaving the government to work for a defense contractor, are you?"

Anya cocked her head. "Why is word *boyfriend* funny? Perhaps he was my boyfriend. I love him."

Gwynn lowered her gaze. "You mean you *loved* him. Past tense, right?"

Anya let her eyes drift to the ceiling and the memory of the sun on her face and the wind in her hair aboard Chase's sailboat. "If you say so."

Celeste's curiosity was suddenly piqued. "You're still in love with him, aren't you?"

Anya almost blushed. "Is for two people only to be *in* love. One person cannot be *in* love, and Chase has Penny for wife now. He is very happy, and I am happy also for him."

Gwynn scoffed. "You almost made that sound sincere, but you're not fooling anybody. If Penny weren't in the picture, you'd pounce on that man so fast it would look like a cheetah attack."

"Is time for changing of subject. Do you want job with Chase or with CIA?"

Celeste swallowed, then took a sip of orange juice. "Why can't I do both?"

Anya said, "Give to me telephone."

Celeste produced her cell and slid it across the table.

Seconds later, Anya pressed the speaker button.

"Hello, this is Chase."

"Chasechka! Is Anya Burinkova. Is serious call for serious reason. Is okay that I called you, yes?"

Chase stared at the number on the screen of his phone. "Two things . . . First, we agreed that you'd stop calling me Chasechka, and second, you don't have to tell me your last name every time we talk. You're the only Anya I know."

She smiled. "Is not real last name anyway. On license for driving and DOJ credentials is Ana Fulton, just like your last name."

He sighed. "You said this was important, so let's hear it."

Anya rearranged herself and brushed a strand of hair from her face as if Chase could see her. "I have person you will hire for job. Her name is Celeste Mankiller, and she is brilliant genius inside laboratory. She can build anything and is technology wizard."

"Can she make a printer work?"

"Why would you ask something like this?"

"Because I'm in a holy war with one that refuses to stay connected to my computer."

"Yes, she can fix this. You must pay her one quarter of million dollars for every year."

Chase let out a long whistle. "That's pretty steep for a printer repair."

"No, silly boy, this not for repairing only printer. She is Technical Services officer at Department of Justice. You know of this department, yes?"

"Yeah, I know what Tech Services is, but I didn't know the DOJ had a branch."

"There are many things you do not know, but this moment is not best time for discussing this. Give to Celeste interview for job. She is here. Ask first question."

"Hello, Celeste. I'm Chase. It's nice to *meet* you."

"Hi, Chase. Sorry, I didn't really mean for Anya to call you right now."

He laughed. "Don't apologize. She's impossible to control. That's one of the things that makes her so irresistible."

Anya's eyes widened into saucers, and she beamed toward Gwynn and mouthed, "He said I am irresistible. You heard this, yes?"

Gwynn pressed a finger to her lips. "Shh."

Celeste leered at Anya. "You obviously know her well."

"You could say that," Chase said. "Listen, now's not a great time for this, but let me ask a couple of quick questions. How much clandestine operations experience do you have, and how's your clearance?"

"I've been with DOJ for six years after earning my doctorate, so I've not worked directly with clandestine services other than to design, manufacture, test, and field covert systems and implements for use by agents of the DOJ. And I have a TS/SCI clearance."

"Why aren't you working for DARPA or the Agency?"

She dug in and swung on the hanging curveball. "Because I want to work for you."

Chase showed no reaction. "One more thing. Is your last name really Mankiller?"

"It really is."

"Then you might fit right in around here. Give me a good contact number for you, and I'll be in touch when I'm not digging a foxhole."

Celeste furrowed her brow. "Did you really answer the phone while digging a foxhole?"

"It's not technically a foxhole," he said. "It'll be a grave as soon as we see our target."

She gave him her number and said, "I really hope you're kidding about the foxhole thing."

He laughed. "You'll get used to it when you come on board. Oh, and tell Ana Fulton I want my UGA sweatshirt back."

Celeste eyed Anya. "I suspect the only way you're getting that sweatshirt back is if she comes with it."

Chase made a sound none of the three could decipher, and the line went dead.

Breakfast ended, and the deliveries from the previous day's shopping trip arrived. They unpacked their dresses, shoes, and accessories, and Celeste said, "I can't believe we're allowed to buy this stuff on the government credit card."

Gwynn and Anya locked eyes, and the Russian pressed a finger to her lips, but Gwynn couldn't let it play out. "We didn't buy these on the government card. Anya bought them for us."

Celeste gasped. "Oh, no! Then I can't keep them. That's not right."

Anya said, "You must keep them. They are gift from me because you are my friend. And I have one more gift."

The tech said, "Anya, that's so sweet, seriously, but this stuff cost a fortune."

Anya said, "When my father died, he left for me some money, and I have made wise investments. Also, I worked with Chase and was paid well. It makes me happy to give to my friends gifts. You will look beautiful in dresses, and this will also make me happy."

Celeste threw her arms around the Russian. "You're too much. I'm really going to miss you."

"Miss me?" Anya said. "Where are you going?"

Celeste said, "If I take the job at the CIA, or even the one with Chase, either way, I'll miss you."

"This is terrible thing to say. Just because you work for other agency, this does not mean we are not friends. We will still see each other and have girls' trips to cities better than Chicago where no one tries to attack us."

Gwynn asked, "What's this other gift you mentioned?"

Anya grinned and squirmed like an excited teenager. "We have day inside spa downstairs for everything to make us beautiful for tonight."

"You have no idea how much I need a spa day. You're the best," Gwynn said.

"Is not really gift from me yet. I charged it to our suite because I want our temporary boss to see it and panic. If is too much, I will pay for, but maybe DOJ will pay bill."

Spa day almost went off without a hitch until the acting special agent in charge showed up inside the plush spa wearing a suit far too nice for any G-Man to have in his closet. "Do any of you want to tell me what's going on here? You're supposed to be working, not getting pedicures and facials."

"We are preparing for work," Anya said. "It is part of our job to look beautiful, so we are becoming beautiful. And speaking of beautiful, that is very nice suit. You look very dapper. This is word, yes? Dapper?"

Johnny Mac shot his cuffs and dusted off an imaginary piece of fluff from his lapel. "You like?"

"Is perfect for you," Anya said. "But your fingernails look like man who works inside car repair garage. Sit, sit. You must have manicure if you are wearing suit so nice."

Johnny curled his fingers and inspected his nails. "I guess they are looking a little ragged. Maybe you're right."

Minutes later, Supervisory Special Agent Johnathon McIntyre's suit was replaced with a soft robe, and he was instantly transformed into one of the girls.

9

POKAZHI MNE TVOI (SHOW ME YOURS)

Back in the suite, Gwynn was the first to emerge from her room wearing a shimmering blue dress, cut lower than necessary at the neck, with a slit almost to her left hip.

Johnny Mac swallowed hard. "You look . . . I mean, that's a really great dress."

She spun on the ball of her foot. "Thank you, boss, but you may want to put your tongue back in your mouth before your girlfriend comes through that door and catches you gawking at your subordinate."

"I wasn't gawking. I was . . ."

Just as Gwynn predicted, Celeste stepped from her room with her long black hair glistening against her skin and an off-the-shoulder dress that looked as if it had been perfectly designed and stitched just for her.

Suddenly, Johnny forgot all about Gwynn and likely forgot his own name. "Wow!"

Celeste grinned. "I'll take that reaction any day. So, you think anyone will notice us at the reception tonight?"

Johnny shook his head. "It would be impossible for anyone *not* to notice you. And you have no idea how glad I am that you're not in my chain of command. I can ogle all I want."

Celeste winked. "Ogling is approved, Supervisory Special Agent."

Everything about the room changed in an instant the moment Anya stepped through her door in a black dress that made her look as if she just stepped off the cover of *Vogue*.

Celeste and Gwynn turned to see the Russian goddess, and Celeste said, "I hate you so much right now. I've never looked better than I do right now, and you had to show up looking like that. Next to you, I'm a troll."

Anya extended her arms toward her partner. "And this is exactly how I feel when I look at Gwynn. If she is not inside room, I can have choice of anyone in there, but when she shows up, I am also troll."

Celeste rolled her eyes, "Yeah, that's exactly how the rest of the world sees you . . . as a troll. Give me a break. I'm not going to lie, though. I'm okay being second runner-up behind you two any day. We're going to knock their socks off tonight."

Johnny leaned toward the tech and whispered, "You can knock far more than just my socks off anytime you want."

She brushed the back of her hand against his cheek. "I know, and that's the plan for later, Supervisory Special Agent."

He cleared his throat and stepped back. "Okay. So, tonight. We've got the van up and ready. You're wearing the signal repeater, right?"

Celeste pulled up her dress to reveal a small black box strapped high on the inside of her thigh, and Johnny wiped a bead of sweat from his brow. "Okay, yeah . . . That's it. And how about you two? Are you carrying?"

Anya said, "I have knives, but not gun. Would you like to see?"

Celeste jumped in. "No! He would not like to see. He'll take your word for it."

Gwynn said, "Same for me, but I'm not showing you."

Johnny sighed. "I may not be cut out for this. I don't know how Agent White does it."

Gwynn said, "You're doing fine, Johnny. Agent White would be proud. Are you going to be in the van?"

"Thank you, Davis. I appreciate that. Yes, I'll be in the van, but we're not going to have comms. There's nowhere to put them. I will have an additional agent inside keeping an eye on you, and he'll have comms with us. Something tells me you'll be glad to see him."

Gwynn cocked her head. "Why would I be glad to see him?"

Johnny said, "I had to go shopping outside the DOJ, and I just happened to stumble upon a particular Air Force Office of Special Investigations officer who needed a little side gig."

Gwynn rose onto her toes. "You got Tom?"

"You know it."

Gwynn threw her arms around him. "Yep, you're doing just fine in command."

Johnny pushed her away. "How about a little professionalism?"

Gwynn chuckled. "You weren't asking for professionalism when Celeste hiked up her dress to show you her . . . transmitter."

He ignored the jab. "Just remember, you're art buyers, not tourists. You're there specifically to buy the *Monakh Tsaritsy*, but you won't be the only ones. We're confident a buyer representing Nikiti Morozov will be there for exactly the same reason. Your job is to photograph the painting and Morozov's buyer. There's nothing more important than finding out who the buyer is. He's crucial for phase two."

Anya said, "Is actually phase three when buyer is crucial. Phase two is . . . Well, everyone knows what phase two is."

Gwynn said, "Everybody except me, apparently."

Johnny let his eyes dance between Anya and Gwynn. "She'll explain it to you when the time comes. For now, just get the pictures and find a way to get lost inside the auction house."

* * *

The driver of the Bentley Mulsanne pulled to a stop outside Sotheby's auction house on North Michigan Avenue, and a gentleman in a top hat and tails held open the rear door of the enormous car. The world seemed to stop turning for the moment it took Gwynn, Celeste, and Anya to step from the back seat and onto the sidewalk.

They accepted flutes of champagne as they entered the gallery, and Gwynn picked Captain Tom Elsmore out of the crowd immediately. His greater-than-six-foot height put him above the crowd, but it was his broad shoulders and sculpted jawline that truly set him apart. Gwynn couldn't suppress the smile, but Tom, in perfect, all-business form, simply gave her a barely perceptible nod.

Anya leaned close to Gwynn and whispered, "He is perfect man, no?"

"He is for me."

They sipped their champagne and strolled by every painting in the gallery. Celeste produced a leather-bound notepad from somewhere and pretended to make notes on several of the masterpieces until they came to the *Monakh Tsaritsy*, where a gentleman stood blocking a third of the painting from view.

Anya laid a hand on his back and gently pushed him aside, and in a voice louder than her typical tone, she said, "You will move from in front of my painting now."

The man turned. "What did you say to me?"

Anya continued pushing him. "You are in front of painting that will be mine. You will now move."

"Look, lady. I don't know who you think you are, but putting your hands on me and ordering me to move is the fastest way to be removed from this preview."

Anya glanced at Gwynn before locking eyes with the man. She spoke in harsh Russian. "This man will either move, or I will write huge check to next gallery that sells this painting instead of this one."

As if summoned from thin air, two men dressed similarly to the doorman stepped beside the gentleman and gently encouraged him to move on.

Anya said "*Spasibo*" as she stepped closer to the painting of the monk Rasputin. She pulled her glasses from her clutch and slid them onto her face. With an index finger on top and a thumb on bottom, she activated the cameras mounted in the frames. The images were transmitted from the glasses to the repeater tucked neatly beneath Celeste's dress, and finally through the walls of the gallery to the receiver built into the skin of the van parked in the alley behind the building.

She pulled the glasses from her face and turned to Celeste. "Have closer look with my glasses. This is maybe fake copy of original."

The tech slid the glasses onto her face and stepped squarely in front of the painting. With her attention focused on the detail of the work of art and not on the hideous monk, she took even more detailed shots than Anya had snapped.

A man with a magnifying glass hanging from his neck stepped beside the painting. "Good evening, ladies. I'm David, the senior international fine arts consultant here at Sotheby's, and I can assure you the provenance of this painting is unquestionable."

Anya peered up as if she herself had been the tsarina Alexandra Feodorovna. "Tell to me, David. How does your provenance begin with painting? Was it counted and catalogued after Tsar Nicholas and his beautiful family were slaughtered, and monk Rasputin castrated and murdered?"

David cleared his throat. "Well, initially, there was some question about the true origin of the piece. However, we have thorough records of its location and ownership since nineteen nineteen. I have every confidence the piece is not only authentic, but also the only known portrait for which Rasputin sat."

"And what is the estimate?"

The man shuffled a bit. "It's hard to put a firm number on an item this rare. You see, this piece has never been offered at public auction until now. I'm sure you know how rare it is for a painting such as this to have existed for a century without a sale at auction."

Anya feigned frustration. "*Your* estimate then, David."

The man stared at the canvas with his hands planted solidly on his hips. "I have little doubt the piece will fetch less than seven figures, madam."

Anya didn't flinch. "Are you authorized to accept private offers before the auction?"

David looked around as if lost beneath a secret he shouldn't tell. "I can entertain such offers, madam, but I must tell you that we already have an offer of eight hundred thousand from a private collector who shall remain nameless."

The man subconsciously glanced to his left and quickly back to Anya as she asked, "Is this only offer, or merely highest?"

"It is the highest."

"I see," she said. "If I were to make better offer, are you required to tell other potential buyers of my offer?"

He shrugged. "I represent the seller, madam. Therefore, I have the fiduciary responsibility of collecting the highest possible price for the piece. I'm sure you understand."

She sighed and turned to Celeste. "Give to me paper and pencil."

Celeste handed her the pad and pen, and she wrote "One million four hundred thousand, and you will tell no one." Then, she folded the paper and slid it into David's hand.

He examined the note, licked his lips, and slid the offer into an interior pocket of his jacket. "You will excuse me for a moment, of course."

Anya laid a palm in the center of his chest. "Five minutes only, then offer is no good, and you will never see me again. So, do not believe you may consider my offer as proxy bid for auction tomorrow. It is one-time offer only, and I will not bid at auction."

He swallowed hard. "I'll be back in a few minutes."

The man sped from the gallery, and Anya whispered, "Watch for someone to disappear. This will be buyer for Morozov. I suspect is small man in blue suit with round glasses and white cuffs and collar."

Gwynn said, "I spotted him, too. He watched us when we stopped in front of this painting."

Anya said, "He not only watched, he made also telephone call for only seconds. He is now inside office at back of gallery."

A waiter collected their flutes and replaced them will full ones. "Is there anything I can get for you?"

"Who is security manager?" Anya asked.

The waiter stood erect and searched the room. "I don't know his name, but he's a tall, thin guy, and he's wearing an ungodly enormous bow tie for some reason."

Celeste cracked a smile. "That's to hide a microphone. He's probably wearing an earpiece, too."

The waiter shrugged. "Don't know. I didn't check out his ears, but the bow tie belongs on a clown. I'll check on you again soon. Is the champagne all right? I can bring whatever you'd like."

In the strongest accent she could force, Anya asked. "You have good Russian vodka?"

He raised a finger. "I'll be right back."

Just as the waiter disappeared, Bow Tie appeared in a doorway at the rear corner of the gallery, and Anya said, "That is him. Watch his eyes. He sees everyone and everything all at same time. I like him."

Gwynn said, "So, are you doing him, or am I?"

"We will do together, I think, but you will have lead."

Gwynn nodded. "Let's go."

The three strolled across the floor and approached the man.

Gwynn said, "We need to speak with the senior security official."

Bow Tie stuck out his hand. "I'm Devon Van Borne, chief of facility security."

Gwynn took his hand and held it longer than necessary. "My name is Davis, and I am security for Ms. Petrovna. We have arranged to purchase a piece prior to the auction tomorrow, but we don't have the local facility to house the piece prior to our transport team arriving. Is it possible to arrange for storage in your vault for two or three nights?"

"Of course, Ms. Davis. Which piece will you acquire?"

Gwynn ducked her chin. "Come now, Mr. Van Borne. We don't discuss such things until the ink is dry, but before Ms. Petrovna dips her quill in the inkwell, I need to be assured that your facilities are adequate."

"Adequate?" He laughed. "Ms. Davis, we hold hundreds of millions of dollars' worth of fine art, jewelry, and rare collectibles every year. We've never lost an item. In fact, we've never suffered a break-in or burglary of any kind in the eleven years I've been chief of security. I assure you there is no safer place for your piece than right here in this facility."

Gwynn ran a hand down his long arm. "I didn't mean to offend you, Mr. Van Borne, but if I took everyone's word for the quality of their security, I'd be a fool, and I assure you that I am not. Let's take a stroll, and you can show me just how secure your property really is."

As if believing himself to be a Secret Service agent, the man lowered his chin and spoke into his obscene bow tie. "Mr. Blair, you have the floor."

Gwynn's eyes fell on the man's right ear, where a tiny, wireless speaker rested well inside the fold of flesh. He listened for a moment and said, "Okay, come with me."

"I'll join you," Celeste said, but Van Borne froze.

"Who would you be, ma'am?"

Gwynn squeezed his arm. "She's the technology side of the house, and I insist she see your facilities as well."

He studied Celeste for a moment. "Okay, but no one else."

Van Borne led the two down a corridor as the furnishing grew less plush with every foot and they came to a pair of heavy doors with a digital cipher lock and thumbprint reader. Beyond the door, the building became industrial, and they passed through two more steel doors with increased security, including a card reader and a biometric iris scanner, but Van Borne ignored the biometrics.

Gwynn asked, "So, is this door single-factor? I noticed you didn't scan your eye."

"No, it's two-factor, just like the others, but my credentials are programmed to bypass the second factor during operational hours. After everyone goes home, it would take the card and the eye scan to make entry. I'm impressed that you noticed, though."

"Don't be impressed, Mr. Van Borne. I'm directly responsible for the protection of millions in assets every day. I'm sure you're equally observant."

He looked down at her. "At least equally observant." With the wave of an arm, he said, "This is the staging area. No one except for Mr. Blair and me is allowed in this area alone. Everyone else must be escorted."

"How about your vault?" Gwynn asked.

He said, "The vault is rarely necessary unless a piece is going to be in residence longer than a few weeks. This exterior staging area serves as short-term warehousing of three days or less, and I'll show the mid-term room next."

Gwynn said, "So, this is where our piece would be held as long as we pick it up within three days, right?"

"That's right, unless you insisted on tighter security. I suppose we could house the piece in the mid-term area, or even the vault if you insisted."

Gwynn stepped closer to him. "Oh, no, that's not necessary. I'm sufficiently impressed with this area, and our transport team will likely arrive tomorrow."

Van Borne sucked air through his teeth. "Tomorrow is going to be a little tricky. As you know, it's auction day, and things will be happening quickly. It would be better, at least from a security standpoint, if you either picked up your piece tonight or the day after tomorrow."

Gwynn said, "We can work with that, but I do have a request. Since tomorrow will be hectic, as you said, I'd like to make sure our piece is protected. Not from theft, of course. That's clearly not a concern. You're obviously very good at what you do. I would, however, have to insist that Ms. Petrovna's piece be crated by our packager and stored well clear of any piece that would likely be moved during the auction."

Van Borne said, "Of course. I completely understand, and I have just the place. Come with me."

He led them around a corner to an alcove, where two crates rested against the concrete wall. "These two pieces will be delivered tomorrow morning, so your piece will be nice and lonely right here."

Gwynn and Celeste turned and scanned the space.

Celeste said, "I don't see motion detectors or even a camera covering this space."

"Very astute," Van Borne said. "But you'll also notice this is a dead-end alcove. There's no way in or out of this area without passing a dozen cameras and two dozen biometric sensors. They're not merely motion sensors. They actually detect body heat, sound, and even airflow. They're impenetrable. I assure you."

10

Idushchiy, Idushchiy, Ushel (Going, Going, Gone)

Back in Sotheby's main gallery after their security tour, Gwynn and Celeste stood across the room and watched David, the man who claimed to be the senior international fine arts consultant, offer his arm to Anya. The Russian slipped her hand inside his elbow and allowed herself to be led from the gallery and into an office on the periphery of the space.

"It must've worked," Gwynn said.

Celeste spoke without taking her eyes off their partner. "Maybe, or he could be schmoozing another hundred grand out of her."

Gwynn smiled. "Schmoozing doesn't work on her. She's immune to most things that work on mortals like us."

Celeste sighed. "It must be amazing working with her every day."

"Oh, it's not an everyday thing. We work these missions, and she disappears. We don't know where she goes or what she does, but when we need her, she always seems to be available."

"She seems to have a pretty good thing going on down in the islands."

Gwynn said, "Yeah, that's pretty cool, but it's weird. It's way out of character for her. I've got a lot of questions, but she shuts me down every time I try to go down that road with her."

"It must be tough for her," Celeste said. "I can't imagine the life she's had. There doesn't seem to be anything in her life that qualifies as normal."

"You're right about that," Gwynn said as she watched the two shapes through the window of the office.

"So, what's the deal with her and this Chase guy?"

Gwynn sighed. "I don't know the whole story, but apparently, he'll always be her person. I mean, she flirts with guys, but most of it is just an act to get them off their game. There was this one guy, Peter, on an op we ran last year. She got a twinkle in her eye when she looked at him, but he didn't survive the op. She's not like you and me. She sees the world through an entirely different lens. I'm not sure I'll ever figure her out."

Celeste squirmed. "Here she comes."

Anya crossed the room as if floating an inch above the floor, and everyone noticed. When she stopped in front of her partners, she whispered, "Watch David."

Four eyes scanned the room until the man emerged from the office. Like a bee drawn to a flower, the man propelled himself directly toward the man in the blue shirt with white cuffs.

Gwynn said, "You nailed it. David is leading white collar to the office."

Anya didn't turn. "This is good. Tell me when they are inside office."

Celeste said, "Okay, they're inside. What's next?"

Anya grinned. "Next is twist dagger."

Celeste furrowed her brow, but Gwynn said, "Relax. You'll love this part. She's really good at this."

Anya turned. "Follow me, and we will have some fun."

If the Russian had gotten attention when she crossed the gallery alone, the three women captivated the crowd of art aficionados on their way back across the floor.

Without knocking, Anya twisted the knob on the office door and leaned inside. "You will now move my painting to secure storage for crating, yes?"

David and the other man looked up, surprise registering on their faces. Neither man seemed to be accustomed to having anyone, especially a woman, barging into an office without at least knocking.

In relatively good English, the man looked up. "Who are you?"

Anya took the question as an invitation, so she pressed through the door with Celeste and Gwynn in tow. "I am Anastasia Petrovna. Who are you?"

The man didn't stand. "I am Anatoly Asimov, and you seem to mistakenly believe you bought my client's painting."

"No, this is not so," Anya said. "I am not mistaken. But which painting do you wrongly believe to be your client's? And who is client?"

Anatoly's face reddened, and his accent thickened. "You know which painting, and you will not get away with this *obman*!"

In her native Russian, Anya said, "I see your English is no good when you are angry. You should not be angry. I am merely better at game than you, and I have more money than your so-called client."

The man slammed a hand on the arm of his chair and leapt to his feet. In furious Russian, he growled, "You have no idea who you're messing with, and you will soon regret this."

Anya smiled. "Tell to Nikiti Morozov that you failed him and you were beaten by girl."

Anatoly turned back to David and jabbed a finger through the air. "You are finished! You will be lucky to have job sweeping sidewalk when this is finished!" He turned his accusatory finger on Anya. "And her, you do not know her. She is mysterious figure making ridiculous offers for painting she does not know."

"I have idea," Anya said. "So you will not feel like you have been beaten behind back, I will do for you this one courtesy. You will now make best and final offer for painting. If it is lower than the price I agreed to pay, game is finished, and I win. If, on other hand, you make offer higher than mine, I will have opportunity to pay your price, plus one hundred thousand dollars. If I do this, game is over, and I still win. This gives to you opportunity to spend more of your master's money, and perhaps he will not kill you for failing."

Anatoly stared between David and Anya before screaming, "This woman has some kind of vendetta against my client. This is obviously some sort of revenge. You cannot let this go on, David. I have made for you many millions of dollars, and now you choose her instead of me. This is unthinkable, and I will see that my client never spends another penny with your company."

Anya continued her mocking smile. "This man has fiduciary responsibility to his seller to capture highest price possible for painting. If he were coward and gave in to your threat, he and all of auction company will lose license. Is very simple matter, really. Surely you are smart enough to understand this, Anatoly."

The Russian exploded from his seat and thundered toward Anya. "I don't care about his license or his fiduciary responsibility. I know exactly how much you offered, but you do not have funds available for such a purchase, so you are guilty of fraud."

Anya turned to Celeste. "Is it done?"

Celeste nodded. "Yes, ma'am. It is done."

Anya motioned toward the computer on the desk. "David, you will now look inside escrow account for my deposit of full amount for my purchase."

David raised both hands. "I don't have to look. I've already been informed the full purchase price has been deposited into escrow."

Anatoly's head was on the verge of exploding. "My client will pay one point nine million dollars with immediate escrow."

David looked up at Anya. "Ms. Petrovna?"

Anya turned to Celeste. "You will make call."

Celeste nodded and motioned toward the phone resting on David's desk.

David rose. "Do you need the phone?"

She stepped around the man and slid onto his chair. With the phone pressed to her ear, she dialed a number and waited. Finally, she said, "It's me. We're at one point nine, and we have the final option at two." She paused, listened, and said, "I'll tell her. Stand by." Celeste covered the mouthpiece. "They say we can close immediately with a wire transfer and no escrow at one point eight."

Anya raised an eyebrow toward David. "Immediate closing at one point eight. What do you say?"

Anatoly was on his feet again. "Wait! This must stop. We had arrangement. One final offer from us with option for one final bid of plus one hundred from her. This was arrangement she made."

David shrugged. "Immediate closing has enormous value for our seller, Mr. Asimov."

Anatoly narrowed his eyes and stared through Anya. "We will wire funds now at one point nine."

Anya's shoulders fell, and she slowly shook her head and extended her hand. "I have been beaten by better man. I cannot apologize for being aggressive, but I will say I have enormous respect for your tenacity. You will understand if I must see wire transfer completed before I fully accept defeat, yes?"

Anatoly pulled his cell phone from an inside pocket and pressed it to his face. In rapid-fire Russian, he spoke into the phone for a few seconds, then he handed the phone to David, and Sotheby's man gave the account information for the receiving account. After pleasantries, he handed the phone back to Anatoly and scanned his computer screen. "The transfer has just occurred, and I have four documents for you to sign."

David produced the documents, and Anatoly hurriedly signed each of them.

Anya leaned toward the desk and spoke barely above a whisper. "I have something to show you. Is there a secure entrance through which my team may bring this item?"

David and Anatoly stared up at Anya, and Sotheby's man said, "I'll have security meet them at door three."

Two minutes later, two men dressed in coveralls carried a shrouded object into the office with a pair of security officers trailing closely behind them.

Anatoly's eyes jerked from person to person as the scene unfolded.

Anya laid a hand on his shoulder. "Congratulations, comrade. I hope Nikiti enjoys forgery you bought for him for almost two million dollars."

She pulled the shroud from the carried object, revealing the framed masterpiece of Grigori Yefimovich Rasputin, the Mad Monk, encapsulated behind sealed glass and framed identically to the painting Anatoly Asimov had purchased for his client, the reclusive Nikiti Morozov. She said, "You see, Anatoly, the real *Monakh Tsaritsy* has been in my family for almost one hundred years, since July of nineteen eighteen. We were once servants in palace, but when Bolsheviks seized Tsar Nicholas and his family, my family seized everything they could carry, including *Monakh Tsaritsy*."

11

Tuk-Tuk
(Knock Knock)

Anatoly Asimov launched himself from his chair and charged Anya with rage pouring from his flesh, but his advance was halted at the gleaming tip of a fighting knife against his chin. In their native language and in the icy tone Russian women inflict so well, she said, "You will sit, or I will gut you like pig."

Asimov froze where he stood with the tiniest trickle of blood appearing in the cleft of his Eastern European chin. Withdrawing an inch, he hissed through a demented smile. "You have just committed suicide, and you do not even know it. My client is not a man to be trifled with."

Anya's eyes never left Asimov's. "This is threat, yes?"

By way of an answer, Asimov extended his left arm and shoved Anya backward. When she stopped, the sleeve of his jacket fell from his arm, having been slit from shoulder to cuff, and his watch lay on the floor at his feet with the band sliced in half.

Through gritted teeth, Anya said, "I am not afraid of Nikita Morozov, but now, you are rightly afraid of me. You will now take me to Morozov, and we will complete business arrangement for real painting of *Monakh Tsaritsy*."

Asimov laughed. "You are foolish girl. You will not live to see him, but you will taste his vengeance."

Anya continued her frozen glare. "I am not person who spent almost two million dollars of Mr. Morozov's money to buy fake painting. I think maybe I am better friend for him than you. Perhaps I will become his buyer because I am not foolish enough to fall for trick like this one."

"You have no idea who you are dealing with."

Almost before he finished the threat, Anya lunged forward with blinding speed and pressed the blade of her knife firmly against the front of Asimov's trousers, just below his belt buckle. "Then you have advantage because you know exactly who you are dealing with. I am Anastasia Petrovna, and you may tell your client there is no need to search for me because he will wake with me standing beside his bed very soon."

Seemingly unfazed by the position of Anya's knife, Asimov said, "You have no idea where he is, and even if you did, you and whole army could not get close to him. I am calling police."

"Perfect," Anya hissed. "Call instead FBI, but be sure to use correct words. Sotheby's sold to you fake painting for almost two million dollars, and other bidder who is woman defended herself from you with knife because she was afraid when you tried to attack her in front of three witnesses. This is truth. Would you like to use my telephone to make call?"

The senior international fine arts consultant trembled in his seat. "No! No! There's no reason to involve the authorities. We can resolve this in-house, and of course, we'll move your payment into escrow until this is resolved."

Asimov spun on a heel to face David. "You'll do no such thing! You'll transfer the entire amount back into my client's account, and you'll do it now. We will not escrow funds to purchase a forgery."

Anya motioned for her team to cover the painting they'd carried in, and they promptly obeyed while David and Asimov fought the battle of one point nine million dollars.

Just as quietly as the painting had been carried into the building, the men carried it down the same corridor, through the sallyport and out the high-security doors, and into the unmarked DOJ surveillance van. Anya, Celeste, and Gwynn followed only steps behind.

Celeste pounded on the console inside the van with both fists. "That was freaking awesome!"

Anya continued her smile. "It was, wasn't it?"

Gwynn, on the other hand, crossed her arms and glared across her glasses. "Just when exactly were you planning to let me in on this little scheme of yours?"

Anya said, "Relax, friend Gwynn. It was necessary for you to be surprised. I did not like hiding secret from you, but I feared Asimov would have to be arrested, and that would be your responsibility. If you knew of secret, situation would be entrapment, and arrest would be invalid, no?"

Gwynn huffed. "Okay, I get that, but I don't like being out of the loop. Did Johnny know?"

Johnny looked up from his seat. "Yeah, I knew, and I'm the one who made the decision to leave you in the dark. It was my call, not Anya's, so don't take it out on her. If you're going to be mad at somebody, point your anger at me on this one."

Gwynn settled onto a stool mounted to the wall of the van. "I get it, but I don't have to like it."

Johnny said, "Okay. Let's move on. We have a long night ahead of us, and I think you're going to like this part, Gwynn. We're going back in when the gala is over, and we're going to steal the authentic *Monakh Tsaritsy*."

Gwynn said, "Okay, you're forgiven as long as I get to be on the penetration team."

Johnny propped his left ankle on his right knee, just like Ray White would've done. "Not only are you on the penetration team, but you're leading the penetration team after the techies part the waters for you."

"I'm starting to like you in charge, Johnny. When do we go?"

He checked his watch. "As soon as the lights go out and everyone else is tucked in bed at home."

Gwynn looked down at her gown. "I'm thinking a wardrobe change is in order, or I'll be the best-dressed cat burglar in Chicago."

Johnny reached behind him and pulled a black duffel from beneath a rack of equipment. He tossed the bag, landing it at Gwynn's feet. "There's your catsuit. You've got at least a couple of hours before things go dark in there, so find something to occupy your time."

Anya tapped the duffel with the toe of her shoe. "Also my clothes are inside bag?"

Johnny shook his head. "Nope. You're not going back in there. You're too important to show up on a security video, and we can't have any more of your fingerprints on this thing. Remember, you're Anastasia Petrovna, but your fingerprints belong to Ana Fulton."

"This is not problem. I will wear gloves."

Johnny said, "You're welcome to wear gloves if you want, but you're not going back inside that building."

Anya said, "Gwynn cannot go alone. She cannot carry painting. Is too big."

"She's not going alone," Johnny said. "She's leading the team. There will be two other agents doing the heavy lifting. Now stop trying to dictate how we're running this op. You can do that once we start playing directly with your fellow countrymen, but for now, it's mine."

Anya took a long breath, preparing to argue, but the memory of Ray White asking her not to be a pain for Johnny played through her head, and she took Gwynn's arm. "You will be careful, yes?"

Gwynn emptied the contents of the duffel onto the floor of the van. "No, I thought I'd go in there all willy-nilly and carefree."

Anya rolled her eyes. "You are being silly. I will need you when we get to Seattle, so do not get hurt."

Gwynn turned her back to Anya. "Unzip me, please."

She lifted Gwynn's hair and pulled the thin zipper down her back until the dress was split to the waist.

Gwynn shimmied from the gown and kicked off her shoes.

The three technicians spun in their seats, determined to catch the show, but Anya stepped between them and her partner. In her best Ray White voice, she said, "You boys better get yourselves some professionalism before I have to shoot all three of you."

The look of utter disbelief shone on their faces as they turned back to their workstations.

Gwynn giggled. "That was pretty good. Between you and Johnny, it's like Agent White never left."

Gwynn stepped into the all-black tactical uniform from the duffel and pulled on her boots. "Do we have anything to eat in here? I'm starving."

One of the techs looked up at Anya. "Can I turn around now?"

Anya gave Gwynn a glance and said, "Yes, you may."

The tech stuck a protein bar toward Gwynn, and she took it from his hand. "Thanks. So, who's going with me?"

Two of the techs raised their index fingers, and Johnny said, "Tim Nash and Glenn Barrow. They both have covert entry experience and have the alarm and security systems memorized. I wouldn't send you in there with a pair of knuckleheads."

Gwynn shook their hands. "I'm Gwynn Davis, resident knucklehead."

"Okay, that's enough. Knock it off, and keep your eye on the prize," Johnny said. "We have to know where they put the painting they now believe is worthless."

Gwynn leaned in to watch one of the eight monitors on the wall of the van and laid her hand on the covered painting case. "Speaking of worthless paintings, where did you get this one?"

"We made it," Tim Nash said. "It was a rush job from the shots you took with Celeste's magic glasses. That's why we had to put it in the case. It wouldn't stand up to any scrutiny."

"Let me see," she said.

Glenn pulled back the shroud.

"Yuck. You're right. That is terrible, but it was good enough to get the job done tonight."

Tim nodded. "We'll slow down the process and paint another one as soon as we get the original in the van later tonight."

"It's on the move!" Glenn said.

Everyone turned to see him pointing toward a monitor, where a pair of men were carrying the authentic *Monakh Tsaritsy* from David's office and down the corridor.

"What are we going to do if they put it in the vault?" Gwynn asked.

Johnny pulled his tie loose. "They won't. They'll leave it out so they can move it to the lab tomorrow for close examination."

"You sound pretty confident about that," Gwynn said.

He motioned toward the screen. "Just watch."

Just as Johnny had predicted, the two men wrapped the painting in blankets and carried it to the same alcove David had shown them earlier in the night.

Johnny snapped his fingers. "What did I tell you?"

Anya scoffed. "Even blind hog finds truffle sometimes."

"That's not how that saying goes."

Anya shrugged. "Maybe not, but is still true."

The next three hours were spent watching the auction preview guests slowly file from the building and disappear with their heads full of fantasies of adding a masterpiece to their collections.

With the guests gone, the staff spent ninety minutes arranging the paintings in the auction gallery under David's direction for the next day's grand event. Each painting was carefully placed, anchored, and locked to its easel, then covered with plastic and a shroud.

"They're going to a lot of trouble just to undo it all in twelve hours," one of the techs said.

Johnny said, "That's somewhere between twenty and fifty million dollars' worth of art. You'd lock it up, too."

The tech looked up. "Yeah, I would, but not with a lock like that. Anya's blind hog could pick that thing with its snout."

Johnny said, "Not everybody has lock-picking on their résumé."

"I guess it's good for them that I'm on the good guys' side."

"Yeah, I guess it is," Johnny said. "Let's let things settle down a little more before we pounce, but it's looking good."

Glenn said, "I've got the decoy video ready to run."

"Have you solved the time stamp problem yet?" Tim asked.

"Yeah, it was pretty simple, really. I just wrote a script to cut out the existing time clock in the video and replace it with a replica of another camera. They're all synced to the atomic clock at the Naval Observatory, so it was simple to set up. Unless someone is watching every monitor simultaneously, they'll never see me switch the feeds."

The third tech finally said, "I'm Craig, by the way. I'll be the one running things from here while you guys are inside. I have control of the cameras, sensors, most of the locks, and the lighting in case it falls apart."

He pulled up a building floor plan and scrolled over it with a mouse. "Okay, you'll make entry here. I'll pop the lock and float the video as soon as you touch the handle. Once you're in, step right and freeze. Don't move until I give the order. From that position, there are nine cameras and environmental sensors that will detect your presence the instant you move more than five feet from the door. I'll need some time to shut those down and launch the bogus video. Remember, stay by the door until I say move. Got it?"

Gwynn said, "Got it. Keep moving."

He pointed out the route until they'd reach the hidden alcove. "This is where it gets tricky. I have no way to know if anyone is in the alcove before you arrive, and I won't be able to see you while you're in there. That means do your work quickly, quietly, and get out of there."

Gwynn asked, "What about the live feed while we're inside? Will you still be able to see it?"

Craig shook his head. "No, that's the greatest weakness of this system. If somebody shows up, I won't see them. I'll only see what the security cameras see, and that'll be the fake footage."

Gwynn sighed. "I don't like that."

Johnny stepped in. "I don't like it, either, but we don't have another option."

Gwynn asked, "What do we do if we encounter resistance?"

Johnny said, "The rules of engagement are simple. Do not engage. If you are engaged, escape, but do not surrender the painting. It is crucial to the remainder of the operation. As a last resort, if you're engaged and it gets physical, put them down, but don't kill them."

Gwynn nodded slowly, then looked up at Anya. "If we get pinned down, how violent can we become?"

Johnny unbuttoned the top button on his shirt. "As violent as it takes, but everybody stays alive. We can deal with some broken bones, but no dead bodies."

Anya said, "I should go inside with them."

"No," Johnny said. "You are not going back in that building, ever."

She leaned toward their temporary boss. "If friend Gwynn is in danger and cannot escape, you will not be able to stop me from going inside building without shooting me."

Johnny closed his eyes and sighed. "It won't come to that. Any more questions?" No one spoke, so he said, "Mount up."

12

Slishkom Mnogo (One Too Many)

Gwynn, Glenn, and Tim stuck earpieces into their ears and tucked microphones behind their collars.

"Maybe we should get some giant bow ties for next time," Gwynn said.

With comms check complete and a scan of the alley done, the city's most high-tech art thieves stepped from the van, but Anya said, "Wait!"

Everyone froze, and she pulled a card from beneath her dress. "I almost forgot. This is security access card from David. I pulled from his pocket while inside office. Maybe you will need, but if no, then drop it on floor before coming out. This way, everyone will believe he dropped it and it was not stolen."

Gwynn tucked the card into a pocket and pressed the van door closed behind her. The instant she touched the access door, the mechanical click sounded, releasing the bolts, and the three stepped through their first choke point without incident.

She said, "We're inside and tight to the door. Kill the cameras and sensors."

Craig said, "Stand by. Give me eight seconds." Time ticked by like an agonizing metronome until he finally said, "Got it. You're clear to move. Report positions at every turn and choke point."

"Roger," Gwynn whispered.

They moved quickly through the space as if they'd trained together for years. The two techs fell in line like baby ducks behind their mother, and momma goose made the calls. "Rounding corner number one."

They moved silently for another fifteen feet. "Corner two."

As Gwynn leaned to clear the corner, she caught a glimpse of a man in jeans and a black T-shirt. She froze and gave the hand signal for the techs to do the same, then watched as the man inched his way down the wall toward the same alcove where her target waited.

Gwynn backed up and lowered her chin. In a whisper, she said, "We've got company. I think it's another thief. He's a single, and he's moving toward the painting."

Craig looked over his shoulder at the operation commander. "What do you want them to do?"

Johnny felt the sting of sudden sweat inside his shirt and on the back of his neck, and he froze.

Craig nudged him. "You have to make a call, boss."

Johnny's eyes darted back and forth between the tech and Anya until the Russian finally curled a finger. Johnny stepped close to her, and she pressed a finger into his stomach.

"Go with gut. Make decision."

He pressed his button. "Trail him to the painting, but do not engage."

Anya felt her heart sink. "No, do not do this. This is terrible plan."

Johnny held up a hand. "Quiet. I'm in charge. But I need you out of that dress."

Anya grabbed the gown at the neckline with both hands and ripped it from her skin. She grabbed the duffel that had contained Gwynn's tactical clothes but found it empty, so she grabbed Craig's collar. "Give to me clothes. Now!"

The tech leapt to his feet and surrendered his clothes to the Russian. They fit well enough but required the belt to be cinched like a drawstring. The pair of fighting knives that had previously been nestled on the inside of her thigh found a new home inside the cinched belt. The tech's shoes were too big to serve their purpose on Anya's feet, so she kicked them back toward the mostly naked technician.

"Stage at the door and stand by," Johnny ordered.

Anya positioned herself by the rear door of the van, ready to explode through the opening the instant the situation demanded her involvement.

Craig said, "I know I'm the naked guy here, but we've got another issue. Whoever this mystery man is inside that building, he's operating in the same environment as us, and he's apparently not afraid of being discovered. That means he has a team like us who has abducted the cameras and alarms, just like we did, or he's not afraid of setting off the horns and sirens."

Johnny said, "There's a third option. He may be a confederate working for the auction company. If they steal their own painting, insurance pays the claim, and they don't have to deal with the fallout from selling what they now believe is a counterfeit."

"That's a good theory," Celeste said. "But at this point, do we care why he's stealing the painting or even *if* he's here to steal *our* painting?"

"Not really," Johnny said. "But we don't want to get tangled up with him if he's not interested in the *Monakh Tsaritsy*. All we can do is wait and watch for now." Johnny pressed the button to activate his comms. "Davis, watch the guy and report any significant action. Anya is standing by to take him down if necessary. We do not want a confrontation inside that building. Do you copy?"

Gwynn whispered, "Roger. He's moving toward the alcove, and he's clearly on a mission."

"Do not intercept. Just observe and report."

"Roger."

Johnny drummed his fingertips on the console. "Does anyone have any theories on what's going on?"

The tech shook his head, and Celeste said, "I think the guy is most likely working for the auction house, like you said, but that's a risky move on their part."

Anya said, "I do not think this is right. I think man is probably working for Morozov."

Johnny said, "Right now, the why doesn't matter, but we can't let him get away with our painting if that's—"

Gwynn's voice came over the speaker. "He's got a painting from the alcove, and he's moving back down the side corridor."

Johnny pointed to Anya. "Go!" He pressed the button in front of him. "Davis, as soon as he's clear, I want you in that alcove. Find out what's missing."

"Roger, moving," came her reply.

"Uh, Houston, we have a problem," Craig said as his fingers flew across the keyboard. "I'm losing control of the environmentals. Get out of there!"

Johnny leaned toward the screen. "What about the cameras?"

"I've still got the cams, but the sensors are coming back online. There must've been a backup system I didn't detect."

Johnny keyed up. "Get out of there, now. It's blown!"

Meanwhile, around the corner of the building, Anya sprang from the shadows and directly into the path of the running man with a rolled canvas in his hand. He shuffled his feet like an all-star running back, but Anya mirrored his every move. Desperate, he pulled a switchblade and thrust it in front of him.

Anya drew a fighting knife with each hand and made the last move the man could've expected. She lunged toward him and threw a hammer fist to the wrist of his knife hand, knocking the blade to the ground. He retreated several steps and studied his avenues of escape. The only two options were back through the door and into the auction house or straight through one of the deadliest Eastern Bloc–trained assassins on the planet.

The man grabbed the handle of a metal trash can lid and held it in front of him as a makeshift shield. Anya, unfazed, continued her advance and planted a bare foot directly in the center of the improvised shield. The kick drove the rim of the metal lid into the man's mouth and nose, crushing and slicing as it went.

Dazed, the man lowered the lid and staggered backward as Anya continued her relentless approach. Two more staggering strides placed the man's back solidly against the wall of the building, and he was instantly a cornered animal. He threw himself toward her, driving the lid through the air as he went and delivering a thrusting strike to her left hand, but she evaded the blow with her right and sent the blade of her knife slicing across the man's bicep. She withdrew and lunged for a stab, but he deflected the attack with the lid in his one remaining usable hand.

Anya pictured the wound she'd delivered and calculated how long her opponent could stay on his feet with significant bleeding.

He seemed to ignore the wound and waved the lid frantically through the air in front of him as he propelled himself forward on determined feet. Anya took the lid across her left shoulder and onto the side of her head. The blow temporarily disoriented her, but she gathered her wits before the man could make his escape.

She turned, mentally measured the distance between them, and let her knife fly. The blade spun through the air, finding its mark at the back of the man's left knee, and he went down hard.

Before his body stopped sliding on the concrete, Anya landed on the small of the man's back, pinning him to the ground. "Who are you?"

He groaned and twisted against her weight, but his inferior position made him little challenge for the Russian.

She growled, "I asked question. Who are you?"

"Get off me, you crazy—"

She grabbed a handful of his hair and pressed the side of his face to the ground at the same instant she laid the razor-like blade against his cheekbone. "This can end one of two ways. You can tell me who you are, or I can cut out your eyes very slowly. Is up to you."

He bucked and squirmed in wasted effort to escape.

Anya leaned close. "I have changed mind. You can keep eyes. I will cut throat instead."

The man's body convulsed beneath her. "Okay, okay. I'm nobody. Somebody paid me to steal this painting, so I did it. You can have it. I don't even know what it is."

"Why did you take from frame?"

The man continued his squirming. "Because it's easier to carry and conceal."

"This man who paid you to steal painting. Describe him to me."

"I didn't see him. It was all arranged on the phone."

"What was his name?"

The man finally gave up his thrashing. "He didn't tell me his name, but he sounded like you."

"Like me? What does this mean?"

The man groaned. "He sounded Russian or something, like you."

"How much did he pay you?"

He twisted beneath her and let out a long breath. "Not enough for this. Look, if you're going to kill me for stealing a painting, go ahead and do it, but something tells me you're more confused than I am. Why don't you just take the painting, and I'll find somebody to stitch up my arm and leg? If you don't get off of me pretty soon, I'm going to bleed to death anyway."

With blinding speed, she dropped her knife, laced her arms around the man's neck and head, and leaned back into a punishing hold that would leave the man unconscious. When his body went limp, she sliced a piece of his shirt and formed a field-expedient tourniquet above his bicep. She then sliced his pants to reveal the wound at the back of his knee, but it wasn't bleeding badly enough to require immediate attention, so she grabbed the rolled canvas and headed for the van.

13

Znachok
(Badge)

Anya stepped through the rear door of the van to find Gwynn and the techs already inside. She laid the rolled painting on the console and turned to her partner. "Did you drop David's access card onto floor as we discussed?"

Gwynn pulled the card from her pocket. "I forgot."

"This is very good," Anya said as she snatched the card from her partner's hand.

She wiped the plastic card with her shirt until she was certain their fingerprints weren't on it, then she held it by its edges and climbed from the van. "I will be right back. Call ambulance for man in alley."

Less than a minute later, Anya was back inside the van, and the driver had them headed south on Michigan Avenue.

"What was the deal with the access card?" Gwynn asked.

Anya said, "I put it into pocket of unconscious man who stole painting. Police will discover and have many questions."

Celeste had the painting rolled out on the console and was studying every inch. "It looks so different out of the frame."

Johnny took a cursory glance at the painting. "Nice work tonight, everyone. So, Anya, other than the painting, what did you get from the thief?"

"He said person who hired him to steal painting had accent like mine. He never saw man, only spoke on telephone with him."

"How much was he paid?" Johnny asked.

"I asked this question, too, but he only said 'Not enough.'"

"You didn't kill him, did you?"

She shook her head. "No, he is very much alive, but I cut him on arm and back of knee. Paramedics will take him to hospital, and he will be fine."

Tim, one of the two techs who'd gone in with Gwynn, stared at Craig. "Why are you naked?"

"It's a long story, but she needed my clothes, and who's going to tell her no?"

Anya removed the tech's shirt and pants and surrendered them back to him. She then pulled Gwynn's dress from a hook on the wall and stepped into it. "Is a little bit small, but is good enough to get inside hotel, yes?"

Gwynn zipped the dress for her partner. "It's good enough to get you into the West Wing of the White House."

"I have already been there. Is boring, and I do not wish to go again."

"That's a story I want to hear someday," Gwynn said.

"Maybe," Anya said as they pulled to a stop outside their hotel.

Johnny said, "Again, good work tonight. Get some rest, and we'll be wheels up at nine tomorrow morning."

Celeste checked her watch. "Nine? That's only six hours from now."

Johnny followed suit and checked his watch. "Would you look at that? She's beautiful and smart, and she can tell time."

Hands landed on hips, and Celeste raised an eyebrow. "Would you look at that? He gets a temporary promotion, and just like that, he's sleeping alone."

* * *

Nine a.m. felt more like three a.m. when the collection of DOJ special agents, Technical Services pros, and one Air Force OSI officer climbed aboard the plane and blasted off for DC.

"How's everybody feeling this morning?" Johnny asked.

He was rewarded with a chorus of grumbles and groans. Gwynn laid her head on Captain Tom's shoulder and drifted back into dreamland.

Anya, on the other hand, slid onto the seat beside Johnny. "I am curious because I do not understand all of American system of criminal justice yet."

Johnny choked on a sip of coffee. "Now, that's funny. Don't feel lonely. Nobody fully understands the American system of criminal justice, but I'll do my best to explain whatever it is that's bugging you."

She stared up at the overhead for an instant. "I think maybe Agent White understands it."

Johnny shrugged. "Okay, maybe him, but he's in the minority. What's on your mind?"

"I have been thinking about what happened last night. We tried to steal painting."

"Yeah, that's right, but somebody beat us to it."

"Yes, but that is not question. Question is, what would happen if we were successful?"

"I'm not sure I understand what you're asking."

Anya said, "I'm asking what would happen when robbery is reported, and we are thieves who took painting?"

"Oh, I get it. The Attorney General knew about our operation, but outside our team, no one else knew, and that's the beauty of it. To everyone except us and the AG, it would appear to be a real art theft amid a scandal over the authenticity of an offered painting. We would've let Sotheby's report the painting stolen, and the FBI would've begun their investigation, but before it got very far, the FBI director would've been briefed in, and the investigation would've stalled until we finished the work we need to do with the painting."

She frowned. "What would happen then to painting?"

"The FBI would miraculously solve the case and recover the painting to be returned to its rightful owner, and the whole world would believe those boys over at the Hoover Building are the best in the world at solving cases."

She let the story sink in. "Who is rightful owner of painting?"

"You wouldn't believe me if I told you."

Anya cocked her head. "Of course I will believe you. Who is owner?"

Johnny glanced over his shoulder and pulled his notepad from an interior pocket. He wrote a name on a small sheet of paper and slipped it to the Russian.

She unfolded the paper and gasped. "The former prime minister of Israel? You are right. I do not believe you."

Johnny shrugged. "I can't make this stuff up. The provenance of the painting even puts it in Adolf Hitler's hands for a short period in the late thirties."

She leaned back and let the information wash over her. "Why is he selling it?"

"How should I know? Maybe the pension for a former PM isn't all that great and he needs the cash."

Almost before Johnny finished his sentence, Anya said, "I want it."

"You want what?"

"The painting. I want *Monakh Tsaritsy*."

Johnny scowled. "Anya, it's worth nearly two million dollars. You can't afford that . . . can you?"

"I will speak with him."

"Who? Him?" Johnny asked.

Anya held up the slip of paper. "Him."

"No! That's not a good idea. Nothing about you talking with the former prime minister of Israel is a good idea."

"I will do this when mission is finished and painting is returned to rightful owner . . . who will be me."

Johnny palmed his forehead. "We'll talk with Agent White about it when he gets back, but—"

"Thank you, but no. There is no *but*. I will do this."

She slipped the paper into her pocket, reclined her seat, and closed her smoky blue eyes.

* * *

After fourteen hours of meticulous work, Dr. Celeste Mankiller's painting robot signed the lower right corner of the canvas of the best forgery of any painting in history.

"That's simply astonishing," Gwynn said.

Celeste brushed off her shoulder. "That's my baby, but believe it or not, the robot isn't the coolest part of this process."

"What could be cooler than being able to create an exact copy of a hundred-year-old painting?"

Celeste said, "Come with me, and I'll show you."

She removed the canvas from the horizontal easel and powered down the robot. "I've had a supercomputer studying every detail of the original painting for over ten hours, and if I wrote the code correctly, it has calculated the exact atmospheric conditions to turn this brand-new painting into a ten-decade-old work of art in a matter of hours."

"How's that possible?" Gwynn asked.

"I'm not certain that it is possible, but we'll soon find out."

She slid the painting into a tube and sealed the opening. After several minutes at the keyboard and a couple hundred clicks of the mouse, the tube issued a series of noises that sounded as if it were on the verge of blowing itself through the roof, and Gwynn recoiled.

"Relax," Celeste said. "It's supposed to do that. Hopefully, my creation will put the new painting through the same treatment the original has endured, but it'll do it in a highly compressed period of time."

"Is this the first time you've tried this?"

"No, I've done it a couple dozen times, and it's worked out, but this is the first time with a full-size painting and a hundred years of history."

"How long will it take?" Gwynn asked.

After a scroll down the page displayed on the monitor, Celeste said, "According to the computer, it'll take just over thirty-one hours."

"Thirty-one hours?" Gwynn grinned. "That means I've got over a full day and night with Captain Tom in DC."

Celeste giggled. "Don't hurt the poor boy. He's delicate like a flower."

Gwynn laughed. "Yeah, that's it. He's a petite little daisy. I'll be gentle."

* * *

Supervisory Special Agent Ray White rolled over and stared at the ringing phone beside his bed as if it were an alien creature coming to life only inches from his head. Perhaps that's exactly what was happening. "Yeah, hello."

"Ray, is Anya Burinkova in America."

He threw his legs over the edge of the bed and yawned. "Hello, Anya. Is Ray White from inside Switzerland."

"You have seen Dr. Müller, yes? What has he said to you?"

"You do realize it's four in the morning over here, right?"

"I am not concerned about time on clock when I am worried about my friend. Tell to me what Dr. Müller said."

The back-handed compliment caught him a little off guard. "It's not great news, I'm afraid. The scans and opinions of the doctors at Georgetown were correct. The diagnosis isn't in question."

"I am sorry for this news, Ray. I wish I could make for you tea and tell to you stories to make you smile."

He cleared his throat. "Yeah, I've not done much smiling lately."

"When is surgery?"

"That's the sixty-four-thousand-dollar question."

Anya said, "I did not ask of price for surgery. I ask for time."

He almost laughed. "That's an old game show. They used to have contestants who had to answer questions . . . Never mind. Forget about that. I'm not sure I'm going to have the surgery."

"What? This does not make sense. You said tumor will kill you quickly if you do not have surgery to remove it. Why would you not have surgery?"

He ran a glass of water from the bathroom faucet and drank it down. "It's complicated, Anya. Dr. Müller says there's less than a five-percent chance of removing all of the tumor, even if I survive the surgery."

"What do you mean, *if* you survive surgery? Of course you will survive. He is brilliant surgeon, and you are young and healthy."

He refilled the glass and deposited himself into the most uncomfortable chair in Switzerland. "It's nice of you to say that, but neither is true. I'm old. I would've been fifty if I lived another eighteen months, but that's not looking good, and I'm not in very good shape. I mean, I'm physically strong, but the tumor is pressing against my spine, and it's only a matter of time before I'll be paralyzed."

"No, Ray. This is not so. It cannot be. I am coming there to be with you and talk to Dr. Müller."

"Stop it, Anya. You're not coming here. There's nothing you can do, and you've got a mission."

She swallowed hard. "Mission can wait, and I can do many things. I can make sure Dr. Müller does perfect surgery, and I can hold your hand while you get better. And I can make for you tea every day. They have wonderful tea in Switzerland and also chocolate. You love chocolate. I remember this."

The line was silent for a long moment. "Anya, listen to me. The chances of me surviving the surgery are less than fifty percent, and I already told you there's less than a five-percent chance of removing all of the tumor. That means the surgery would only delay the inevitable."

"Yes, maybe all of this is true, but maybe is possibility of removing all of tumor, and you can be alive for many more years, and we can have tea and honey, and I will even allow you to drive my car."

For the first time in days, he cracked a smile. "That's not your car, Anya. It belongs to the taxpayers."

"I pay taxes. So, see? It is my car. I will go to airport now, and I will be there as soon as flight will come."

Ray moved from the torture device of a chair and plopped onto the bed. "No. Listen to me. You're not coming over here. I talked with Johnny, and he briefed me up. It sounds like the op is going great. I knew you guys could handle it without me."

"You are trying to make change of subject, but this will not work. Ray, you are my friend, and . . ."

Silence claimed the space between them again until Ray pressed his lips together in a tight horizontal line and forced back the tear lingering in the corner of his eye. "Anya, I'm scared."

Suddenly, the tears that Ray wouldn't cry fell from Anya's face. "Please have surgery, Ray. Please."

He let himself sink into the billowing covers of his bed. "There's an experimental drug that has slowed the rate of growth in these kinds of tumors. It's in clinical trials, and—"

"I will call Dr. Müller, and you will have surgery. This is not question. If I had tumor and you did not, wouldn't you want me to have surgery?"

"It's not the same," he said. "I've stood toe to toe with men who could tear me apart, and when the fight was over, they were in cuffs, and I was having a beer with my buddies. I wasn't smart enough to be scared back then. I've had the president of the United States point his finger in my face and tell me I'd be homeless in thirty seconds, and I never broke a sweat. I've never been scared of anything, Anya, but when I heard the desperation in your voice, I felt something I'd never felt before that moment. I'm scared for the first time in my life, and it had to happen right here at the end of my life."

Anya sank her teeth into her bottom lip and fought back the break she knew would come when she opened her mouth. Finally, without the Slavic bite, she whispered, "I've been scared every day of my life since I watched that horrible man kill my mother when I was four years old. The only time I've not been afraid has been when I've stood beside Johnny Mac, Gwynn, and you, Ray White. With you, I am an American with a badge you gave me, and a knife I trust, and a purpose that is good. I will not wear this badge for anyone else, Ray. Only for you. Without it, I am an animal again—a savage with no purpose. Do not take this badge away from me. Do not take away my purpose. Tell Dr. Müller you want the surgery, Ray. Tell him."

14

STRANNYY KAK RASPUTIN
(WEIRD LIKE RASPUTIN)

Dr. Celeste Mankiller released the pressurized seal on the chamber she designed and built and pulled the counterfeit painting from inside. She carefully placed the painting on an easel beside the original and stepped back to admire her creation.

She studied both paintings with a critical eye. "Not bad, huh?"

Special Agent Gwynn Davis stepped within inches of the two paintings. "You've done it. This is unbelievable."

Anya sat on a folding chair in the corner of the room, wearing the cold look of Eastern Bloc women with too much on their minds, and her inaction wasn't lost on the temporary leader of the team.

Johnny perched himself on the corner of a chair beside the Russian. "Are you okay? What's going on in there?"

Well outside her typical demeanor, she said, "I am worried about Ray."

Johnny frowned. "Why are you worried about him? It's just a family thing, and he'll be back in a few days."

She raised her chin and met Johnny's eyes. "This is not true. He told to you this story so you would not worry while you are in charge of operation."

"What are you talking about?"

She laid a hand on Johnny's knee, and he flinched.

She squeezed and didn't look away. "Ray is very sick, and he has gone to see specialist doctor in Switzerland."

"What? That's crazy. There's nothing wrong with him. He would've told me if there was."

She sighed. "Normally, he would have told you, but this is not normal situation. We have mission, and he needs you to focus on this mission. He told to me truth, and I arranged for him to see best neurosurgeon on Earth. This is where he has gone."

Johnny swallowed hard. "Neurosurgeon? What's wrong with him?"

Anya felt like an icepick had been driven through her ear. "He told to me in confidence, but has gone too far. You must know. He has tumor at base of skull where spine begins. Tumor is cancer and is very difficult to remove, even for greatest of surgeons."

Johnny slid himself fully onto the seat and disappeared behind disbelieving eyes. "When is the surgery?"

"This I do not know, and also I do not know for sure if he will agree to surgery."

"Agree to it? I thought you said he was the best neurosurgeon in the world. Why wouldn't he do the surgery?"

"No, Johnny. This is not problem. Doctor will perform surgery if Ray agrees, but I do not know if he will agree. I pleaded with him to say yes, but I do not know if he will."

Johnny leaned back and searched the ceiling for answers that wouldn't come.

Celeste spun and said, "Are you two going to at least take a look at what I've done?"

Johnny glanced down until his eyes landed on Gwynn. "Does she know?"

Anya swallowed the indecision and chose the truth. "Yes, Gwynn knows, but only because she is not important to mission as you. Your mind must be clear and focused. This is only reason Agent White would keep you outside of truth. Even when he is possibly dying, mission is still most important thing to him."

Johnny let the weight of the situation settle on his shoulders and stood. After thirty seconds of examining both paintings, he cleared his throat. "Let's see them under blacklight and X-ray."

Celeste lowered her chin. "No 'Good work, Celeste'? No 'You're amazing, Celeste'? Nothing?"

Johnny said, "There's no time to tell you things you already know. Let's see them under blacklight and . . ."

Celeste said, "Yeah, yeah. And X-ray. Fine."

She laid both paintings on their backs on a table and turned off the overhead fluorescent lights. She brought the blacklights online and lowered them into place above the paintings.

Gwynn gasped. "Celeste! They're identical."

"Not completely identical," Johnny said. "The signature area appears to have been repaired in the original."

Everyone leaned in and examined the lower right corner of the original painting.

Celeste said, "It's subtle, but you're right. It is different."

"Why didn't that show up on the copy?" Gwynn asked.

Celeste shrugged. "I don't know, but maybe the X-ray will give us some answers."

She brought the lights back up and replaced the blacklight apparatus with an overhead X-ray machine. "Let's step behind the wall for this. Who knows? One of us might want children someday."

They moved behind a partial wall, and Celeste manipulated a few controls on a panel. "Okay, that's it. Let's take a look."

They moved to a table of computer monitors, and Celeste brought up the X-rays. "The one on the left is the original."

Johnny motioned toward the screen. "Zoom in on the signature."

She brought the image to ten times its original size and centered the signature on the screen.

"Does anybody want to explain what I'm seeing?" Johnny asked.

"It's called an overpaint," Gwynn began. "Instead of scraping off the old image or removing it with solvents, an art restoration expert sometimes paints over a damaged area of a painting in the restoration process. Sometimes, when artists didn't have the means to buy a new blank canvas, they'd paint over a piece of work they didn't particularly like."

Johnny scratched his chin. "Okay, I get that, but what is that image beneath the overpaint?"

Celeste blew up the image until it consumed the screen. She studied every line and curve. "It's another signature."

"Another signature?" Johnny said. "Whose?"

"I don't know. Give me a minute to enhance it." Celeste stroked the keys until a dark line filled the original signature. "That's definitely a K and an M, but the rest is gibberish."

Gwynn snapped her fingers. "I know who it is. I need a computer with an internet connection."

Celeste pointed to the table. "Pick one."

She typed furiously, and Johnny asked, "Who is it?"

Gwynn ignored him and kept working.

"Who is it?" he demanded.

"Give me a minute. His name won't come to me, but I can find it. I know that signature from somewhere."

A few minutes later, Gwynn slapped the table. "I knew it! It's Kazimir Malevich. He was a painter from the eighteen nineties through the twenties. His parents were most likely Polish, and he was probably born in Ukraine, but he's considered Russian for some reason. Who cares? Anyway, he was a big part of the Cubist movement."

"Cubist?" Johnny said. "Portraits are done by Cubist painters, aren't they?"

"They were before Cubism was a thing. Painters painted whatever would pay the rent most of the time. Although Malevich became a Cubist, he painted everything before then."

Johnny said, "So, here's the real question. Was he important enough to matter when Rasputin had the painting done?"

"Oh, yeah!" she said. "He was one of the darlings of the day. His stuff has sold for millions. In fact, his painting, *Suprematist Composition*, still holds the record for the highest price ever paid for a work by a Russian artist. Here it is."

Everyone stared at the screen, and Johnny said, "It's just a bunch of rectangles and lines. What makes it so special?"

Gwynn said, "Sixty million dollars makes it pretty special. That's what it sold for in two thousand eight."

Johnny took a step back and examined the *Monakh Tsaritsy*. "So, you're saying that painting of Rasputin was done by this Russian guy, Malevich, and somebody painted over his signature?"

Celeste said, "That's what it looks like."

"If Malevich was truly the darling of the day, as Gwynn said, who would paint over his signature like that?" Johnny asked.

Anya spoke up. "Rasputin would do it. Remember, the monk claimed the painting was done by *Ugly Neba*, Angels of Heaven, so he would have to cover Malevich's signature to support this claim."

Johnny squeezed his temples. "You Russians are weird people."

Anya said, "I do not claim all you *Americans* are weird because Charles Manson is American."

"Not the same," Johnny said.

Anya pushed Gwynn away from the computer and brought up a new picture. She pointed toward the painting and back at the computer screen. "Look at painting of Rasputin and picture of Charles Manson."

Johnny stared between the bearded faces and wild hair of the two men. "Okay, okay. I get it. I'm sorry for calling you weird."

"Is okay," Anya said. "We are weird, but not weird like Rasputin."

"Wait a minute," Gwynn said. "This changes everything. If Kazimir Malevich painted *Monakh Tsaritsy*, and we can prove it, the value of the painting goes through the roof, especially to Nikiti Morozov."

Johnny said, "So, let's hear it. How do we get this information to Morozov, and more importantly, how do we get in front of him?"

"I have perfect way," Anya said. "First, we must find Anatoly Asimov, man from auction who works for Morozov. If we can find him, I can explain to him what we found, and he will give to me key to Nikita Morozov."

Johnny shook his head. "No way. That guy will never give up access to Morozov. It's worth too much to him, and if Morozov is the recluse we believe him to be, there's no chance Asimov would risk losing his business."

Anya smiled. "Every person has price. If this painting is worth enough to make Asimov wealthy beyond all imagination, he will lead us directly to Morozov and walk away rich and happy with only finder's fee. This is what is called, yes? Finder's fee?"

"Yeah, that's what it's called," Gwynn said, "And that's brilliant."

Celeste groaned. "I don't know. It's not like we can just walk up to Asimov and say, 'Guess who painted the crazy monk?' He'll need proof, and we can't exactly bring him here to the DOJ so he can take a look at a painting we stole from a guy who stole it from Sotheby's."

"Not so fast," Johnny said. "Maybe we can. Like you said, if it's enough money, Asimov will give us the keys to the castle. Why would he care that we're the feds as long as he gets paid?"

"No, this is no good," Anya said. "Asimov is criminal and is greedy..."

Gwynn said, "Wait a minute. What makes him a criminal?"

Anya conceded. "Okay, maybe he is not criminal, but he is at least shady in world of maybe stolen art. Perhaps he does not steal it, but he will gladly have commission for delivering stolen piece to Morozov. I believe we must treat him like criminal because this is world he understands."

"What are you saying?" Johnny asked.

"I am saying we must kidnap him, bring him here with blindfold and hood, and show to him painting and X-ray of overpaint."

"What if he's not a criminal?" Celeste asked. "We'll freak him out and scare him to death."

"This is also fine. If he is scared, he will tell to us everything we want to know if we agree to let him live."

Johnny shook his head. "That's not how we do things at Justice. We're not in the kidnapping and threatening business."

Anya crossed her arms. "Then tell to us *your* plan."

He shook his head. "I don't know, but it doesn't involve kidnapping."

Gwynn said, "Maybe we can come up with a legitimate reason to arrest him and bring him in."

"If he's clean, that might work," Johnny said. "But if he's dirty, like Anya suspects, he'll just lawyer up and be back on the street in an hour."

The temporary supervisor paced the floor with his head squeezed between his palms. "What would Agent White do?"

Anya stepped beside him and laid her arm across his shoulder. "Let's go ask him."

15

Uydi s Yeye Puti
(Get Out of Her Way)

The chartered Gulfstream jet touched down at Aéroport International de Genève, and the four Americans climbed into the waiting car for the thirty-minute drive to Clinique de Genolier on the northern shore of lac Léman.

Gwynn stepped from the car. "How can you afford all of this?"

Anya took her hand. "This is not for you to worry about, and money was not collected by illegal means. Is perfectly legal, so is no problem."

"I wasn't suggesting you're a criminal. It's just that a private jet to Switzerland costs a ton of money, and I feel bad you're spending that kind of money for us."

Anya squeezed Gwynn's hand. "Is friendship, and this is why we have money . . . to share with people we love."

At the reception counter, in flawless German, Anya said, "We are here to see a patient named Raymond White. We are his family."

A few keystrokes later, the lady behind the desk said, "Mr. White is still in surgery, but you can wait for Dr. Müller in the lounge if you'd like."

Anya covered her mouth with both hands and stepped back from the counter as relief washed over her.

Gwynn watched in disbelief as her friend and partner was overcome with emotion. "Are you okay, Anya?"

The Russian turned and stepped through a closing door and into a corridor. By the time Gwynn pushed her way through the same door, she was sitting on the floor with her knees drawn to her face.

"Anya, what's going on? What do you need?"

She caught her breath. "Please wait for me away from here. I need moment or two. I do not know what is happening, and I am ashamed."

Gwynn fell to her knees in front of her friend and took her hands. "Anya, it's okay. I understand."

"No! You do not understand this. Is not possible for you to understand. I am not this person. I am not. Please, Gwynn . . . please. I need moment alone."

Gwynn squeezed her hands and stood, then she stepped back through the door and into the reception area.

Johnny said, "What's that all about? What's going on with her?"

Gwynn held up her palms. "Just give her a minute. She's having a girl moment."

"A girl moment? She doesn't have those. What's going on?"

Gwynn locked eyes with him. "Just give her a minute."

Johnny turned back to the reception counter. "Where is the lounge to wait for Dr. Müller?"

The lady motioned to a corridor and fumbled through the English. "Go to end . . . and uh . . . links abbiegen. Uh . . . I am sorry . . ."

Anya stepped beside Johnny and continued the conversation in German. After the instructions, she said, "*Danke*," and led the others down the corridor.

Once ensconced in the waiting lounge, Gwynn made a mug of tea and placed it into Anya's hands. "I get it, and we'll talk about it later."

Anya took the mug and laid a hand across Gwynn's. "You do not, and no, we will not, but thank you for tea. Is very kind of you."

The television offered only German, French, and Italian language channels, so it remained silent while the hands of the clock moved as if dragging themselves from the mud. Finally, after four agonizing hours, a surgeon wearing green scrubs stepped through a concealed doorway and into the lounge, and Anya bounded to her feet. "He is okay, yes?"

Dr. Müller reached for Anya and took her in his arms. In German, he said, "It's wonderful to see you again, Anastasia."

"Ray is okay, yes? You removed tumor, yes?"

He stepped back and motioned toward Celeste, Gwynn, and Johnny. "*Sind sie bei dir?*"

"Yes, yes, they are with me. Tell me Ray is okay."

He pulled off his surgical cap and spoke in English. "Your friend is going to be just fine. The surgery was a great success. I had to remove a small amount of the occiput bone and fuse the atlas and axis, which are the first two cervical vertebrae. It is typical in this type of surgery for us to remove less than eighty percent of the tumor, but the structure of Mr. White's tumor made it possible to access more volume than normal, and I am confident I removed one hundred percent of the tumor and a significant amount of the surrounding material, including the blood vessels that were feeding the growth. It was, most certainly, malignant, but the lab will confirm that later today. We're going to wake him up and perform a few simple motor skills and cognitive tests, but we will most likely induce a coma for three to five days to allow the trauma of the surgery to heal without swelling. He'll be closely monitored during that time, but I have every reason to believe he will return to normal life with limited restrictions for a few months and full recovery within six to eight months."

Anya said, "We can see him while he is awake for testing, yes?"

Dr. Müller studied the four of them. "One of you may see him while he is awake, but only briefly, and you will not do or say anything to upset him."

Anya beamed. "I will not upset him. I promise this."

Johnny said, "Wait a minute," but Gwynn gripped his wrist and whispered, "Unless you're writing the check to pay for the surgery, Anya is going in."

Johnny slumped in surrender, and Gwynn said, "Exactly."

Dr. Müller said, "Come with me."

Anya walked in locked step with the doctor as they passed through several double doors and into a private room where Ray White lay with a heavy brace around his neck and shoulders. His hair was disheveled, and his face looked pale and dry.

Anya hurried to the side of his bed and took his hand. "You chose to have surgery, and this makes me so very happy. Thank you, Ray."

"I didn't do it for you."

His voice was froggy and weak, but Anya didn't seem to notice.

"The others are here also."

"What others?"

She said, "Johnny Mac, Celeste, and of course, friend Gwynn."

"Johnny?" he mumbled. "He doesn't know."

She laughed. "He does now, and I told to him small lie that you did not tell him because you needed him to focus on mission and not on you. This is maybe true, yes?"

He smiled. "Maybe."

"Dr. Müller says you are cured."

Ray's eyes shot immediately to the doctor, and Müller said, "That is not precisely what I told her, but we do have very good news."

He went through the procedure with Ray until he'd shared the good news about removing all of the tumor, and a tear rolled from Ray's eye. "I don't know how to thank you."

Dr. Müller tilted his head. "You don't have to thank me, Mr. White. It's my pleasure. Cases like yours are the ones that keep my team and me encouraged to never stop."

Ray seemed to blush. "I do appreciate everything you've done, doctor, but I was talking to Anya."

Dr. Müller spun on a heel to see the beautiful Russian wiping a tear from her eye. "He is federal policeman inside United States and could not afford private clinic. I will pay for cost of surgery."

The doctor looked between Ray and Anya. "There is no cost for this one. After what you did for me, I could never consider charging you for any service I can provide. I will forever be in your debt."

"This is not true. Was only small thing I did for you. Of course I will pay."

"We'll discuss it later, but for now, I need to perform a few tests, and you're a distraction. Is there anything else the two of you want to discuss before we let you sleep again?"

"There is one thing," Anya said. "Johnny does not know what to do about one small thing in case inside America. I told to him I will handle and is only small matter. I will tell to him you said to stay out of my way. This is good with you, yes?"

"Yeah, that's good with me. And Anya, seriously . . . thank you."

She took his hand again. "Next time you wake up, mission will be over, and you will be ready to come home."

Dr. Müller eyed them. "Are the two of you, uh . . ."

Anya said, "No, we are only friends, and I sometimes work with him on police missions. This is all."

The doctor grinned. "Whatever you say."

Anya stepped from the room and followed the corridor back to the lounge, where she found Gwynn sitting alone and cradling a cup of coffee. "Where are others?"

"They've gone to find something to eat. Did you get to see him? How does he look?"

Anya nodded. "Yes, I saw him, but he would be ashamed if he knew how badly his hair was messed up."

Gwynn giggled. "His hair is always perfect."

"Not today. He looked like man who just had brain surgery, but Dr. Müller said he is doing perfectly well. I trust him. He will not lie to me."

"How do you know the doctor?" Gwynn asked.

"Is long story, but he needed my help, and I gave to him help. We are now friends."

Gwynn closed one eye. "Something tells me that's only part of the story, but I'll let you get away with it for now if we can talk about what happened earlier."

"No, friend Gwynn. I do not want to talk about this. Is embarrassing for me, and I do not like it."

"Anya, don't be embarrassed. You were overcome by emotion. It happens to all of us sometimes. It's nothing to be ashamed of. It just means you're human."

"No, this is not what it means. It means I am weak, and I cannot be weak. It is just that . . ."

She paused, and Gwynn said, "It's okay. You can tell me. It's just you and me."

Anya took a long, deep breath. "It is hard to explain what Ray does to me."

Gwynn gasped and covered her mouth. "You're in love with him, aren't you?"

Anya's eyes exploded. "No! I am not. This is not reason I was surprised."

"Surprised?" Gwynn said. "That wasn't surprise. That was relief on your face. Trust me. I know the difference."

"Okay," Anya said. "Maybe it was relief, but is more than this. You must understand, and is very difficult to explain. I was innocent child when my mother was taken from me. From that moment, I had no one. I was only tool for Soviet Union to shape and hammer and form into stronger, sharper tool. I was treated as thing, not as person."

Gwynn was enraptured by Anya's out-of-character sentiment.

"When you and Ray captured me in St. Augustine, I was animal. I killed without regard for life. I preserved myself at all costs with no consideration for anyone or anything outside myself. That is way of wild animal—not proper way for person to behave."

Gwynn frowned. "But you were . . ."

Anya laid a hand on Gwynn's arm. "Please let me finish. When I agreed to work with Ray and with you, I did also this to preserve myself, but as time passed, and I came to know and understand you and Ray and Johnny Mac, I was slowly no longer wild thing. I was person with friends and people who care for me. This is you, friend Gwynn. When I spoke with Ray yesterday, he said to me he was not going to have surgery, and I felt terrible pain inside heart. I did not want him to die. I pleaded with him to tell doctor to do surgery, but he would not agree for this."

She paused, caught her breath, and continued. "When we came to this place and woman said to us Ray was in surgery, it was like my heart was too full of happiness and it would explode."

Gwynn leaned toward her friend. "That's the most beautiful thing I've ever heard. This is a side of you I've never seen, and it's gorgeous. Why haven't you ever told me how you felt before today?"

Anya bowed her head. "Maybe is because I did not know this side of me existed until today."

Celeste and Johnny slipped through the door with Styrofoam cups and paper bags.

Celeste held up a bag. "We found this great little shop, and we brought back goodies. How's Agent White?"

Anya looked up. "He is pleased and is going back to sleep. Oh, and there is one more thing. He said to tell to you to get out of my way and let me do what Avenging Angel does best."

16

Ostrova v Potoke
(Islands in the Stream)

Back in DC, Johnny Mac steepled his fingers behind the desk he claimed as his. "First, I don't believe you that Agent White said for me to get out of your way, but I've been giving a lot of thought to what we should do next. I've come up with a plan that's sort of a hybrid of the two extremes we discussed before our little field trip to Switzerland."

Anya perked up. "Maybe he did not say exactly what I told you, but I was—what is word?—paraphrasing."

Johnny rolled his eyes. "Yeah, I figured. Anyway, here's the plan. We're going to approach Anatoly Asimov and cut him in. There's no way for us to know exactly what his agreement is with Morozov, but he's in the business of buying and selling art. I'm quite certain he understands commissions. We'll buy his cooperation."

"What if this does not work?"

"If this doesn't work," Johnny said, "I'll get out of your way."

This brought an enormous smile to Anya's face. "Do we know where he is?"

Johnny opened a file on his desk. "We don't know exactly where he is today, but he has dinner reservations for Tuesday night at Canlis in Seattle."

Gwynn said, "It looks like we're moving from one Washington to another."

Johnny checked his watch. "Get packed, tidy up any strings you've got dangling here in DC, and we'll be wheels up at nine tomorrow morning."

"What about Celeste?" Anya asked.

Johnny said, "I'll brief her, and she'll be on the plane, also." He turned to Gwynn. "And before you ask, Tom is packing, too. He'll meet us there."

Anya stuck out her bottom lip. "I am only person without date. Perhaps Anatoly is lonesome."

***

At precisely 9:00 a.m., the wheels of the federal government jet left the runway with two crewmen, three special agents, two electronics technicians, and one Mankiller. They touched down four hours later at Seattle-Tacoma International Airport, where a pair of black SUVs waited on the tarmac. As they descended the stairs, two men stepped from the SUVs, and Anya chuckled. "I think those two could not look any more like FBI agents."

Gwynn joined her friend in laughter. "I think you're right. They could've been sent over from central casting in Hollywood."

"Cut it out, ladies." Johnny stepped past them and stuck out his hand. "Johnny McIntyre."

The two agents shook hands and introduced themselves. "If you wreck our Suburbans, it's coming out of your budget."

"Noted," Johnny said. "Now, if you'll excuse us, we've got work to do."

They spent ten minutes loading their gear into the Suburbans and climbed inside. Arrangements had been made for a pair of adjoining apartments just north of the Space Needle, and it didn't take long for the team to settle in. By nightfall, the second apartment looked more like an operations center than a residence, and the techs had all three of Anatoly Asimov's cell phones under surveillance.

Anya and Gwynn watched the tracking screen as the three phones left dry land and seemingly hovered over Puget Sound.

"What do you see?" Johnny asked.

Gwynn pointed to the screen. "It looks like he got on a boat of some kind."

"Perfect," Johnny said. "Let's get some eyes down there."

Tom Elsmore, their borrowed Air Force OSI officer said, "I'll go."

Gwynn followed immediately behind him. "Me, too."

They grabbed two bags of video surveillance equipment and headed for the Suburban.

Twenty minutes later, Johnny's cell rang. "McIntyre."

"It's Gwynn. Are you still tracking the cell phones?"

"Affirmative. They're loitering about a thousand yards offshore. Can you see anything?"

Gwynn said, "We're setting up now. I think I see the boat, and it's a lot more than just a boat. It's somewhere between a yacht and a ship."

"Keep your eyes on it, and let me know as soon as your video gear is up and running."

"Tom's on it now, and it's active," Gwynn said.

Johnny said, "Celeste has it, but it's pretty dark."

"It'll improve when they move back to the dock . . . Wait a minute!"

"What is it?" Johnny demanded.

"Stand by."

"That's a chopper," Johnny heard Gwynn say before she returned to the phone.

"We've got a chopper climbing off the helipad."

Johnny squeezed the phone. "Get the tail number!"

"We're trying. I'll get the cleanest video we can, and then we can clean it up."

Johnny said, "Do what you can, but don't abandon the surveillance. Asimov may not be on the chopper."

"You got it. We'll keep sending video."

Johnny said, "Call if anything significant changes."

Anya eyed the video screen and turned to Celeste. "Can you track helicopter?"

Celeste didn't look up from her computer. "I'm on it, but no promises."

She worked furiously, and Anya silently wished for Skipper's skill on the mission. Chase Fulton's analyst would have the shoe size of everyone on the chopper by now.

"Got it!" Celeste almost yelled, and everyone in the room turned to see her monitor.

She pointed toward a small symbol on the screen. "That's it. They're flying due north, and they're doing well over a hundred knots."

The symbol flickered on and off in irregular patterns, and Johnny asked, "What's that flashing about?"

Celeste said, "I'm using mosaic satellite data, and it's not perfect."

"We need to know where he lands," Johnny said.

"I'm doing the best I can."

The cell phone rang, and Johnny thumbed the button. "What do you have?"

Gwynn said, "The yacht is almost back to the dock. You should have good, clean video."

Johnny turned to the video monitor. "Yeah, we've got it. Watch for Asimov to come off the yacht. We need to know if he's on that chopper."

"We're on it."

Johnny glanced at Celeste's monitor. "Good. Stay on it. We're tracking the chopper. He's headed due north for now."

Celeste looked up from her keyboard. "What if he goes to Canada?"

Johnny didn't hesitate. "Then we'll sic the Border Protection boys on him."

Gwynn said, "Asimov is coming off the boat. Do you want us to pick him up?"

Johnny considered the question. "Not yet. Just follow him, and let's see where he goes."

"What if he goes to the airport?" Gwynn asked.

"He won't. He's got dinner reservations, remember?"

"Ah, that's right. We're packing up. I'll call you when he makes his next stop."

Johnny said, "Perfect. We're tracking both of your cell phones." He disconnected and spun to watch the helicopter on Celeste's monitor. "Is he still heading north?"

Celeste said, "He turned slightly to the west and appears to be headed for Port Susan."

"What's Port Susan?"

"It's a bay off Puget Sound."

Every eye was glued to the monitor until Johnny's cell phone rang again. "McIntyre."

Tom's voice came through the speaker. "We've got him."

"Got him? What do you mean? I told you to just follow him."

"Sorry," Tom said. "We don't have him in custody. We just shadowed him to his house."

"How do you know it's *his* house?"

"His remote opened the garage, and he took the dog for a walk two minutes after pulling in, so he's either walking somebody else's dog, or this is his house."

"Good work," Johnny said. "Put him to bed and get back here. We're close to having a fix on Morozov."

"Will do," Tom said. "See you in a few."

Gwynn and Tom remained concealed and waited for Asimov and his pooch to return from their walk. Ten minutes later, they were back, and every light in the house was dark.

When they made it back to the apartment, Celeste was working feverishly over her keyboard.

Johnny said, "Nice work out there tonight, guys. As you can see, Celeste is trying to triangulate exactly where the chopper landed."

"I've almost got it," Celeste mumbled.

Gwynn and Tom settled onto the sofa at the same instant Celeste declared, "Winner, winner, chicken dinner! You're never going to believe this."

Everyone hit their feet and crowded around Dr. Mankiller.

"Check this out," she said. "It landed on a pretty small chunk of land just north of Hat Island."

"Bring up some daytime satellite images," Johnny said.

The screen filled with a bird's-eye view of the small island.

"That's it," Celeste said. "What better place could there be for a hermit? He's got his own island, and now we know exactly where he sleeps at night."

Anya said, "This is dangerous thinking. We know only this is where he will likely sleep tonight. We do not know where he will sleep tomorrow night."

"Okay, I'll give you that one," Celeste said, "but you've got to admit that's an ideal hidey-hole for a hermit crab like Morozov."

Anya nodded. "Is very good place, and not so easy for us to get inside."

Johnny propped himself on the edge of the table. "We can call in HRT to get us on the island."

Anya laughed. "This is terrible idea. Hostage Rescue Team is very good at breaking things and gaining entry, but is horrible at being quiet. I can get inside island without making sound. You will see."

Gwynn gave Anya a playful shove. "You're the coolest chick on Earth. Do you know that?"

Anya winked. "Yes, of course I know, but is nice of you to say."

Celeste held up a finger. "Wait. Before you declare Anya queen of the world, I just placed a satellite tag on Morozov's island. If there's movement big enough for the eyes in the sky to see, it'll be recorded on this very computer right here on my lap."

Gwynn said, "That's pretty close to queen-of-the-world quality right there. Celeste is catching up to you, Anya."

Celeste said, "I wasn't finished. Not only will it record everything, but it will also send me a text message letting me know it's happening."

Anya stood, walked with perfect posture to Celeste's side, removed her make-believe crown, and placed it with great ceremony on Dr. Mankiller's head.

Celeste took a small bow. "Thank you, my lady."

"At your service, my queen," came Anya's perfect reply.

That got a good laugh, but Celeste said. "I'm afraid we'll have to share the crown. I can't do that whole breaking-into-the-fortress thing she can do."

Anya grinned. "Is okay. I cannot do that whole making-satellites-obey-my-command thing."

Johnny slapped his forehead. "I've been given a court full of jesters. Go to bed, people. We've got a big day ahead of us tomorrow. We'll rattle Asimov's cage early tomorrow morning, and if he doesn't want to play ball, we'll hit the island."

Anya motioned for Johnny to follow her to her bedroom, and Celeste noticed. "Is not what you think, silly queen. Is only tactical question."

"In that case," Celeste said, "be gentle and send him back to me when you're finished."

Johnny stepped into the small room with Anya.

She said, "I think is best plan to access island and Morozov's home during night instead of day if Asimov is unusable. You are in charge, but we have many advantages inside darkness we do not have when is light."

Johnny said, "I agree. If Asimov won't come on board, we'll recon in the afternoon and knock on Morozov's door after bedtime. How's that sound?"

"It sounds like you are brilliant leader. Good night, Supervisory Special Agent."

17

Otvedi Menya k Svoyemu Lideru
(Take Me to Your Leader)

With dawn still lingering two hours beyond the eastern horizon of Puget Sound, Tom doused the lights of the Suburban and rolled to a stop four houses down from the house where Anatoly Asimov walked the dog only a few hours earlier.

Anya leaned forward from the back seat. "This will do. Keep the house in sight, but do not approach unless we call. We have no reason to believe Asimov is dangerous."

Tom met her gaze in the mirror. "What about the dog?"

"I will have him eating from my hand before Celeste disables alarm."

Tom scoffed. "Okay, whatever you say. I'm just a mic click away."

Anya, Gwynn, and Celeste slipped from the SUV like serpents and disappeared into the darkness while Tom situated the Suburban perfectly behind a landscaped island, giving himself a perfect line of sight to the house and an unobstructed course to intervene should it become necessary.

Reaching the side door of the house, Anya knelt and pulled her pick kit from a pocket. The deadbolt and knob lock surrendered in seconds, and Celeste slinked through the opening.

Anya followed her through the opening with Gwynn only inches behind. As they reached the living room, Anya gave the signal to hold in position. She crossed the carpeted floor in utter silence and lay prone beside the plush bed on which Asimov's Golden Retriever lay in peaceful sleep. From her pocket, she pulled out three pieces of Polish sausage containing a gentle drug that would encourage Goldy—or whatever his name was—to continue dreaming of frolicking in a peaceful meadow—or whatever dogs dream of—while his owner endured the most shocking morning of his life.

Anya stood and motioned for Gwynn and Celeste to follow as she approached the stairs. Placing each foot on the outer extremes of each stair tread, they climbed inch by inch without the wooden framework uttering so much as a sigh. The first door rested with barely an opening between its edge and the jamb. Anya squeezed the knob in her palm and gently lifted, taking the weight of the door from the hinges. Pushing inward at a snail's pace, she swung the door into the room barely far enough to peer inside. The gentle hum of a computer's cooling fan resounded from the darkness, and Anya pulled the door back to its original position.

The three continued down the second-floor hallway to the end, where an identical door waited. Anya gripped the knob and gave it a twist, but it didn't budge. She knelt and withdrew her pick kit for a second time and inserted a small metallic probe into the mechanism. The spring-loaded lock shot from its bolted position with a click that sounded like a clap of thunder inside Anya's head, and she froze.

Listening for any movement beyond the door, she silently scolded herself for allowing the cheap lock to unload so violently. Thirty seconds later, convinced Asimov hadn't heard the gong, she twisted the knob and carried the weight of the door in her palm as she pressed into the bedroom.

Celeste and Gwynn followed, and Anya pressed the door back to its closed position. Anya and Gwynn approached the bed while Celeste stood by the door awaiting the signal. When it came, she flipped the light switch, illuminating the room with brilliant white light and causing each of the three to squint against the assault.

Asimov didn't flinch. He lay on his side, breathing softly and rhythmically, even with the overhead light beaming into his face. Anya smiled, relishing the moment. She motioned for Gwynn and Celeste to move into position at the foot of the bed, and they followed her silent command.

She then gently lowered herself onto the mattress behind Asimov and moved with the patience of a stalking cat until her body was pressed against his back, then she whispered into his ear. "Anatoly . . . Anatoly . . . Wake up, Anatoly. Is time for school."

He rustled and groaned until his eyelids fluttered open and the world around him poured into his freshly awakened mind. He jolted, but Anya's arm around his chest held him in place.

She spoke softly in the man's native tongue. "It's okay, Anatoly. We're not going to hurt you. We simply need to have a conversation."

"What? Who are you?" He bucked and jerked against Anya's grasp until she released him and leapt to her feet.

Asimov lunged for his nightstand, and Gwynn reached for her Glock, but Anya laid a hand against her wrist. Asimov slapped the surface of the bedside table until his hand fell on his glasses, and he shoved them onto his face.

With disbelief and confusion flooding his senses, he shook his head and raised a hand against the offensive light from above. "You. What are you doing here? What is going on?"

Anya continued her calm, measured tone. "Let's speak English, Anatoly. This way, we can all understand each other."

He retreated against the headboard, pulling the blanket tightly beneath his chin, and Anya sat on the edge of the bed. "I told you do not be afraid. We are not going to hurt you unless you make us. Is okay to relax. We are here only to have conversation."

The man trembled. "What do you want? What is this all about?"

"We are here to talk about painting."

He shoved his glasses onto his forehead with both fists and buried his knuckles into his eyes in a desperate attempt to clear his vision and force the scenario to make sense. "The painting? Which painting?"

Anya leaned closer. "The *Monakh Tsaritsy*."

His hands dropped from his eyes, and his glasses fell back into place. "That painting was stolen."

Anya smiled. "Yes, but not by the person you believe."

"What?"

"We have the painting, and we know the truth."

He let the blanket fall onto his lap. "What truth?"

Anya slowly shook her head in small, fluid motions. "Do not try to play games with me, Anatoly. I know everything, and I am most dangerous person you know."

The man laughed. "That's a good one. You are buyer of art, like me. We are not dangerous people. We are businesspeople."

Anya lowered her chin. "We are not what you are, Anatoly. Person Nikiti Morozov sent to steal painting failed. I made him fail. You can read police report from Chicago if you like. Man was found unconscious outside Sotheby's with no identification and no painting. This is because I have painting."

The look on Asimov's face said he was fully awake but still unsure of what was happening around him. "You have *Monakh Tsaritsy?*"

Anya smiled broadly. "I do, and I know secret of painting."

He furrowed his brow. "What secret?"

"I told to you do not play games. I know painting was not created by Ugly Neba."

He grimaced. "Everyone knows this is lie. Angels do not create paintings, even for Rasputin, but no one knows who painted the portrait."

Anya held her expression. "I know who painted it, and I believe your benefactor knows also. This is why he hired unidentified man to steal painting from gallery."

For the first time, Asimov almost smiled. "You are playing dangerous game. It is not wise to press Nikiti Morozov. He has dangerous allies."

"Not as dangerous as me."

He closed his eyes. "You have no idea what you are doing, and you will not survive this foolish endeavor. I do not know what you are talking about. To my knowledge, the painting has no authentic creator, and Nikiti Morozov is a legitimate businessman."

Anya asked, "How much were you to be paid for ruse in Chicago?"

"I take only a modest acquisition fee and nothing more."

"But you were not acquiring painting in Chicago. You were providing plausible deniability for theft. This is why you were so aggressive in pretending to prevent me from buying painting. You are poor actor, Anatoly. You will now take me to Nikita Morozov, and for this I will pay you modest acquisition fee."

He cleared his throat. "I am not foolish enough to do that, and if I were, you do not have enough money to convince me to do it. You will have no audience with Mr. Morozov, but I am willing to act as liaison and representative for him. If you truly have *Monakh Tsaritsy*, I will broker sale, but you must stop with foolishness of knowing true painter. No one will ever know who painted it."

Anya turned to Gwynn and extended a hand. "Give to me papers."

Gwynn produced a folded collection of papers and placed them in Anya's palm.

The Russian then laid the papers on top of the cover in Asimov's lap. "Read."

Asimov adjusted his glasses and lifted the papers. "What are these?"

Anya said, "It is federal search warrant to search your home, automobiles, business, and storage areas. On back page, you will see my affidavit swearing you tried to sell to me stolen painting of Rasputin. FBI will search, and they will find *Monakh Tsaritsy* because I will place it inside one of places in search warrant. You will be arrested, and you will go to prison."

"Why?" he groaned. "Why would you do this to me?"

"There is other option," Anya said. "You can take me to Morozov, and warrant will disappear. Is up to you."

He closed his eyes and sighed. "You will never get away with this. My security system will—"

Celeste cut him off. "Oh, yes, please rely on your PGS Secure-Alert system. Your account number with PGS is seven two seven four one one six one, and your de-arm code is your favorite aunt's birthday in reverse order. Please tell us again how your security system will be of service to you."

He stammered, "How . . . ? How did you . . . ? This is not possible."

"It is not only possible, Anatoly, but is happening. You have only choice to do as we wish."

"You do not understand," he said. "I cannot do this for you. He will have me killed. The only choice for me is prison or death."

Anya paused to reconsider their approach, and Asimov held up the warrant. "Are you FBI?"

Anya snapped. "No! We are not. Do I look or sound like FBI to you?"

He studied the papers. "Then how do you have a copy of a warrant before it is executed?"

"We are not FBI!"

Something about the man's expression and tone rang inside Gwynn's head, and she asked, "Why do you want to know if we're the FBI?"

Asimov dropped the papers, and they scattered on his bed. "ATF or some other government agency I do not know?"

Gwynn strengthened her tone. "Why do you keep asking this question?"

Asimov stared into Gwynn's face and began to sob. Special Agent Gwynn Davis took control of the room, pulling Anya from the bed and sitting even closer to Asimov than her partner had. "Listen to me, Anatoly. We have nothing against you. You are caught in the middle of something you probably don't understand, and that's a terrible situation for anyone. Tell me what's going on inside your head."

He wiped his face with the sleeve of his sleeping shirt. "I never wanted to be part of this. I am an art buyer. I came to this country with nothing, and . . ." He paused, wiped his face again, and stared nervously around the room. "Did you kill Sacha?"

"Who is Sacha?"

"My Golden Retriever."

Gwynn said, "She's just sleeping. We gave her a mild tranquilizer on our way in, but she'll be fine in a couple of hours. Tell me what you want."

He choked out the words. "I want to be back in Moscow, poor and hungry again."

"Tell me why you want to know if we are feds?"

He squeezed his eyelids closed until flashes of orange and red exploded across his vision. "I will cooperate and tell you everything I know about Nikiti Morozov if it will keep me alive and outside of prison."

Gwynn swallowed hard and stood. "Get up, get dressed, and I will take you to my supervisor. You will tell us everything you know, and if it rises to the level of significant prosecutable information, we will protect you and provide you with a new home and identity."

18

Vsya Pravda
(The Whole Truth)

While Anya guarded Anatoly Asimov through his morning regimen to ensure he didn't disappear, Gwynn thumbed her phone.

"McIntyre."

"Johnny, it's Gwynn. We've had a dramatic turn of events. We're bringing Asimov in."

Johnny fumbled his coffee cup. "What? You're bringing him in where?"

"Sorry, that was abrupt. Everything was going smoothly until he broke down and decided he wanted to spill his guts."

"Spills his guts? About what? He's an art dealer. What guts does he have to spill?"

"Apparently, Morozov is involved in a lot more than just stolen art, and Asimov knows where the bodies are buried."

"What did you promise him?" Johnny demanded.

"I didn't promise anything. I told him *if* his information rose to the proper level, we would protect him. And I emphasized the *if*."

Johnny suddenly forgot what made him lust for the position and power of supervisory special agent. "Give me a minute to think."

"We don't have a minute, Johnny. You need to make a decision. Where are we taking this guy?"

Johnny grunted. "Take him to the FBI field office, and I'll meet you there. What's your ETA?"

"Less than thirty minutes," she said, and the line went dead.

Her next call was answered by a man with no indecision in his voice.

Tom Elsmore said, "Go for Tom."

Gwynn wasted no time. "Pull in front of the house and open the back door. We're coming out with a cooperating witness."

"Roger. Moving."

With Asimov dressed and on his feet, Anya led him from the door to the waiting SUV and hustled him inside. Almost before she could get him buckled in, Gwynn and Celeste followed them inside, and they were moving.

Tom looked up into the mirror. "Say destination."

Celeste said, "Eleven-Ten Third Avenue."

Gwynn gave her a sideways glance. "Do you have the address of every field office memorized?"

Celeste nodded. "Yeah, don't you?"

"No, I barely remember my own address."

Asimov said, "I knew you were FBI."

"We're not FBI," came four voices as one.

Tom pulled the Suburban into the garage at the FBI field office and into the secure reception area, where Gwynn walked Asimov in as if she'd done it a thousand times. "Supervisory Special Agent McIntyre."

The reception officer motioned down the hall. "Interview four."

Seconds later, Asimov was seated in a comfortable chair beside a small table in a carpeted, well-lit room that looked nothing like the interrogation room he expected.

Gwynn asked, "Would you like some coffee or tea?"

"Am I under arrest?"

Gwynn took a seat in an identical chair as Asimov's. "No, Anatoly, you're not under arrest. If you were, you'd be wearing handcuffs and sitting on a hard metal chair. With your willingness to assist in our investigation, we're on the same team. You have nothing to fear."

He sighed. "I have everything to fear, Special Agent. You could never understand."

"My name is Gwynn, and I'll be with you all the way. You've got nothing to worry about as long as you tell us only the truth."

A gentle tap came at the door, and Johnny stuck his head into the room. "Do you need anything?"

Asimov glanced up at him and back to Gwynn. "Tea would be very nice."

She patted the table. "Sit tight. I'll be right back with your tea, and we'll have a few questions, all right?"

He nodded, and she vanished.

The psychological game was afoot, and Asimov—even in his comfortable chair—began to sweat.

"He wanted tea," Gwynn said.

Johnny nodded. "Give it to Anya. I want her in the box with me in case we run into language hurdles."

Gwynn made the tea and slid the cup toward Anya. "I've been building rapport, so I'd like to start the ball rolling."

Johnny considered her request. "Okay, let me Mirandize him and swear him in. That'll put the bad-cop hat on me, and you can play good cop."

Johnny stepped into the interview room with his best Ray White expression and dragged the chair directly in front of Asimov. "Are you Anatoly Nikolaevich Asimov?"

"Yes, I am."

"My name is Supervisory Special Agent McIntyre with the U.S. Department of Justice, Mr. Asimov. I'm in charge of this operation, and I don't have time for you to make this day longer than it has to be. You're either going to cooperate fully or not at all. There is no in-between. Do you understand?"

"Yes, sir."

Johnny nodded. "Good. I need you to listen closely. You have the right to remain silent. Anything you say can be used against you. You have the right to speak with or have an attorney present with you during questioning. If you cannot afford a lawyer, we have no obligation to provide one for you. If you decide to cooperate and answer questions now without a lawyer present, you have the right to stop answering at any time. Do you understand your rights as I have explained them?"

Asimov said, "I do."

"Very good," Johnny said. "Now, we're going to question you under oath. The penalty for perjury is up to five years of imprisonment for every count. That means if you lie to us, we will prosecute you to the fullest extent of the law. Do you understand?"

"Yes, I understand. I will tell only truth."

Johnny said, "Good. Now, raise your hand and repeat after me. I, Anatoly Asimov, do solemnly swear to tell the truth, the whole truth, and nothing but the truth, withholding nothing related to the questioning, so help me God."

Anitoly repeated the oath, and Johnny slid two pages across the small table. "Sign at the bottom of each page."

Asimov signed, and Johnny retrieved the paperwork and left the room.

"He's all yours, good cop."

Anya poured a second cup of tea and followed Gwynn into the interview room. Each laid their credential pack on the table beside Asimov.

Gwynn said, "Anatoly, I am Special Agent Gwynn Davis, and she is my partner, Special Agent Ana Fulton. We are with the U.S. Department of Justice. We're investigating Nikiti Morozov for numerous offenses against the people of the United States. It is our job to speak with you to strengthen and narrow our investigation. Should you provide information that bolsters our position and leads to the arrest and conviction of Mr. Morozov, the United States is prepared to offer considerable compensation including, but not limited to, relocation, assignment of a new identity, and lifetime protection under the provisions set forth in the Witness Security Program as administered by the U.S. Marshals Service. Are you now willing to speak with us concerning your knowledge of Mr. Morozov?"

Anya placed a cup of tea in Anatoly's hand, and he said, "Thank you, but I do not believe your name is Ana Fulton."

She took a small sip of her tea. "I was not given this name at birth, but is my name now."

He took a timid sip and licked his lips. "I will tell you everything I know, and I will trust you to keep your word concerning my safety."

Gwynn opened her notebook. "Let's start with a question you asked this morning. You specifically asked if we were ATF. I'd like to know what prompted that question."

Anatoly cocked his head. "Because of the guns, of course."

Gwynn shot a glance at Anya and bluffed. "Of course we know about the guns, but tell us what you know, and we'll compare notes."

Anatoly said, "I am sure you know Morozov provides black-market weapons to street gangs throughout California, but that is only drop in bucket, as you Americans like to say."

Gwynn scribbled a note. "Keep talking."

"He is now exporting across border to Victoria."

"British Columbia?"

"Yes, but that is not limit of his network. He also provides weapons in Midwest in cities of Chicago, St. Louis, Kansas City, Cincinnati, and Detroit. I am certain there are more, but I cannot think of names of places right now. You have to understand. I am very nervous. If it is known that I provided information to you, I will be a dead man within hours."

Gwynn shrugged. "I don't know, Anatoly. So far, you haven't given us anything we didn't already know. You need to step up your game, or I'll be powerless to protect you."

"I am sorry, but I cannot recall more names. But I will tell you when I remember them. I swear to this."

Gwynn smiled and softened. "It's okay, Anatoly. Just relax. Nothing bad is going to happen to you. I promise you that."

"Is impossible to relax," he said. "My life is over no matter what happens next. I will either be killed, imprisoned and killed, or become someone I am not."

Gwynn gave him a gentle smile. "You're doing the right thing, Anatoly. Just keep talking. Tell me everything you know about the guns, then we'll move on to the next topic."

Anatoly took a longer sip of his tea that was rapidly approaching room temperature. "That would be the girls, yes?"

Gwynn had to bite the inside of her jaw to retain her composure. "Yes, naturally, but we'll get to them. Let's talk some more about the weapons trafficking for now."

Anatoly talked until Gwynn had four full pages of notes on the details of Morozov's weapons-trafficking network.

When he paused, she asked, "How do you know so much about the weapons scheme?"

He lowered his chin. "I was forced to have weapons and ammunition packed inside crates of art I delivered to clients across country. I was one of Morozov's delivery drivers, but I was only one of dozens. Coffee is his favorite cargo for hiding weapons and especially ammunition. Dogs cannot smell gunpowder through strong smell of coffee beans."

Gwynn continued writing. "We'll need a list of all the companies you can think of who carried weapons and ammo for Morozov."

Asimov spat several names out, then said, "Just like before, I cannot remember every name, but I will tell to you when it comes to me."

"That's fine," Gwynn said. "Let's take a little break so this doesn't become overwhelming for you. If you need to use the restroom, you're welcome to do so. We'll bring more tea and continue in ten minutes or so. Is that okay with you?"

He nodded. "Yes, this is fine, and perhaps I will remember names while we are having break."

Anya stood and smiled down at the man. "*Spasibo, Anatoliy, ty ochen' smelyy.*"

He said, "No, this is not brave, comrade. This is terrible."

Gwynn and Anya left the room together and stepped into the booth where Johnny and Celeste had been listening to every word.

Gwynn almost squealed when she spoke. "Can you believe this? Does anybody care about the art anymore?"

Johnny couldn't hide his excitement. "It's a goldmine, for sure. What do you think he's going to tell us about the girls, whoever they are?"

"I suspect it's prostitution, but I don't know."

Anya said, "I think it is something worse than merely prostitution. He made terrible look on face like eating something sour when he mentioned the girls."

Johnny said, "We'll see. I wish Agent White could be here to see this. It's a goldmine, I tell you. Our very own goldmine."

With their elation under control—at least temporarily—Gwynn and Anya returned to the interview room, and Gwynn reopened her notebook. "Okay, Anatoly, was the break long enough?"

He nodded. "I suppose now you wish to talk about hundreds of young girls being brought into United States through Arizona and Southern California for work in sex business."

19

Nastupit' Yemu na Golovu (Step on His Head)

Maintaining her confident, nonchalant demeanor, Gwynn choked back the surprise and sudden rage.

Anya, on the other hand, did not. She bolted to her feet. "I will conduct interview now."

Gwynn held up a hand in a wasted attempt to control her partner.

Anya ignored the hand and stared through Anatoly Asimov. In their native Russian, she asked, "What role do you play in child sex trafficking?"

"None. I know of it only because sometimes weapons and girls come to America in same containers."

Anya scowled. "You are under oath, and if you tell lies, there will be no protection for you. You understand this, yes?"

Anatoly nodded. "Once, several months ago, I . . ." He stopped, and his chest rose and fell as his sobbing returned. "I am sorry. It was only once, I swear."

"What did you do?" Anya demanded.

He wiped his face. "I drove twelve girls from Los Angeles to Las Vegas."

Gwynn laid a hand on Anya's shoulder. "That's enough."

Anya made no acknowledgment of her partner's hand nor her command. "Where, precisely, did you take them in Las Vegas? Who did you give them to? Do you have daughter? Do you?"

Gwynn tightened her grip on Anya's shoulder. "I said that's enough. Step outside."

Anya said, "I am not finished with questions."

"Yes, you are," Gwynn said. "Step outside. I will join you in a moment."

Johnny stepped into the interview room without a knock. "Anya, come with me. Now."

She narrowed her icy stare. "If you are lying, or if you do not tell everything you know about selling little girls, no one can protect you. This is solemn vow from me."

"Anya!" Johnny ordered. "Now!"

After a stare that could melt stone, Anya turned and followed Johnny from the room.

"What the hell was that about? You know better than to interrupt an interview while it's yielding fruit."

Anya focused on his determined eyes. "You have never been little girl with hands of men doing things you cannot understand. There is no greater hell than for innocent child to experience this evil, and is something your mind cannot comprehend because it never happened to you."

"I get it," he said. "But we can't let our emotions get the best of us during an interrogation. You have to understand that."

Anya stepped to within inches of her temporary boss. "Imagine Celeste giving to you beautiful baby girl and then that man selling her to men who will rape, torture, and destroy her. Imagine this, and try keeping emotion from getting best of you."

Johnny closed his eyes and devoted every ounce of strength he possessed to banish the scene Anya painted from his mind. "I'm sorry."

Gwynn stepped from the interview room. "We're in over our heads. You've got to bring in the FBI and Homeland Security."

"I'm already on it," Johnny said. "Is Asimov writing a statement?"

Gwynn nodded. "Yeah, but it's just busywork. We've got everything recorded."

Johnny sighed. "I know . . . including Anya's threat."

"Was not threat," Anya said. "Was assurance he would tell all of truth. Fear is wonderful motivator, and is also something I am very good at putting in hearts of prisoners."

Johnny said, "Yes, you are, but that's not how this works. Asimov isn't a prisoner. He's a cooperating witness. And speaking of cooperation, we need to know if he's going to be missed if we tuck him away somewhere nice and safe for a while."

Gwynn said, "I'll find out, but I can't let Anya back in that room after the stunt she pulled in there."

The Russian said, "I will tell to you same as I told to Johnny Mac..."

Gwynn said, "It's not necessary. I get it, and I understand, but you blew your top in there, and having you back in that room would only serve to frighten him and limit the quality of information he's spewing."

Anya said, "I did not mean to mess up interview, but only thing I care about right now is stopping trafficking of little girls. Art, guns, I do not care. Innocent children, about them, I care, and if I have to break his fingers one at a time to get to truth, I will do this gladly and with smile on face."

Gwynn said, "I know. Like I said, I get it, but we can't put you back in there."

"What if question of language comes up? You will need me."

Gwynn shook her head. "There are at least a dozen people in this building who speak Russian. What I need from you is to watch him for lies. Listen and watch. Let me know every time you even think he's lying or hiding anything. You're staying out here with Johnny, and I'll wear an earpiece. If you hear or see something that I should probe, tell me. Got it?"

Anya said, "Yes, I can do this."

Gwynn turned to Johnny. "How far do you want me to push this?"

Johnny said, "Let's change gears and find out if he'll be missed and how to get in front of Morozov. Do you want me in there with you?"

"No, not yet. I've established trust, worked through some tough admissions, and I yanked Anya when she got scary. That bought me some goodwill, I'm sure. Let me keep going."

"Okay, it's your show, good cop."

Gwynn steadied herself and pushed back through the door and into the interview room. "How are you coming on the statement?"

Asimov looked up. "It is harder than I expected."

"That's okay," Gwynn said. "We can work on that later. For now, I want to talk about keeping you safe."

Asimov's posture softened, and his eyes took on a refreshed look. "Does this mean I have told you enough to place me in Witness Security?"

"Don't think about that right now," she said. "Let's focus on the short term. If you disappear, will Morozov miss you? How often are you in touch with him?"

Asimov said, "I must be available to him. With *Monakh Tsaritsy* supposedly stolen, he will burn down all of world to find it, especially if he hired original thief. I will be expected to start many of those fires myself."

Gwynn made a few notes. "Okay, so here's the big question. How do we get in front of Nikita Morozov?"

Asimov studied the floor beneath his feet. "You cannot, but I can."

Gwynn lifted her pen from the page. "I think you're underestimating us, Mr. Asimov. We know where he lives and how he travels."

"Because you think you know where he lives, you believe you can walk into house like my house and put dog to sleep?"

"No. You were a soft target, Mr. Asimov. We know Morozov is not. However, we are very good at what we do."

"You do not know where he lives. Fewer than five people know where he lives. I am not one of those few."

Gwynn let the possibilities roll through her mind until Anya's voice sounded in her ear. "Ask him how he can get in front of Morozov."

Gwynn said, "Tell me, then. If *we* can't get in front of Morozov, how can you?"

Asimov smiled. "First, you must tell to me who painted *Monakh Tsaritsy.*"

"This isn't a negotiation, Mr. Asimov. Please don't mistake my kindness for weakness. We are many things, but weak will never be one of them."

"Forgive me, Agent Davis. I did not mean to imply you are incapable. It is my belief that if I can present *Monakh Tsaritsy* to Morozov and prove to him who original painter is, this will be bait your prey cannot resist."

Anya's voice was replaced by Johnny's. "Step on his head, Davis."

Gwynn hardened her expression. "Cooperating witnesses do not dictate our operations, Anatoly. You waived your right to legal counsel and confessed to numerous felonies. We are prepared to keep our word and provide protection for you. However, you must first prove to us that your information is thorough, true, and adequate to acquire an arrest and conviction. You've yet to fulfill your requirements. Sit tight."

Asimov began to speak, but Gwynn stood, turned on a heel, and stepped from the room.

Johnny waited until Gwynn settled onto a chair far less comfortable than the ones inside the interview room before saying, "Maybe you should've been the bad cop. Well done."

Anya stood. "I will make him understand he is not in position of power. Stop recording."

Celeste leapt from her seat and slammed herself against the door. "Uh, I'm just the tech here, but that sounds like a terrible idea."

Johnny pointed toward Anya's vacant chair. "Sit down. You're not going back in there for any reason, especially not to teach him a lesson."

Anya sat, but everything about her posture said she wanted to be in fisticuffs with Anatoly Asimov.

Johnny steepled his fingers. "We can't let him call the shots, but his idea isn't a bad one."

Gwynn smirked. "You're right, but a lot can go wrong."

Anya said, "I am not questioning your authority, Johnny Mac, but attorney general or someone close to her must make decision, yes?"

Johnny nodded. "Yeah, I'm certainly not making it. There's too much at stake, but we do need to get the ball rolling. Celeste, we need a new painting that is an exact copy of the original with Kazimir Malevich's signature painted over it. How long will that take?"

Celeste grinned as if she'd just hit the jackpot. "I thought you might ask for that, so it's already cooking in the oven. It should be ready by tomorrow morning."

Johnny sighed, "And that's why we can't afford to lose you to the CIA."

Celeste and Anya shared a glance.

"It may not be the CIA who gets me. We'll see."

Johnny made a mental note to explore that statement later. "Davis, see if they've got a holding cell that resembles a hotel room in this place. I think we need to hold on to this guy. He's too flakey to let him back out into the wild."

Gwynn nodded and stepped from the room as Johnny said, "Okay, Anya, let's have it. What do you see?"

She didn't hesitate. "I see worthless piece of garbage who helped put little girls in hands of terrible men. This is all I see."

Johnny sighed. "I know. That's eating me, too, but there's a lot more to this. We can bust Asimov now, but that doesn't do anything to stop the trafficking. We need to get to Morozov. From him, Homeland Security can follow the chain to the top and bust the ringleaders."

Anya licked her lips and tried to expand her focus. "Asimov is frightened, and this is normal, but he is also on edge of feeling important. Is dangerous balance, no?"

Johnny nodded. "Indeed, it is. That's why I had Davis crush him a little. We can't let him believe he's our only avenue of access to Morozov. We have to keep him leaning toward the side of being afraid."

"I can make sure of this. Just let me back inside for two minutes."

Johnny leaned back. "What would you do if I let you back in there? I mean, what *exactly* would you do?"

Anya said, "I would whisper into his ear things that would keep him awake for rest of his life."

"Can you do it without physically hurting him?"

"I can."

Johnny shook his head, incapable of believing what he was about to do. "If you touch him, you're out of the investigation. Do you understand?"

Anya smiled. "You are letting me do this, yes?"

Johnny said, "Yes, but only words. Nothing else." He turned to the panel and shut off the audio and video recording in the interrogation room.

Anya stood, opened the door, and slipped inside.

Celeste said, "This is a terrible idea, Johnny. What if she kills him?"

Johnny held up a hand. "It was a judgment call."

Anya perched on the edge of the chair in front of Asimov and spoke softly in Russian. "Listen closely to me, Anatoly. I was innocent girl child in Moscow in hands of men with power. They did things to me that would kill most children. Part of me survived, but my innocence was trampled beneath their boots. The part of me that survived is strong, and deadly, and evil. I have no ability to feel pity or sorrow for men who hurt children, or men who make it possible for others to hurt them. I would love nothing more than to gut you like pig for what you have done, but as long as you are obeying the people I work for, I cannot do this. So, I am praying you disobey and turn away. I vow to you, Anatoly, that you will suffer pain beyond anything you can imagine, and I will put inside you the same fear that is inside those innocent girls you transported to Las Vegas. I have only one loyalty, and that is to destroying men like you and the men who tore my childhood from inside me. I make solemn vow to tear your heart from inside your chest if you turn your back on what is good."

She stood with her eyes still locked on his, and with a blindingly fast strike, she splintered the small wooden table beside Asimov. "Doubt me if you will, Anatoly, but this would be worst decision of life. I am not like the people on other side of mirror. I am simple and unafraid. This should terrify you."

20

DRUGIYE RUSSKIYE
(OTHER RUSSIANS)

Special Agent Gwynn Davis, dressed in a blue suit with her badge clearly visible and her Glock readily detectible behind her right hip, stepped through a secure sallyport and knocked on the apartment door. Anatoly Asimov opened the door, and Gwynn studied her cooperating witness. "It would appear someone made a poor estimation of your size."

Anatoly stretched against the constraints of the button-down shirt the FBI had supplied and tugged at the obviously oversized pants. "These certainly do not qualify as tailored for me."

Gwynn motioned with an open hand into the corridor. "Come with me. We'll get you some better-fitting clothes, and I have something to show you."

Inside a makeshift laboratory where Celeste erected the equipment necessary to examine the painting her team back in DC created and aged, Johnny, Anya, and Dr. Mankiller awaited their guest of honor.

Johnny checked his watch. "What's taking her so long?"

Anya said, "Maybe Anatoly is still sleeping. I will go and find her if you would like."

Johnny waggled a finger. "Oh, no, you don't. I can't have you running loose in an FBI field office. God only knows what havoc you'd create."

Anya laid a hand across her chest. "This breaks my heart. You do not trust me, temporary boss?"

Celeste giggled, and Johnny did not.

He said, "No one in his right mind trusts you."

"Friend Gwynn trusts me."

Johnny rolled his eyes. "She doesn't count. You two have got some sort of bond that nobody understands."

"This is called *druzhba*. Word is *friendship* in English."

Gwynn led Anatoly through the door, and Johnny checked his watch again.

Gwynn said, "I know. I'm sorry. The knucklehead FBI agents who picked out Mr. Asimov's clothes thought they were dressing a pigmy. We had to get him some clothes that fit."

"I'm in no way surprised," Johnny said. "Good morning, Mr. Asimov. Dr. Mankiller has something to show you that you'll find quite interesting."

Celeste pulled the drape from the painting resting on the easel, and Asimov gasped.

"Is that the original frame?"

Celeste shook her head. "No, we had it reframed. Your thief ripped it from its original housing and broke the canvas frame. Fortunately, the painting itself wasn't damaged."

He took several steps toward the painting and examined it with a practiced eye. "It is truly a magnificent work of art. I can almost feel Rasputin's insanity."

Celeste shrugged. "If you say so, but that's not exactly what we brought you here to see. I assume you're familiar with the process of X-raying paintings to find overpaints, restorations, and flaws."

"Yes, of course," Asimov said.

Celeste handed him a thick, lighted magnifying glass. "Take a good look at the signature in the lower right corner."

He took the glass from her hands, knelt in front of the painting, and examined the corner for several minutes. "It does appear a restoration may have been done, but it is very good work."

Celeste motioned toward a monitor. "Take a look at this. It's the X-ray of the signature area."

Asimov stood and frowned at the image.

Celeste asked, "Do you recognize that signature?"

"No. I cannot make it out."

"Let me give you a hand." She added some definition to the image and traced the signature with the same dark lines she'd used the first time they discovered the painter's true identity.

When she finished, Asimov choked out the words, "That is Kazimir Malevich. This cannot be authentic."

"I thought you might say that," Celeste said, "so, I've arranged for an X-ray machine so you can watch it in real time."

Asimov gasped. "No! Do not expose it to more radiation. I will believe you for now because this makes everything make sense. Of course Morozov wants this painting so badly."

Celeste said, "You're right. Further exposure to X-ray isn't good for the painting, but there's one lingering question. How does he know about the signature overpaint?"

Asimov froze. "I do not know answer to this, but I have other question. How did you know?"

Gwynn fielded that one. "You can be assured that Morozov didn't find out the same way we did, and we'll leave it at that."

The look on Asimov's face said his wheels wouldn't stop turning based on such an answer. "How can you be certain of this?"

Gwynn grinned as if she had a secret Asimov would never know. "Because we are very good at what we do. Otherwise, you wouldn't be here."

Asimov stared into the painting as if mesmerized, and Gwynn touched her finger to her lips to stop Johnny from breaking the trance.

When it appeared Asimov would never pull himself from the painting, Gwynn stepped beside him and let their shoulders touch. "Breathtaking, isn't it?"

He added barely detectable pressure to their touch. "Russian word is *zavorazhivayushchiy*. I think there is no English word so strong. It is beyond my mind to believe both Mad Monk, Rasputin, and great master Kazimir

Malevich held this painting in their own hands. I would give everything I have to know who made overpaint of signature."

Gwynn let the moment continue, dragging Asimov further and further into the trap. Men from every corner of the world had found themselves ensnared in the classic Russian honeytrap of irresistible women, like her partner. Those men surrendered their morality, their profession, and oftentimes a piece of their souls when they found themselves in the arms—and in the bed—of one of the most beautiful women on Earth, but carnal, lustful yearning wouldn't be the undoing of Asimov and Nikita Morozov. For them, the irresistible draw of the rare masterpiece with enormous historical significance in the lives of both men's families and their countrymen was beyond allure, beyond desire, and worthy of obsession. That obsession would be the cord from which she would spin the twine, tie the snare, and choke her prey into submission and ultimate demise.

She allowed Asimov the moment as he drew ever closer to the trap of the huntress. Finally, she gave Johnny a small nod.

He cleared his throat. "Okay, Anatoly. Here's what happens next. You get Morozov on the phone and tell him you've been approached by the people who possess the *Monakh Tsaritsy*, and that those people revealed the truth behind the creator of the painting. You are to tell him you've examined the painting and seen the X-ray. Make him understand that you are certain it was originally painted by Kazimir Malevich and overpainted by someone before Rasputin showed it to the tsarina. Every word of that is the truth. Don't you agree?"

Asimov still couldn't take his eyes from the painting. "Yes, all of it appears to be true."

Johnny continued. "Here's what I now need from you. Tell me how much that painting is worth now that we know the true master behind its creation."

Asimov ran his hands through his graying hair and allowed his eyes to fall closed. "Is impossible to know value. Is truly one of kind, and I can think of no other painting with such intrigue and deceit. Tell to me who is owner of painting."

Johnny said, "It's in the custody of the United States at the moment."

"No, no. I do not wish to know custody. I wish to know who would have been paid if painting was sold at auction last week."

"That doesn't matter," Johnny said.

"Oh, but it does. If painting is owned by Kremlin, it has no value."

"No value?"

Asimov opened his eyes and faced Johnny. "Kremlin is shrouded in secrecy and has long history of elaborate schemes to change truth of many things. If Kremlin is responsible for overpaint, this means no one will buy painting for more than a few thousand dollars. If is owned by some oligarch, maybe is five million. If owned by person or gallery with no political ties to Kremlin, is maybe twenty million."

Johnny tried not to gasp. "Twenty million?"

"I say this maybe. In private sale not at auction, maybe twelve to fifteen million."

"How much will Morozov pay for it with your assurance of its authenticity?"

Asimov examined the ceiling. "If he has liquid asset to do so, I am confident he will now pay fifteen million. But there is better way . . ."

"What better way?"

"If you wish only to capture and convict Nikita Morozov for any serious federal crime, approaching him alone to purchase painting is fine, but if you want to play also game with him, maybe have private auction on black market. This will make him pay more and will also deliver to you other people who may be also criminals. You understand, yes?"

Johnny motioned toward a chair. "Please have a seat and tell me about how to run a black-market art auction."

"Is simple. Let word filter into world of black-market art that finally, true painter of *Monakh Tsaritsy* has been discovered, and painting is available for highest bidder. But this is not auction like you are thinking."

"Keep talking," Johnny said.

"This is one-time-only bid for each buyer. When auction is over, person with highest bid is new owner of painting."

Johnny said, "And you think it could go as high as twenty million, right?"

Asimov shrugged. "Maybe."

"How do we guarantee Morozov will be the high bidder?"

"You cannot. This is why we must first know how much liquid money he has."

Johnny stood. "Would you like some time alone with the painting, Anatoly?"

The man's eyes lit up like a child's on Christmas morning. "You would do this for me?"

Johnny said, "Dr. Mankiller, set up the painting in the interview room, and start the cameras."

Celeste did as she was instructed, and Johnny motioned toward the door. "She's all yours, Anatoly. If you damage it, try to take it from its frame, or do anything we don't like, our deal is off, and you're going to federal prison. Capisce?"

"Yes, I understand, and thank you for kindness."

Gwynn escorted Asimov into the same interview room in which she'd conducted his initial interrogation. "There's a black light and a magnifying glass on the table. Make yourself at home, but don't put your oily fingers on the government's painting."

"I will not touch. This I promise to you."

She motioned toward four of the sixteen cameras that had every angle of the room covered. "We're watching."

When she stepped from the room, Johnny had the team huddled around a small table.

Gwynn joined. "What did I miss?"

Johnny said, "Nice work with the shoulder thing."

Gwynn took a small bow. "I made that up on the fly, thank you very much."

Anya huffed. "I taught this to her long time ago. She is wonderful student."

Gwynn rolled her eyes. "Trust me, sister, you didn't have to teach me what a woman's touch can do to a man's brain."

Johnny said, "So, here's what I'm thinking. I want to put Anya and Anatoly in front of Morozov. I don't like the black-market-auction idea. There are too many variables we can't control. Let's hear what you've got."

Anya spoke up. "This is wonderful idea. Room full of Russians is perfect way to put Morozov on guard. Nobody trusts Russians—especially not other Russians."

Gwynn asked, "Are you sure you can be in the same room with that guy and not gut him like pig?"

Anya shrugged. "We will see."

Johnny turned to Celeste. "Are you sure Asimov won't be able to tell that painting in there is a counterfeit?"

Celeste smiled and leaned back in her chair. "How do you know that's not the original?"

21

U Menya Yest' Plan
(I Have a Plan)

The buzzer in the room sounded, startling everyone at the table except Anya.

"What was that?" Johnny blurted.

A second later, the door opened, and the head and shoulders of a guy who looked like he belonged somewhere between Woodstock and Haight-Ashbury appeared. "Hey, guys. Mind if I come in?"

Johnny said, "That depends on who you are."

The man stepped through the door and stuck out his hand. "Kent Geller, FBI Art Crime Team."

"FBI? What are you doing here?"

Geller pulled up a chair. "I don't know. The AG sent me. She said you'd brief me up."

Johnny narrowed his gaze. "The AG, you say?"

Geller nodded. "Yeah, that's what I said. So, what do you guys have going on here? It looks like a little tea party of some kind. Mind bringing me up to speed?"

Johnny instinctually glanced behind the man's ear, half expecting to find a joint. "You're an FBI agent sent here by the attorney general?"

Geller threw up his hands. "Yeah, I thought we covered that."

Johnny pulled his phone from his pocket. "You'll have to excuse me for a minute, Agent Geller. I need a little independent confirmation on exactly who you are and why you're here."

Geller crossed his legs and inspected his fingernails. "Go ahead, but call me Kent. We're all friends here. There's no need to be so formal."

"Agent Rousch, this is acting Supervisory Special Agent Johnny McIntyre."

Geller glanced up and mouthed, "Acting supervisory special agent."

"Yes, ma'am. I'm on assignment with my team in Seattle, and a Special Agent Geller just checked in saying he was dispatched by the AG to liaise on my operation."

"Hold on a moment, Agent McIntyre."

Johnny covered the mouthpiece and waited for Rausch to return.

Geller raised a finger. "Are you on hold?"

Johnny nodded, and Geller said, "Good. You have the wrong impression. I'm not here as a liaison. I'm taking over the case."

Anya bored holes through Geller's skull. "This would be terrible plan and will not happen."

Geller perked up. "Is that a Ukrainian accent I hear?"

Anya lowered her chin. "Is Russian, and you will not replace Agent McIntyre."

Geller slid a fingertip across a nail and examined it more closely. "Oh, you misunderstand, too. I'm not here to replace Agent McIntyre. I'm here to replace all of you."

Johnny slipped his hand from the receiver. "Yes, ma'am. I see. That's interesting. Let me ask you this . . . Has the AG reassigned the case to the FBI?"

"I see. So, until then . . ." He paused and listened. "Thank you, ma'am. I look forward to hearing from you again soon."

Johnny hung up and pointed toward the door. "Get out."

Geller said, "Oh, no. They can stay. They'll likely have something meaningful to add to the briefing."

"Not them," Johnny said. "You. The AG didn't send you. You're not taking over our case. In fact, you're not joining our case until I get official notification from DC."

Geller grinned. "That's cute, acting Supervisory Special Agent. You see, you've been using the facilities of the FBI for two days without an official order from your beloved DC. What that means is this. Since the FBI has cooperated fully with your investigation and provided critical support"—he glanced around—"I think all of this counts as critical support. Otherwise, you'd be housing, feeding, clothing, and interrogating your perp in the parking lot at the mall. That gives the FBI jurisdiction and responsibility for what you keep calling your 'operation.' It's not an operation, by the way. It's a case. You would've known that if you were a real supervisory special agent."

Johnny licked his lips. "You can either get out, or we'll throw you out. It's up to you, but either way, you're leaving this room and this operation until I get official notification from the Office of the Attorney General."

Geller's grin widened. "That's adorable. You think you're going to throw *me* out of an FBI facility *you* are borrowing."

It was Johnny's turn to grin. "Special Agent Fulton, would you please remove this person from the room?"

Anya stood, buried two fingers in Geller's armpit and two more under his opposite jaw. An instant later, the man was on his heels and being dragged from the room.

With Geller in the hallway and the door closed, Anya said, "Thank you. That was fun."

"You're most welcome," Johnny said. "But he'll be back. I just bought us a couple of hours, so we don't have any time to lose."

Gwynn hit her feet. "I'll get Asimov."

Celeste followed. "And I'll get the painting. The techs can collect the gear."

In short order, the team, their cooperating witness, the painting, and their gear were crammed into two of the three SUVs the FBI provided, and they were on their way to the airport.

Asimov read the SEA-TAC sign. "Where are you taking me?"

"Believe it or not," Johnny said, "we're taking you home, but not in the FBI's vehicles."

Johnny rented two Suburbans from the airport rental counter and abandoned the two FBI vehicles in the parking lot. When they stopped again, it was in Asimov's driveway.

"Invite us in," Johnny said.

Anatoly nodded. "Please come in."

The team filed into the house and set up their temporary operation center in the dining room.

When Asimov finally sat down, Johnny slid a sheet of paper toward him. "Read that four times, then call Morozov. Don't quote the script verbatim, but make sure you include every point. Got it?"

Asimov read as he'd been told. "I can do that."

When Morozov answered, Anatoly began in Russian. "Nikita, is Anatoly Asimov. I have found your painting. It is in the hands of the woman named Anastasia Polovna, and she wishes to offer it at auction for our friends."

Anya listened closely and translated for the team as Asimov continued down the list of elements from Johnny's script.

"You will never believe the original signature on the painting, Nikita. It is Kazimir Malevich. I saw the X-ray myself, and I examined the painting to exhaustion. I assure you, it is authentic." He listened for a moment and then answered Morozov's question. "She took it from the man who was trying to steal it in Chicago."

Asimov covered the mouthpiece. "Can you print an image of X-ray?"

Celeste said, "Yes, of course."

More Russian, and then Asimov said, "He says he will meet Ms. Petrovna, but only with painting."

"Where and when?" Johnny asked.

Asimov said, "Jefferson County Airport. Five o'clock today."

Johnny said, "Does anybody know where the Jefferson County Airport is?"

"I do," said Asimov. "It is northwest of city on Puget Sound. With little traffic, maybe one hour by car."

Johnny ran the numbers, checked the time, and met Anya's gaze. She gave him a nod.

"Tell him it's on," Johnny said, "but Ms. Petrovna never travels alone. She will have a personal assistant, and there is no negotiation on that point."

Asimov spoke, listened, and disconnected the call. "He says is okay, but something in his voice sounds maybe . . . nervous."

"Of course he's nervous," Johnny said. "He's about to buy a twelve-million-dollar stolen painting."

Asimov examined the floor beneath his feet and then spoke softly. "I must warn you. Meeting is not at airport."

Johnny recoiled. "What? You just said it was at the airport when you were on the phone." He shot a look at Anya. "That's what he said, right?" She nodded, and Johnny said, "Care to explain?"

Asimov sighed. "Yes, initial meeting is at airport, but Morozov will not be there. He will have two people waiting for you. First person will be pleasant at first, and second person will be pilot."

"Pilot? What are you talking about?"

"He will never have meeting with anyone he does not know unless he is completely in control of everything. He will insist that you fly on helicopter to some place he can control and where he has every advantage. This is what he does."

"Where will he take us?" Anya asked.

Before Asimov could answer, Johnny said, "Nowhere. You're not getting on a helicopter unless we know the destination."

As if Johnny hadn't said a word, Asimov said, "Perhaps somewhere in mountains. Maybe Canada. Perhaps yacht somewhere in Puget Sound. There are many possibilities."

Johnny pointed at Celeste. "You and Tom get a GPS tracker on that yacht. Go now!"

Celeste bolted from her seat and through the door, leaving the three federal agents, one Russian art broker, and most importantly, her painting behind.

Anya furrowed her brow. "If you will not permit Gwynn and me to get onto helicopter, why do you care where yacht is?"

Johnny smiled. "Because I have a plan."

"What is this plan?" Anya asked.

"You'll see."

Gwynn pulled off her glasses. "Whatever this plan is, you have to remember we just spit in the face of the FBI, so we're all alone on this one."

Johnny held up a finger. "That's not entirely correct. Just because we brushed off the Feebs doesn't mean we're alone. We're still copacetic with Homeland Security, but we're betting on the come. If I'm wrong, we're right back where we started. But if I'm right, this op will be one they study at the Academy."

"Are you going to let us in on this plan of yours?" Gwynn asked.

Johnny eyed Asimov. "Not with him in the room. I'm sorry to do this to you, Anatoly, but I need to have a huddle with my team."

The Russian said, "I understand. I can go into bedroom."

Johnny nodded down the hall, and Gwynn rose with Asimov.

She removed the telephone from the bedroom and pulled a pair of handcuffs from her belt. "Sorry, but I can't let you hop out the window and warn Morozov."

Asimov nodded and extended his hands.

Gwynn said, "I only need one."

She cuffed his left wrist to the bedframe. "Just in case you've ever fantasized about having a woman handcuff you to the bed, you can let your filthy little mind run wild." She turned on a heel and headed back for the dining room.

The team huddled closely, and Johnny briefed the plan in exquisite detail.

When he was finished, Gwynn raised an eyebrow. "I've got to hand it to you, Johnny. That's a great plan. Agent White would be proud."

"I'm not worried about Agent White being proud," he said. "I'm worried about locking up an art thief, a gunrunner, and a human trafficker in one fell swoop."

"If this doesn't do it," Gwynn said, "I don't know what will."

Johnny asked, "Do you have any concerns, Anya?"

She shook her head. "Is good plan."

Johnny glanced down the hall. "Go get your boy. I need to use his 'office' to make some calls."

Gwynn uncuffed Asimov and brought him back to the living room while Johnny shut himself inside the bedroom.

Asimov said, "Would you like a drink? I have excellent selection of wine, and of course, vodka."

Gwynn said, "Thank you, but we're on the clock. Perhaps when all of this is over, we can all have a drink in your new home wherever you land."

Asimov's eyes lit up. "This means I have done enough?"

Gwynn said, "Maybe. If we pull this off and you continue to cooperate, I don't see how the government could tell you no."

Relief seemed to overcome the Russian as he relaxed for the first time in days.

22

Sverkayushchiye Pushki (Guns a Blazing)

Air Force OSI Officer Tom Elsmore and Dr. Celeste Mankiller returned to Asimov's house at the same instant Johnny emerged from the bedroom.

He said, "Everything's in place, and Homeland is on board. As long as you two got the tracker in place, the op is a go."

Gwynn said, "It's in place, but just barely. They were shoving off when we got to the marina."

Asimov said, "If I am right, you are rolling dice that Morozov will be on yacht, and you will board yacht unexpectedly."

Johnny said, "That sounds like a pretty good plan, but it also sounds like a plan that has a lot of potential to get a lot of people hurt."

Asimov said, "Perhaps Russians are more daring than cautious Americans."

Anya gave him a wink. "Perhaps we are."

Johnny's phone chirped, and he stuck it to his ear. "McIntyre."

The universal look of dread fell over his face as he stood and moped from the room.

Celeste asked, "What do you think that's about?"

Gwynn leaned to make sure the bedroom door was closed. "If I were guessing, I'd say it's somebody from the Attorney General's office chewing him out for brushing off the FBI."

"Do you think it'll change our mission?" Celeste asked.

Anya said, "If Agent White were here, mission would not change."

Celeste giggled. "I love Johnny, but he's no Agent White . . . Not yet anyway."

Asimov scanned the room with uncertainty in his eyes. "What is happening? This will not change my agreement with government, right?"

Gwynn said, "Relax, Anatoly. Your deal is solid. This is just some bureaucratic posturing from DC. It's Johnny's job to protect us from that sort of thing. He'll take the hit, and the show will go on. It always does."

Johnny returned to the dining room without the phone stuck to his face. He clapped once and rubbed his palms together. "Okay, troopers. Let's go to work."

Gwynn hesitated. "Are you sure everything's okay?"

Johnny nodded. "Yep. Everything with the op is a go. Let's make this happen."

Celeste stood and rifled through her gear bag. "I have gifts." She pulled four small pouches and passed them out. "These are satellite comms. I'm still perfecting them, but they'll work well enough."

Gwynn pulled her set from the pouch and stuck it in her ear. "Where's the mic?"

Celeste pointed toward her own unit. "It's built into the earpiece. They're still a little muffled, but I'll work out the kinks."

"What's the battery life?" Tom asked.

"That's the biggest issue," Celeste admitted. "There's only about twelve minutes of actual transmit time. Since receiving is pretty much a passive function, they can listen a lot longer than they can talk, so keep your transmissions short and to the point."

Johnny said, "What about me?"

Celeste pulled another pouch from her bag. "This is the base station, and it's for you. As long as it's connected to power—either batteries or a wall socket—it's essentially unlimited transmission. Are you running the op from here?"

Johnny plugged in the base station and brought the unit to life. "We'll do comm checks as we spread out."

Tom said, "Hey, Anatoly, are they going to frisk us before they put us in the helicopter?"

The Russian said, "They have never frisked me, but I do not know."

Tom turned to Johnny. "What's the call, boss? Are we going strapped or not?"

Johnny considered the question. "Everything inside me wants to say strap up, but if they search you and find a gun, we're blown."

"We can't risk it," Tom said. "Anya and Gwynn can bring us some firepower when they show up."

The Air Force officer and Tech Services genius hit the road, and Johnny's plan was in motion. Almost before Tom and Celeste were out of the driveway, the tech team arrived with their laptops and gadgets galore. They set up shop in the dining room, and suddenly, Asimov's house morphed into a tactical operation center.

The tech who appeared to be in charge spoke without looking up. "Everything's up and running, and we're tracking all four operators."

Johnny said, "Okay, Xena and Gabrielle, you're up. Make it count."

Gwynn grabbed the painting Celeste had removed from its frame and rolled into a tube. "Ready, partner?"

Anya cocked her head. "Who is this Xena and Gabrielle?"

Gwynn chuckled. "Just pretend you're a warrior princess in a leather bikini and I'm your much hotter sidekick, and everything will work out just fine. Let's go!"

"This is ridiculous thing to pretend. I do not understand."

Gwynn hit the door. "Let's go catch a really bad guy. How's that?"

"Now this, I understand."

When they reached the marina, Gwynn checked in on her cell phone on speaker to save the battery life in her earpiece transmitter. "We're ready to hit the water. The Homeland Security guys are here in an unmarked boat that looks way faster than any helicopter."

Johnny said, "We've had an unexpected wrinkle. The yacht left Puget Sound, and it's headed for international water off the coast."

"We're still going, right?"

"Yes, but the mission parameters have changed. We're making the sale and bailing out. There are some tricky jurisdictional issues offshore. The AG's office is working on an opinion, and we've got a federal judge standing by, but I don't think we can bust him offshore. We have to wait until he's back in U.S. waters or on land."

Anya said, "I can simply kill him and put his body in ocean if you want."

Johnny coughed. "Yeah, let's keep that idea as a last resort. That's not really what we do."

"But is what we can do if becomes necessary."

Johnny said, "Davis, keep her under control, and don't let her kill anybody who isn't actively trying to kill you."

Gwynn scoffed. "Yeah, I'll get right on that. Controlling Anya . . . That's funny."

"Do the best you can, okay?"

Gwynn turned all business. "Send the coordinates for the yacht. We're shoving off."

The coordinates followed within seconds, and the DHS boat operator entered them into the GPS. "Have a seat, ma'am. We're going to go pretty hard. We've got a lot of water to cover."

She and Anya settled into a pair of seats behind the boat pilot and pulled their hair into tight ponytails.

"They weren't kidding," Gwynn said. "We're truckin'."

Anya leaned in and yelled over the roar of wind and engines. "Chase has Mark-Five patrol boat from Navy that is even better. You will someday see it."

"Why would I ever see anything Chase has?" Gwynn yelled back.

She lifted Gwynn's hand and placed it in the center of her chest. "Sometimes, I think he still has my heart."

Gwynn pulled her hand away. "Now's not the time for this, Anya. We've got work to do. You can be lovesick and sentimental later when we don't have a bad guy to bust."

"We are not busting bad guy today. We are only setting up for busting him. I cannot promise I will not kill him if I think about what he does to little girls."

Gwynn yelled, "I feel the same way, but we'll get him legally, and he can spend the rest of his miserable life being somebody's federal prison plaything."

Anya brushed a stray strand of hair from her face. "This is very good thought."

One of the boat crew turned and yelled, "It's going to get rough. We're leaving the sound into open ocean. Do you have updated coordinates?"

Gwynn pulled out her phone and opened the screen. "Not yet."

"Get some. We're on the coordinates you gave us originally."

Gwynn texted Johnny, and in short order, a new set of numbers appeared and she tossed the phone to the crewman. With the new position of the yacht programmed into the nav system, the crewman handed back the phone, and his prediction of rough water came true.

The massive speedboat left the water several times as they crested wave after wave, causing the engines to race and the hull to shudder every time they landed back on the roiling surface of the North Pacific. Gwynn and Anya held on and tried to absorb the shock of the pounding.

The crewman pointed at the radar and yelled, "There they are. Eight miles."

Gwynn stood and grabbed everything she could find to steady herself as she stumbled toward the console. "I need you to stop the boat for thirty seconds so I can check in with the ops center."

"Yes, ma'am. Stand by."

She held on while the man commanded the stop. With the engines barely above idle speed, the pounding and roar of the wind stopped. Gwynn thumbed Johnny's number, but the call failed.

The crewman said, "There's no cell service out here. We've got a sat-phone if you need it."

Gwynn shook her head and pressed the tiny button on her earpiece. "Ops, Davis."

"Go for ops," came Johnny's reply.

"We're less than eight miles from the yacht. We can be on them in . . ."

She looked up, and the pilot said, "Less than ten minutes, ma'am."

"Less than ten minutes. What's Tom's and Celeste's status?"

Johnny said, "You should see them any minute. They're less than five miles behind you. Stay out of sight until they've had time to land and get inside before you make your grand entrance."

Gwynn glanced into the eastern sky. "There they are. We'll follow them in."

"Hey, Gwynn," Johnny said. "Don't let any good guys get hurt, okay?"

"I'll do my best, boss." Gwynn pocketed the phone and watched the helicopter soar overhead on a direct course for the yacht. She pointed skyward. "Follow him inbound and put us on deck three minutes behind them. Can you do that?"

The crewman said, "Consider it done, ma'am."

The chopper got smaller in the sky, and the helmsman shoved the throttles forward, but the bow was pointed well behind the yacht.

Gwynn pointed toward the gleaming ship. "Isn't that the yacht over there?"

"Yes, ma'am," answered the crewman. "But I thought you wanted to arrive incognito."

"I do."

"I thought so. We'll maneuver behind the vessel and approach dead astern. That'll give us the best angle to avoid as much of their radar sweep as possible and get you two on deck ASAP."

As they approached, the helicopter slowed to a hover above the stern deck.

The crewman said, "Every eye on that boat is focused on the chopper and not us. Are you ready to go?"

"We are."

He turned to the helmsman, and they maneuvered exactly as he'd described. The chopper landed and shut down. Tom and Celeste stepped from the bird with their heads lowered and moved toward the main salon of the massive yacht. The remaining crew on deck set about securing the chopper with no thought of the speeding boat rapidly approaching from the east.

The crewman cupped his hands around his mouth and yelled, "We'll lay alongside the port stern quarter and match their speed. The longer we're there, the higher the probability of being detected, so I need you two off my boat and on theirs double-quick. Got it?"

"We've done this before," Gwynn said. "We won't hang you out to dry, but stay close. We may need you as a QRF if things go south up there."

"Quick Reaction Force?"

Gwynn nodded. "Yeah, you guys are Homeland Security agents, right?"

"Yes, ma'am."

"Armed?"

"Well armed."

Gwynn plucked the earpiece from her ear and handed it to the crewman. "Good. Then stay within striking distance, and shove this in your ear. Don't transmit. Just listen. If you hear a voice on that thing asking for help, I expect you to come in guns a blazing."

The crewman smiled. "Yes, ma'am!"

23

Litsom k Litsu k Litsu
(Face-to-Face-to-Face)

The Homeland Security helmsman performed the maneuver flawlessly, and Gwynn and Anya leapt from the starboard gunwale and onto the yacht's swim platform. Almost before their feet hit the deck, the boat peeled away and vanished to the south.

Anya caught a stainless-steel handle on the back of the yacht at the same instant her feet hit the deck, but Gwynn did not. She landed with one foot turned beneath the other and went down hard on the teak and fiberglass platform. Anya grabbed her partner's wrist with one hand while gripping the handle with all of her strength with the other.

Gwynn landed on her side and came to rest with both feet dangling from the platform, her right hand hoisted above her head and gripping the rolled painting tube like the prized possession it was. Anya stared down at her friend and then up at the tube. If she released her grip on the yacht to grab the tube, both of them and the painting would end up in the Pacific.

The Russian set her feet and leaned back against Gwynn's weight, pulling her partner closer, but only by inches. "Pull feet onto deck!"

"I'm trying!" Gwynn yelled back, but her eyes shot above her partner in an instant, and a voice echoed from above.

"Hey! What are you doing down there?"

Gwynn didn't take her eyes off her partner but tightened her grip on Anya's wrist, tucked the tube beneath her chin, and drew her Glock with her free hand. Aimed only inches from Anya's head, the pistol belched twice, and orange flame billowed from the muzzle.

She holstered her pistol and grabbed Anya's wrist with her gun hand. They pulled against each other until Gwynn had both feet firmly beneath her, but as she relaxed from the tension of the moment, the tube fell from beneath her chin, and both women's hearts leapt from their chests.

Gwynn let go of Anya and batted the tube like a cat playing with a ball of yarn. The surge of the ocean wasn't as punishing as it had been on the much smaller boat, but the ride was still a roller coaster on cocaine. Anya released her grip on the handle and dived to the platform with both arms extended. She covered the tube like a hockey goalie smothering a puck on the ice.

Gwynn planted a knee beside Anya's shoulder to keep her on the yacht. "Nice save!"

Anya cradled the painting and bounded back to her feet. "Thank you. Who did you shoot?"

Gwynn looked up. "I don't know. It was some guy with a rifle pointed at us. We should get up there and see how badly I've kicked the hornet's nest."

They climbed the ladder and stepped over the transom to find a single body lying on his back with two holes where his nose had been only minutes before. They dragged the body to a corner of the deck and tucked him behind the controls for the overhead crane used to deploy the tender.

Anya tapped the button on her earpiece and reported, "We are aboard and moving to interior of ship."

Johnny's voice filled her ear. "Did you leave an earpiece on the boat?"

"Yes, Gwynn left hers with boat crew in case we need QRF."

"Roger."

They moved as one along the gunwale and slipped through the door and to the interior where they found themselves alone in a sitting area. Anya pointed down a set of stairs at the forward end of the compartment, and Gwynn followed. They descended the stairs just as they'd practiced thousands of times together and separately, stepping slowly and intentionally on the outsides of the treads and letting their eyes lead the way.

Halfway down the stairs, Captain Tom Elsmore's voice rang through the air. "We didn't bring the painting because we have no way to know if you have the money."

In choppy, Russian-accented English came, "Look around you. Does it look to you like I do not have money?"

"How am I supposed to know if this is even your boat?" Tom said.

"You are wasting my time. Throw them both overboard," the Russian voice commanded.

Anya took off, and Gwynn stayed only inches behind. The pair stepped into the salon just as three men who looked a lot like the dead guy on deck grabbed Tom's and Celeste's arms.

Anya stomped a foot. "You will take your hands from them immediately. I have painting, and you have made price even higher with threat."

Every eye in the room was fixed on the statuesque Russian and her partner, who was still wet from the knees down.

"Who are you?" demanded a bulbous man consuming well over half of the well-stressed settee beneath him.

Anya glared into his deep-set eyes. "I am Anastasia Petrovna, and you are Nikita Morozov. I am here for only one reason. If you wish to play childish game and get people hurt, I will take painting and walk away."

The man said, "We are on boat. You cannot walk away."

Anya glared at him. "How I got onto boat is mystery to you, so be careful telling me how I will leave."

Morozov turned to the man who clearly spent far too much time in the gym. "Search her."

Before the musclehead could take a step, the overhead light glistened from the razor's edge of Anya's fighting knife as she drew the weapon. "If you touch me, I will slice hands from arms and feed to you. Do not test me."

The Sloth consuming the settee growled. "Take her!"

Muscle Boy took two strides toward Anya, and she pinned his left foot to the deck with a blinding throw of her knife and produced a second blade seemingly out of thin air. "Next one goes into eye."

Anya reached toward Celeste, encouraging her to move behind the three well-trained agents, and the tech happily obeyed. She turned her attention back to Morozov. "You are wasting time and disrespecting me. Do you want to see painting or not?"

Muscle Boy bellowed like a wounded bear and yanked the knife from his foot as blood pooled around him. Anya stepped toward him and struck the back of his hand with the pommel of her knife, sending the blood-covered blade clanging to the deck. She recovered her first knife and shoved the guard backward. "You are ruining beautiful carpet with blood from foot. Go away and clean yourself. You are disgraceful."

The beast of a man staggered backward and turned his full attention to Morozov, obviously awaiting instructions.

Nikita waved a swollen hand. "Do as she says. Go away."

Morozov ignored the man's departure from the salon. "Show to me painting, and when I am finished inspecting it, you and I will talk privately about many things. Having someone like you working for me could be very promising for both of us."

Gwynn stepped toward Morozov and stuck out the tube. He took it from her hands and fumbled with the latch. Once the painting was free from the case, he unrolled it as slowly as his awkward hand could manage.

Anya sheathed her knives. "Person you hired to steal painting was weak and sloppy. I should have killed him, but I left that honor for you."

Morozov never took his eyes from the painting. "Maybe you can kill him for me and we will both have reward. You are obviously very dangerous woman and without fear."

Anya gave no response and watched with pride as her protégé moved to the opposite corner of the salon to cover all angles should threats appear. A glance behind her reassured her that Tom had the exterior door well covered. Celeste held her position of safety right behind the knife-wielding Russian.

The Sloth continued to make noises like a curious animal until he finally said, "I will have painting examined and give to you my offer in few days."

Anya motioned to Gwynn. "Put painting back inside case. I believed him to be serious Russian art collector, but I was obviously mistaken."

Morozov drew the canvas close to his engorged body. "Wait! Do not come onto my boat with demands and insults. Is not courteous."

Anya took a step toward him. "Is not courteous to have man try to shoot us on back of boat and have your gorilla try to attack me minutes ago. Courtesy is not part of this. You wish to purchase painting, or you do not. Is not negotiation. Painting is for sale at my price for only you, but if you do not have assets to make purchase, is okay. I will have auction after revelation of true creator of painting, Kazimir Malevich."

Morozov held up a meaty hand. "Do not continue with insults. Of course I have assets to purchase painting. What is price?"

Anya continued her gaze. "Is twelve million, and is only yes or no."

A sound escaped Nikita Morozov's mouth that began somewhere deep inside his enormous body. "This is ridiculous price! No one will pay such outrageous number."

Anya leaned in, grasped the edge of the canvas, and laid her hand against the man's monstrous shoulder. "This is very good for me. There will now be auction, and you can bid with everyone else. Release painting now!"

Morozov abandoned English, and his gravelly Russian felt somehow like an assault. "I will pay two million and not a penny more."

Anya continued in English. "If this is truth, you will never see this painting again."

He tightened his grip on the edge of the canvas, and Anya drew her knife again. "You will release painting, or I will cut your fingers from it. Is your choice."

He coughed as if his death were imminent. "Three million."

She laid the tip of the gleaming blade against the second knuckle of his index finger and pressed barely enough to open the flesh. "Shall I continue?"

He looked down at the blood oozing from the thin wound on his bulging finger. "Five million now, and I will not have you hunted and killed."

Anya moved the blade from Morozov's finger to his chin. "I told to you price is twelve million, and I will not slice your throat right now."

He narrowed his eyes. "You have no idea who you are playing with, little Russian girl. I could have you driven into ground with simple brush of my hand."

Anya hissed, "Twelve million."

"You have just ordered your own death."

She laughed aloud. "I will deliver to you heart of anyone you send who believes he can kill me. Now, let go of my painting." Morozov didn't move, so Anya stepped away and said, "Take photograph quickly."

Celeste pinched the frame of her glasses four times in rapid succession, and Anya lunged back toward the man with her blades leading the way. She paused only inches from him. "Twelve million or you will never see painting again."

"Take the filthy rag, you *shlyukha*. You will soon beg for my money."

Anya thrust her blades forward with unimaginable speed and sliced the painting into shreds no bigger than dollar bills. When her knives stopped moving, the first came to rest just beneath Morozov's left eye and the other against the rolling flesh of his neck. Her face hovered inches above his. "Now no one will have painting, and I cannot wait to do same to men you send to die at my feet. They will fail, and I will find you in your sleep when you do not expect, and I will remove pieces of you like butcher until nothing is left."

She allowed the tip of her knife to sink into Morozov's cheek, parting the flesh to the bone. "This will make perfect scar for you to never forget what you have done and who left permanent souvenir." She holstered one knife and tapped her earpiece. "Come for us now! We are four, and be prepared for possible gunfire."

24

Myaso
(Meat)

Aboard the Homeland Security boat, the helmsman shoved the throttles to their stops and leaned forward against the acceleration of the fiberglass and steel rocket beneath him. A crewman pulled on his body armor, mounted an M240 machine gun near the bow, and manned the weapon.

A third man pressed binoculars to his face. "I see four on the starboard stern."

The crewman with Gwynn's earpiece tapped the button. "We're thirty seconds out."

Tom Elsmore tapped his earpiece. "We're pinned down. Put some suppressive fire in the air!"

The M240 belched to life, sending 7.62 x 51mm rounds into the upper decks of the yacht in thunderous bursts.

Tom yelled, "Keep walking them down, but stay above the stern rail on the first deck above the waterline."

Three pistol-wielding security men continued firing as the incoming automatic fire hammered into the yacht and moved lower with every pounding round. Gwynn and Anya returned pistol fire, but the heavy weapon on the rapidly approaching Homeland vessel ruled the night. Glass, fiberglass, and teakwood shards filled the air as the rounds slammed into the vessel, sending the three gunmen retreating for the relative safety of the interior.

As he grew nearer, the helmsman hit the switches, illuminating his vessel just as he pulled alongside the yacht at eighteen knots. Gwynn was first over the rail and landed in the waiting arms of a crewman below. The gunner swept the upper decks with his muzzle in case a target of opportunity presented itself.

Anya tossed her Glock to Tom and stepped over the rail. She landed like a cat on the deck of the Homeland Security vessel and immediately turned to see Celeste hesitate on the rail above.

"Jump!" she yelled over the combined roar of the two vessels just as the M240 gunner pressed the trigger, driving torturing lead into the starboard side of the yacht. Anya shot her gaze to the gunman's target and watched a security guard melt to the deck and his pistol fall harmlessly into the North Pacific.

Tom shoved the pistol into his belt and turned to Celeste. "You have to jump. They'll catch you. You have to go!"

Celeste turned with tears of fear and disbelief in her eyes. "I can't."

The Air Force officer turned back and drew the pistol, scanning the deck for any aggressors. Seeing none, he shoved the pistol back into his pants and stepped onto the rail. With a powerful arm, he lifted Celeste and stepped into the night.

Although his landing wasn't as graceful as Anya's, Tom and Celeste found themselves safe and uninjured as the helmsman peeled away from the yacht.

The gunner spun the weapon astern and yelled, "Do you want me to take out the chopper?"

Gwynn yelled through the rushing wind. "Yes! Cut it down!"

Anya waved both arms. "No! No! No! Do not kill helicopter!"

The gunner looked between the two women, unsure of who he should obey. "Kill it or not? I need to know now."

Anya laid a hand on Gwynn's shoulder. "No! Do not kill!"

Gwynn stared up into her partner's determined eyes. "Why not?"

"Is all part of plan. I will explain when we are back on shore."

Tom set Celeste on a well-cushioned seat and took a knee between her feet. "Are you okay?"

She shook her head violently. "No. I'm not okay."

"Are you hit?"

She continued shaking her head. "No, but that's insane. I'm never doing that again."

Tom relaxed. "It's okay. You don't have to."

"How?" Celeste demanded. "How do you ever get used to . . . whatever the hell that was?"

Tom chuckled. "You don't. You just learn a little more every time it happens, and the longer you stay alive, the more you learn how to continue the trend."

Celeste laid her head back, stared into the heavens, and screamed like a wild animal.

Anya and Gwynn spun to see what was happening, and Tom said, "She's okay. It was apparently her first gunfight."

Both women nodded and turned away.

Back at the marina, the crewman who appeared to be in charge asked, "Which one of you is in command of this mess?"

Tom looked at Anya, Anya looked at Gwynn, and Celeste laughed hysterically.

Gwynn said, "I guess I am."

"You guess?" the crewman asked.

Gwynn shrugged. "The actual commander is in the ops center, but I'm the ranking agent out here."

"That's good enough for me," he said. "I need to know what to put in my report. We fired on a civilian vessel in international waters with at least one casualty. I'm not sure that needs to be on paper anywhere . . . ever."

Gwynn screwed up her face. "You must be mistaken. We cruised Puget Sound in search of a suspect accused of multiple federal offenses, but we were unable to determine his location."

She glanced around the boat. "That's what you guys remember, right?"

Everyone nodded, and an echo of agreement resounded. "Absolutely. Yes, ma'am."

The crewman stuck out a hand. "I'm Special Agent—"

Gwynn slapped the offered hand from the air. "I don't care what your name is, but I really appreciate what you guys did for us tonight. I don't have a card on me for obvious reasons, but if you ever need anything from Justice, just ask for Special Agent Ana Fulton."

They climbed from the boat and into the waiting SUV.

Gwynn said, "Okay, Anya, spill it. What's this grand plan of yours, and why did you go all chop-a-matic on the painting?"

The Russian said, "Plan is to follow tracking device Celeste made and I attached to Morozov's shirt collar. This is reason for keeping helicopter airworthy. They will fly him home, and we will know exactly where he goes."

Gwynn softened her tone. "Okay. I like it so far, but what about the painting? Why did you cut it to ribbons?"

"I did this to make certain Morozov would search for me and try to kill me. If we cannot gather enough evidence of art thievery, gun running, and human trafficking, we can arrest him for conspiracy to kill federal agent . . . me."

"What if whoever he sends is better than you?"

Anya laughed until she almost lost her breath. "You are now comedienne, friend Gwynn. I am hungry. We should eat."

Gwynn rolled her eyes. "What we should do is check in with the ops center."

Johnny answered on the first ring. "Well, that sounded exciting. Is everybody okay?"

"We're fine, Johnny, but we can't say the same for everyone on Morozov's yacht."

"I'm not surprised. I'm also not concerned. I don't anticipate them filing any official complaints with the Coast Guard. Do you?"

Gwynn said, "No, I don't think that's an issue, but we do have a few things to report."

"Save it until you get back to the house. I'd rather hear it face-to-face."

Anya jumped in. "I am hungry. We will eat soon, yes?"

Johnny huffed. "Give her a cracker or something, and get your butts back here ASAP."

The line went dead, and they pulled into the drive at Asimov's house twenty minutes later.

"Okay, let's hear it," Johnny said before they could sit down.

Gwynn cleared her throat. "Here's the abridged version. We climbed aboard. Anya killed a guy trying to kill us. We hid the body. We met Morozov. He's a swollen cow, by the way. Another guy tried to get tough, but Anya stuck a knife through his foot. Morozov examined the painting and made a lowball offer. Anya stuck a tracking device to his shirt and cut the painting into bite-sized pieces."

Gwynn eyed the team. "Did I miss anything?"

Celeste said, "Yeah. You left out the part about me wetting my pants and crying like a scared child. You guys are like superheroes or something. I don't know how you do it."

The concern showed on Johnny's face, but Tom spoke up before Johnny could console Celeste. "The machine gunner on the Homeland Security vessel put a few dozen rounds of suppressive fire into the boat and took out at least one bad guy trying to pick us off when we disembarked from our luxury cruise."

"Where were you when all of this happened?" Johnny asked.

"At least fifteen miles offshore, but the lights of the city were still visible."

Johnny closed his eyes as he processed the information. When he rejoined the team, he stared at Gwynn and Anya. "I wonder if there are any other SSAs who have to deal with anything close to the insanity the two of you pull off."

Anya said, "This means you are unique, and every other supervisory special agent wants to be you. Oh, and I am also still hungry."

Johnny ignored her and leaned toward the two techs hovering over their computers. "Any luck tracking Morozov?"

"Yes, sir. He's been airborne for"—he checked his watch—"seven minutes, and he appears to be heading for the same island as before."

"Keep on it," he ordered. "And let me know if he lands anywhere other than the island. We're going to dinner, and we'll bring something back for the two of you. Any preferences?"

"Meat," the first tech said. "My wife is a vegetarian, and I'm losing my mind in that house. For the love of God, please bring me some meat."

"Meat it is," Jonny said, and a phone chirped from somewhere nearby.

Anya said, "That is mine." She lifted the phone from the counter. "Is Switzerland!"

She thumbed the button and stuck the phone to her ear. "Ray?"

The voice from the other end said, "Ms. Burinkova?"

"Yes, is Anya Burinkova. Who is this?"

"My name is Doctor Yuna Vogel. I'm a neurologist with Dr. Müller's team from Clinique de Genolier. I'm calling with an update on Mr. White's condition."

Anya gasped. "He is okay, yes?"

"Yes, ma'am. He's doing very well, but we still have him in a medically induced coma. There is very little swelling, and we expect to wake him up in forty-eight to seventy-two hours. Dr. Müller wanted me to let you know in case you wanted to be here. It is sometimes very comforting to patients when their loved ones are the first faces they see."

"Two, maybe three days?"

Dr. Vogel said, "Yes, forty-eight to seventy-two hours. Will you be here?"

Anya said, "You must wait a moment." She covered the receiver with her palm. "I have on phone doctor, and she says Ray will be awake in two maybe three days. Will you come?"

Johnny said, "We're in the middle of a critical case. We can't just . . ."

Anya pressed the phone back to her ear. "Yes, we will be there." She disconnected and said, "Is better if Ray sees people he cares for when he wakes from coma, so we will go."

"That's not how this works," Johnny said. "I'm in charge of this operation until Morozov is in custody."

Anya ducked her chin. "Think about what operation has become. Is now only game of waiting for Morozov to send men to kill me. I will stop them, of course, and they will tell to us that Morozov hired them."

"Why would they admit that?" Johnny asked. "It's not like you have some magical power over men to make them . . ."

Anya smiled. "Is not magic, Johnny Mac. Is fear for life. I will trade to them their lives for them to tell truth. If they do not want to tell truth, I will kill them until we find one who will talk."

Johnny shook his head. "That's not at all how this is going to work. We are agents of the federal government, and as such, we don't plan to kill anyone. If we're forced to defend ourselves or others from imminent significant bodily harm or death, we are justified in the use of deadly force, but planning to kill people until we find a cooperative witness is not how we operate."

Anya spoke softly. "Come with me and have conversation privately, Johnny."

He let himself be led into a bedroom, and the two sat on the edge of the bed.

Anya said, "Listen to me. Ray White captured me for only one reason. He threatened prison for me, but this was never what he wanted. He wanted me to find and eliminate Russian mafia in this country. He knew who and what I was. That is why he chose me. Maybe he did not explain this to you. Probably he thought you are very smart agent and you would see truth without explanation. Name of operation is Avenging Angel. This is me, so give to me vengeance and let me remove Nikita Morozov from world. Maybe we arrest him and he spends rest of life in prison. This is best ending for mission, but he is terrible man with God complex. Men like this sometimes will not allow themselves to be arrested. I will probably not kill him, but is possible he will kill himself when I frighten him to edge of life. This is what I do better than anyone else on Earth. This is why I am now federal agent with you. If you have other plan, we will discuss with Ray when he wakes up in Switzerland in two maybe three days. Now, we will go back into other room, and you will make decision. This way I will not look like bully, and you are still in charge."

Johnny closed his eyes, took a long, deep breath, and sighed. "I'm pretty sure I just got handled. But thanks for doing it privately."

25

Nam Nuzhno Pogovorit' (We Need to Talk)

Johnny spent several frustrating minutes on the phone with the Marshals Service arranging for a babysitter for Asimov. "I'm sorry, Agent McIntyre, but we can't simply dispatch a team of deputy marshals at the drop of a hat. We will, however, coordinate with local police to sit on your witness until we can get deputies in place."

Dinner was exactly what the team needed after a long, stressful afternoon and evening, and when it was over, Gwynn took Tom's hand and said, "We need to talk."

Tom groaned. "Those are the four most terrifying words any man ever hears."

Gwynn looked up at him. "No, don't be afraid. I just want to make sure I understand a few things."

They walked from the restaurant and to a park bench beneath a pair of trees arching toward each other as if longing to touch.

"Okay," Tom said. "What did I do?"

"No, it's not that," Gwynn said. "I mean . . . Well, it is something you did, but maybe I took it wrong. We're getting off on the wrong foot. I'm not accusing you of anything. I just want to understand. So, let's start over."

He shrugged. "I'm listening."

She stared at her hands for a long moment. "Tonight, out there on the boat when we were running for our lives, I saw you do some things that bothered me a little bit."

She paused, and Tom's mind raced through the list of possible things he could've done wrong. He slid his hand into hers. "I'm still listening."

She squeezed his fingers. "When Celeste froze on the rail, you grabbed her and jumped into the Homeland Security boat."

"Yeah. She was exposed, and like you said, frozen. Somebody had to do something to get her off that rail."

"It's not that," Gwynn said. "It's what you did once you were in the boat with the rest of us."

He replayed the scene in his mind. "Okay . . . And?"

Gwynn let out a huff. "It's silly, and it's probably nothing."

"No, what is it?"

She took another long pause. "When you were consoling her on the seat, it looked pretty intimate, and I want to know . . . I mean, what are we, you and me? Are we dating, just having fun, or what?"

Tom relaxed and leaned back on the bench. "Take a breath, and let me tell you a story."

She breathed and tried to relax, and he started talking.

"When I was in Germany, I worked a case investigating a contractor who worked for the company that provided rapid supply of aircraft parts when the Air Force jets needed emergency repairs. The way the budget worked with them was a little flaky because the maintenance guys had to have the parts as quickly as possible to get the jets back in the air. That meant the contractor had a lot of freedom to spend Air Force money without a lot of oversight."

Gwynn frowned. "I don't see how this has anything to do with what we're talking about."

"Hang on. You'll understand soon. I'll make a really long story as short as possible."

Gwynn pressed her lips into an impatient horizontal line, and Tom kept talking.

"The guy we were investigating got greedy and found a way to skim a little money for himself while ordering parts from one particular supplier. By *a little*, I mean almost a million bucks over an eighteen-month period."

Gwynn let out a groan. "A million bucks?"

Tom nodded. "Yeah, it was just over nine hundred K. The details are too complicated to keep short, so let's just say things escalated quickly. The guy ran, and we chased him down. My partner at the time was a fresh-out-of-training second lieutenant named Merideth Cole. I wanted her to get some real-world experience on a real case, so I assigned her to work with me."

Gwynn patted his leg. "If this is a story about somebody else you were in a relationship with, I really don't want to hear it."

"No, it's not like that at all. Just let me finish. We finally cornered the guy, and he decided to fight. I'd never been to the range with Lieutenant Cole. In fact, I'd never done any real training with her at all. I made assumptions that she'd been trained to operate under fire, but you know what they say about assumptions. Anyway, as you know, there are three keys to winning a gunfight: shoot, move, communicate."

Gwynn said, "Yeah, we're all taught that at the Academy."

"Right. Well, Lieutenant Cole returned fire, but when it came time to move, she stepped from behind cover and took a round to her body armor. Of course the impact hurt, but she wasn't injured. The problem came when her brain couldn't process being shot and continuing to move. She froze, and I stepped around her to continue to cover."

He stopped talking and drummed his fingertips against his knee. After a moment of silence, he said, "The guy apparently realized Cole was wearing body armor, and he put a round in her right ear. A twenty-two-year-old Air Force officer died in the middle of the night, ten feet away from me, because I didn't shove her behind cover. I stepped around her and left her out there to die."

Gwynn gasped and grabbed Tom's hands. "I'm such an idiot. I'm so sorry, Tom. I didn't mean—"

He squeezed her hands. "When Celeste froze on that rail, it all came rushing back, and I wouldn't make the same fatal mistake twice. That's what happened out there tonight."

Gwynn laid her head against his shoulder and breathed. "I was such a jerk. I'm sorry."

He pressed his cheek against her forehead. "If we need to label our relationship, I'm fine with that. Here's how I see it and what I want. You're beautiful, smart, funny, sexy, and bad-ass when knives and bullets start flying. I love all those things about you, but what I love most is the part no one else gets to see. I love the tender, hopeful, bright-eyed girl who still lives inside you and refuses to become jaded in spite of the evil you see every day. Gwynn, I love you, and I want to be together. That's what this is to me."

She forced back the tears. "I'm so sorry for being a jealous idiot tonight. I love you, too, and I want to do what it takes for us to be together."

He took her face in his hands and pressed her lips to his as they let the moment wash over them.

From behind the leaning tree to her left, Gwynn heard Anya's voice. "Gwynn, is happening. I need you."

She pulled away from Tom and slinked behind the tree with her partner. "What's happening?"

Anya said, "Do not look, but I am being watched by man near black van in parking lot. He has been watching me for several minutes."

"Who do you think he is?"

"I do not know, but I need to borrow Tom while you move into position to confront him. This is okay with you, yes?"

Gwynn couldn't hold back the smile. "Yeah, it's fine with me. You play with Tom, and I'll flank the creeper. Where's Johnny?"

Anya said, "He and Celeste caught cab back to hotel, but I do not think we need to call him until we know who is watching me."

"Agreed."

Gwynn stayed low and circled behind the restaurant to the darker side of the parking lot while the Russian sparrow took Tom's arm as if they were lovers out for an evening stroll.

Gwynn moved silently between cars, keeping as many vehicles as possible between herself and her target. She ducked behind a pickup truck and peered over the tailgate to see her partner clinging to Tom's arm, and the bitter taste of jealousy she'd known earlier was long forgotten.

She slipped within ten feet of the van and crept behind it until she was mere feet from the stalker. Silently, she drew her pistol and stepped from behind the cover of the black van. "Federal agent. Freeze."

The man obeyed and turned his head to see Special Agent Davis bearing down on him with her government-issue Glock. He said, "Relax, Agent. I'm on the job."

In spite of the man's use of the common police term to let other officers know they're cops, too, Gwynn didn't lower her weapon. "Place the binoculars on the ground."

He followed her instructions but said, "I'm FBI. I'm going to draw my cred pack. Don't shoot me."

"Keep your hands where I can see them, and get on your knees."

The man huffed but did as Gwynn ordered.

As if materializing from thin air, Anya appeared beside the front fender of the van, only inches from the man on his knees. He flinched and cursed. "What's wrong with you people? I told you I'm FBI."

Gwynn said, "Interlock your fingers on top of your head."

"Would you chill out?"

Anya laced a hand behind his neck and shoved the man's face against the van's front tire. Holding him in place, she frisked him with her free hand and came up with an authentic FBI credential pack.

She studied the credentials and compared the photograph to the man still pressed to the tire. "Okay, is really you."

She let him go, and he leapt to his feet with his finger in her face. "I identified myself as an FBI agent, and you put your hands on me. You're under arrest."

Anya laughed and swatted the finger from her face. "Yes, please do this. Please arrest me and put me in handcuffs. You will be laughingstock of unemployment line tomorrow morning."

"I'm not messing around. Don't make me take you down."

Simultaneously, Tom, Gwynn, and Anya drew their cred packs and held them in the air in front of their faces.

Anya stepped toward the FBI agent. "Why are you stalking me?"

"I'm doing my job, lady."

"Your job?" Anya asked. "Spying on other federal agent is your job?"

"I'm just doing what I was told to do. Nothing more."

"Who told you to follow me?"

"My supervisor," he said through gritted teeth.

"And what is supervisor's name?"

"Special Agent Peterson, Seattle Field Office."

Gwynn already had her phone in hand and Johnny's number dialed when Anya tossed her the agent's credentials. "Johnny, it's Davis. We just rolled up a Feeb who says SSA Peterson out of the Seattle office put him on Anya."

"Please tell me she didn't hurt him."

"Only his pride," Gwynn said. She read the guy's name and credential number to Johnny.

He said, "Hold tight. I'm on it." A minute later, Johnny said, "Cut him loose, and tell him his mommy said it's time for him to come home."

She tossed the credentials onto the ground beside the agent. "You should probably skitter on back to the hole you crawled out of, Agent. Your boss is about to have a really bad night, and I suspect he'll take it out on you for getting busted. Next time you plan on creeping on another federal agent, you might want to learn some camouflage techniques."

Back at the hotel, they had a good laugh at the FBI agent's expense.

Johnny said, "The AG's going to come down pretty hard on the FBI director, and I'm sure it'll flow downhill to the Seattle field office, so that means one of two things will happen. The local agents will either pretend we don't exist and leave us alone, or they'll double-down and come at us even harder. I'm hoping for option number one, but we did spit in their Cheerios, so I can understand them being upset."

26

Chelovek po Imeni Khammer
(A Man Called Hammer)

Back at the hotel, Johnny called a huddle. "Tonight's excitement with the local FBI guys has me a little concerned that they're going to blow our cover if we don't put some time and space between us, and we can't afford for that to happen. We're too close to lose this big fish. Does everyone agree?"

Heads nodded, and he continued. "I think the best way to make that happen is to head back to DC tomorrow morning, report in with the AG, and be in Switzerland when Agent White comes back from the spirit world. But there's a caveat. I want Tom and the tech team, including Celeste, to remain on station and monitor the Feebs while they bounce around looking for us."

Tom said, "I'm good with that. The Air Force made it clear that I was all yours until you sent me back."

Gwynn said, "I have a timetable I'd like to propose for that."

Johnny said, "I'll bet you do, but this isn't a democracy. We'll keep Tom on board as long as we can, but unless it starts falling apart, it looks like we'll have a nice case built in a matter of days, thanks to the four of you."

* * *

Thirty-six hours later, Johnny, Gwynn, and Anya boarded the flight from DC to Switzerland.

"Any news from Seattle?" Gwynn asked.

Johnny said, "Not yet, but it's only five a.m. out there, so I'm not expecting anything to happen for several hours. You've not heard from Tom, have you?"

Gwynn said, "He called last night, but it was just personal. He didn't mention anything operational."

"Things are going pretty well with him, huh?"

She almost blushed. "Yeah, he's pretty great. I had a stupid girly moment the night of the yacht incident, but I apologized, and we put it behind us."

"That's not like you," he said. "What happened?"

"It was nothing, really. It's all behind us now."

Johnny said, "You know you have to tell me if something is going on that could disrupt the investigation."

"It won't. I promise. But I do have a question."

"Shoot."

She said, "If Tom leaves the Air Force and comes to work for DOJ, how does that work if we're in a relationship?"

Johnny clicked his tongue against his teeth. "It's touchy, honestly. There's a no-fraternization policy, but it isn't generally enforced if you work in different branches."

"I know about that policy, and I guess I agree with it. On the down-low, can you tell me if there's a move in the works to get Tom on board?"

Johnny said, "If I knew, I'd tell you. That's above our paygrade. Is he certain that's what he wants to do?"

"He seems pretty set on the idea. He's been in the Air Force almost six years, and he's ready to chase real bad guys instead of catching airmen with a dime bag of pot."

"Let me ask you this . . . If you weren't in the picture, would he still be interested in coming to Justice?"

She said, "If I weren't in the picture, he wouldn't even know we exist. He'd be lobbying the FBI and Homeland."

"I get it. He's a bright guy with a bright future. Everybody likes him, and if he wants to turn in his captain's bars for a federal badge, it'll happen. I just don't want him to think he's coming to our division."

"I'll talk with him about it, but I'm sure he's ready to make the move professionally."

Just before the door of the airliner was closed, an airport police officer stepped aboard and picked up the handset to the PA system. "Can I have your attention, please? If there is a Supervisory Special Agent McIntyre aboard, please come to the boarding door."

Johnny shot a look to Gwynn, and she shrugged. "Don't look at me. You're the guy they want."

He unbuckled his seat belt and made his way to the front of the first-class cabin, where the officer waited. "I'm Special Agent McIntyre. What can I do for you?"

The officer said, "Come with me, please. You have an urgent phone call."

Johnny followed the man up the passenger boarding bridge to the airline counter. The officer lifted a receiver from its cradle and handed it to Johnny.

"McIntyre."

A voice sounded through the phone, and Johnny knew he'd heard it before, but he couldn't place it.

"Is this Supervisory Special Agent McIntyre?"

"It is, and who is this?"

"This is Kent Geller from the art division at the Bureau. We met briefly in the Seattle field office until you and your team pulled your disappearing act."

Johnny said, "We're holding up an international flight, Geller. What do you want?"

"You'll want to cancel your flight, Agent McIntyre. Your cooperating witness was murdered just after midnight, and a piece of an oil on canvas was shoved deeply into his throat. If I had to guess, it was a piece of *Monakh Tsaritsy*. What time can I expect you back in Seattle, Supervisory Special Agent?"

Johnny slammed down the phone and sprinted back down the boarding bridge and onto the airplane. "Davis, Fulton, let's go!"

The two women shared a glance and jumped from their seats, following Johnny from the plane.

"What is happening?" Anya asked in a dead run through the terminal.

"Asimov is dead, and somebody shoved part of the painting down his throat."

Gwynn struggled to keep pace with the long strides of the others. "Where were the marshals?"

"I've told you all I know," Johnny said between heaving breaths.

"Who was on telephone?"

Johnny slowed his pace. "It was Geller, that hippy-looking guy from the art division."

Anya asked, "How did he know where to find us?"

Johnny motioned toward the Delta counter and shoved his way past several waiting passengers. He slammed his credentials on the counter. "When is the next non-stop to Seattle?"

The counter agent typed quickly as passengers behind Johnny groaned and cursed. "It's not until one-fifteen this afternoon."

Johnny checked his watch, shoved his cred pack back in his pocket, and headed for the doors.

A uniformed airport police officer stepped in front of the three sprinters and held up his hands. "Hey! Hey! Slow down. What do you think you're doing?"

Johnny badged him. "Do you have a car?"

"Yeah."

"Good. Take us to Andrews, immediately."

The officer examined Johnny's credentials and pointed toward his car. Gwynn and Anya slid onto the back seat, and Johnny jumped in the front. With lights and sirens blazing, the airport cop proved he could drive.

Johnny spent the trip on the phone with the Attorney General's office, and there was a government business jet waiting on the tarmac when they pulled up. An agent met them at the boarding stairs with weapons and a change of clothes. They climbed aboard and blasted off on a direct course to Seattle.

The five-hour flight felt as if it would take days, and Johnny's expression of fury never softened. "I should've seen this coming."

Gwynn said, "There's no way you could've known, Johnny. Don't beat yourself up. Asimov knew what kind of man he was dealing with, and he willingly climbed into the hole with him."

"I know, but he was trying to climb back out of that hole, and we were supposed to protect him."

The bevy of phone calls continued from the jet as they pieced the puzzle together.

Johnny got off the phone. "There's one dead deputy marshal and one in critical condition. Whoever this guy was, he bested two U.S. deputy marshals."

Anya asked, "Was anything missing from Asimov's house?"

"What kind of question is that?" Johnny asked.

"If killer—or maybe killers—were inside Asimov's house, perhaps they stole something that could make connection for me. Russian hit men are strange people with strange fetishes."

"I don't know, but we'll ask when we get there." He leaned back in his seat, and the energy drained from his body. "Everybody wants to be the boss 'til a witness gets killed."

When they landed and taxied to the ramp, Tom and Celeste were waiting beside the black Suburban. They sprinted for the SUV as Tom held open the door.

Once inside, Johnny said, "Let's have it."

Tom pulled the Suburban into gear and sped away. "Marshals, FBI,

Homeland, and Seattle PD. Those are the people who are pretty pissed off right now."

Johnny said, "You can add me and the attorney general to that list. What do we know about the killer?"

Tom rounded a curve, and the tires chirped as he accelerated away. "He was definitely a pro. No fingerprints, no DNA, no vehicle tracks or footprints. He was in and out, and the security system was still armed. A neighbor across the street reported a man lying beside a parked car around two a.m. It turned out that guy was a deputy U.S. marshal. His partner was unconscious and barely alive by the time SPD showed up. Celeste and I were on the scene about twenty minutes after the first black-and-white showed up."

"Was anything missing from house?" Anya asked.

Tom furrowed his brow. "I don't know. We didn't do an inventory, but like I said, whoever did this is a pro. He's not a burglar. He's a killer."

"I know this," she said. "But is strange part of Russian brain. It makes us require a small object—always same object—when we kill."

Tom leaned in. "You said *we*. Were you talking about Russians or Russian killers?"

Anya lowered her eyes. "I have sixteen small buttons from shirt. I do not understand why I took buttons, but when SVR sent me to kill enemy of Russia, I did almost always with knife. Maybe having knife made it easy to cut button from clothes. I don't know, but for me is buttons."

Tom leaned back, closed his eyes, and replayed the scene. Seconds later, he threw open his eyes. "I think it's the salt shaker."

Johnny recoiled. "What?"

"Anya asked if anything was missing. I think either the salt shaker or pepper shaker is missing. I don't know why that image stuck in my head, but there's only one shaker on the stove."

Johnny held up his palms toward Anya, and she said, "If this is true, is very bad. How was Asimov killed?"

Tom said, "The coroner hasn't made it official yet, but it looked like a single nine-millimeter to the forehead."

"Is not bullet. Is mark of man called Razgromit', and he did not take salt shaker."

Tom squinted as he reached deeply into the part of his brain where he stored his foreign language knowledge. "Razgromit'? Isn't that a hammer?"

Anya slowly nodded. "Yes, this means sometimes hammer, but is more like punishment with hammer. This man strikes victim in face with welding hammer with very sharp point. Sometimes is inside eyes, but is most often in forehead. Strike happens with so much force, skull is punctured, and brain is destroyed."

"You said he didn't take the salt shaker, though."

"Coroner will find it inside body, but it will be empty. Razgromit' takes only contents of shaker and uses it to season his food. When he runs out of salt, is time for more killing."

Gwynn shuddered. "That's horrible."

"Yes, but is true."

They pulled into Asimov's driveway and climbed from the Suburban. Once they badged their way through the crime scene tape and pulled on their paper booties, Anya stepped through the door and turned for the kitchen. Just as she'd feared, a single pepper shaker rested atop the stove, and tiny grains of white salt speckled the range.

27

KRUSHENIYE POYEZDA V BOLOTE (TRAIN WRECK IN A SWAMP)

Anya and Gwynn scoured Asimov's house in search of anything out of place, and aside from the salt shaker, nothing appeared to be missing.

Gwynn said, "I'm no expert, but there's about a million dollars' worth of art in this place. Why wouldn't the killer at least take the paintings?"

Anya said, "There is something you can never understand about Russian assassins. We are like no other killers in all of world. We are trained from childhood to have what you call 'single focus.' The assignment is to kill, sometimes leave or take token as message, and vanish. If one million dollars were in middle of floor in cash, a proper *Russkiy ubiytsa* would step over and around it to make kill and escape. We do not have greed inside mind when on mission. We have only mission and nothing more."

Gwynn squeezed her temples between her palms. "It'll always be weird to think of you as an assassin . . . a *ubiytsa*."

"I am no longer *ubiytsa*, but I have still skills inside to do this when is necessary."

Gwynn took one final look around the room. "Is it necessary now?"

The somber look on Anya's face told the story Gwynn didn't want to hear.

"Where's Johnny?"

Anya said, "I do not know, but we should find him. This is not going to be good, and we should support him just like we would support Ray."

Gwynn giggled. "It's weird to hear you say that. You usually go to great lengths to get around the directions of our SSA."

"This is different circumstance. We are team, and we cannot let fault for this fall only on Johnny."

As they stepped from the house in search of Johnny, Tom appeared.

"There you are. I'm not sure what's going on, but I just got recalled back to Nellis."

"The Air Force recalled you?"

"Yeah. Like I said, I don't know what's going on, but it's getting weird."

"Weirder than a dead guy with part of a painting shoved down his throat?"

Tom said, "There's not much weirder than that, but I have to report back to Nellis today."

"That doesn't sound good. What do you think it means?"

He shook his head. "No, there's nothing good about it. And if I had to guess, it means we need to find Johnny, now. This operation is falling apart under our feet."

They found their temporary boss sitting on the ground and leaning back against the right front tire of their SUV with his head in his hands.

Anya took a knee beside him. "Are you okay?"

He shook his head. "No. It's over."

"What is over?"

"My career."

Gwynn knelt beside her partner. "What are you talking about? This isn't the worst thing that's ever happened."

Johnny looked up. "We stole a stolen painting and didn't return it to its rightful owner. Then we made an illegal counterfeit copy of that painting and tried to pass it off as the real thing. I blew off the FBI and skated from under their thumb twice. I dropped a cooperating witness in the marshals' lap with zero notice. That witness and one U.S. marshal is dead, and a second marshal probably won't live through the day. I instructed a Homeland Security boat crew to fire on a civilian vessel in international waters, resulting in at least two dead civilians at sea. Two of my agents rolled up a third Feeb and slammed his head into the tire of a van. One of my agents planted an unapproved electronic tracking device on a suspect without a warrant. I put an unarmed, untrained Tech Services officer on a yacht, where she was nearly killed by gunfire. Oh, yeah. I almost forgot. I paid for dinner and cocktails with a government credit card."

Gwynn's headache reappeared. "So, what happens next?"

Johnny groaned. "I'm suspended without pay. You and Anya are on administrative leave with pay until the investigation into my offenses is complete. Tom got yanked back to the Air Force base. Celeste is suspended without pay, pending the investigation. I screwed up everything I touched on this mission. Everything."

Gwynn said, "That's not true, Johnny. You—"

He huffed. "Go ahead. I . . . what? Name something I did or some decision I made that was the right choice. Can you do that? Huh?"

Anya rolled from her knee and sat beside him. "Is my fault. I do not play inside rules, and I made you do same. I will tell them I am responsible for everything, and they will understand."

Johnny rocked back and forth. "That's not how it works. An SSA is supposed to be able to control the agents under his command. Letting you drag me outside the regulations is just further proof that I can't be an SSA."

Gwynn asked, "What are we supposed to do now?"

Johnny said, "We're supposed to brief the FBI and step away."

Anya hooked a finger beneath Johnny's chin. "Look to me, Johnny. I would follow you into any mission any day. You are brave, determined, and calm in fight. These words from me are . . . I think word is *rare*."

He gave her knee a playful shove. "Thanks, Anya. That's a huge compliment coming from you, but it's not going to pay my mortgage, and car payment, and health insurance. My whole life is upside down."

She leaned toward him and whispered, "Do not worry about such things. We are team, and we do not let teammates suffer alone. I have money and faith in you. Do not worry."

He cocked his head. "That's nice, and I know you mean it, but—"

A gruff voice interrupted. "Are you McIntyre?"

Johnny looked up and nodded.

The man standing beside the Suburban wore a suit that hadn't seen an iron in weeks. "Come with me."

Johnny got to his feet and looked down at Gwynn and Anya. "I'll let you know what's happening after whatever this is."

The man said, "No, that won't happen. You two are on the next thing flying east. The FBI's in charge now, just like it should've been all along."

He led Johnny away, and Anya watched them go. When they were well out of earshot, she said, "Is pivotal moment in career."

Gwynn nodded slowly. "Yeah, it's going to be tough on him. This job, and especially a promotion to SSA, is his whole world. I don't know what it'll do to him, but that was way cool of you to tell him you wouldn't let him lose his house or car."

Anya looked across the lot at Johnny and the FBI agent. "I was not talking about pivotal moment for him. His decisions will be made for him. This is biggest moment of life for you."

"I'll be fine. I didn't really do anything wrong. I'll come out of this whole thing squeaky-clean, and I'll be back on the task force before you know it. I'm worried about Johnny, though."

Anya said, "You do not understand. Official Task Force Avenging Angel is gone forever. Ray will never come back to work. Johnny is finished. And they will send me away. You will be assigned to another division, but I'm trying for you to understand you must now make decision."

"What decision?"

Anya checked again for prying ears. "I am going after Razgromit' and Morozov. If you come with me, you will also be fired."

Gwynn's eyes turned to giant orbs trying to explode from her head. "What? What do you mean you're going after them? What are you talking about?"

"I will say to you same thing I said to Johnny. I have money, and I have job you can do. It does not maybe have retirement plan like government job, but is more fun."

Gwynn smiled. "You're sweet, Anya, but you know I can't take you up on that."

"So, your decision is to go back to Washington instead of going with me to catch man who is trafficker of young girls into this country for prostitution and dirty movie work? This is your decision, yes?"

Gwynn said, "You're serious, aren't you? You're really going after them, right under the FBI's nose."

"Yes. I am not afraid of FBI."

"And you want me to come with you?"

Anya said, "What I want does not matter in any of this. If you come with me, your career is over, but not your life. Is up to you, but you must make decision now before they force us onto airplane."

"You mean we're going, like, right now?" Anya nodded, and Gwynn said, "Let's go."

The Russian didn't hesitate, and seconds later, the crime scene grew smaller and smaller in the rearview mirror of the Suburban.

Gwynn buckled her seat belt and felt free for the first time since her first day of college over a decade before. "You know we can't keep this truck, right?"

Anya said, "Yes, of course, but it will get us far enough away from Asimov's house so we can operate without being noticed. First hour is most important. After this, they will believe we are on flight for Washington."

Seventy-five minutes later, they had wired fifty thousand dollars in cash to themselves at a Western Union office, purchased four burner phones, and bought a twenty-year-old Jeep. Gwynn followed Anya south to Tacoma where they left the rented Suburban in the parking lot of an Enterprise Rental office with the keys still in the ignition.

Anya climbed into the Jeep. "They will find Suburban here in one or two days and maybe believe we went south."

"That should be the end of the easy-to-follow trail, right?"

Anya said, "Yes, and maybe our work will be finished by then."

"It sounds like you've got a plan."

"Of course I have plan. Is simple. We know what FBI will do, yes?"

Gwynn thought for a moment. "I guess they'll probably get a warrant based on the testimony we took from Asimov, and they'll hit Morozov's house with HRT or maybe local SWAT."

Anya asked, "How long will it take to get warrant?"

"It depends on how they run the investigation. From their perspective, it's a train wreck in a swamp right now, so they'll spend a couple of days sorting through the details that Johnny tells them before they do anything. So, I'd say it'll be at least two days before they get the warrant, and maybe twenty-four hours after that before they can get the Hostage Rescue Team in place to hit the island."

"This is wonderful news for us. We will have perfect alibi in three days."

"Alibi?" Gwynn asked.

Anya smiled. "You will see."

"Okay, but keeping secrets isn't cool. What's next on our list?"

Anya said, "We need construction site or military base and boat."

"The Naval Station and Puget Sound Naval Complex are on the water up in Everett. Will that do?"

"Do they have Navy SEALs at Naval Station?"

"How should I know? I've never heard of there being any SEALs stationed there."

"If no SEALs, is no good."

Gwynn said, "The other option is Joint Base Lewis-McChord. It's less than thirty minutes from here."

"This is Army base, yes?"

Gwynn nodded. "Yeah, it's a joint-use base for Air Force and Army, I think."

"This is perfect. Take us there."

Gwynn turned the Jeep around and headed south. Traffic was light, and they made the trip in twenty minutes. Approaching the main gate, Gwynn stuck out her hand. "Give me your cred pack."

Anya produced the wallet, and Gwynn badged the gate guard with their matching DOJ credentials. He waved them through.

"That was easy."

Anya took back her credentials and pocketed them. "Yes, but second part of mission will not be so easy. Find armory for Army, not Air Force."

"Okay, I'll do my best."

They drove every road on the base until they both had the entire facility memorized.

On their second lap past a building claiming to be the small arms armory, Anya said, "Find place to hide until sun goes down."

Gwynn backed the Jeep between a pair of Conex containers across the road from the armory, and Anya said, "This is perfect position."

"Yeah, until the MPs show up and roust us out of here."

"Maybe this will not happen."

Just as the sun was sinking behind the western horizon, Gwynn said, "It's time for you to come clean about what we're doing. We're not DOJ agents anymore. We're vigilantes, and I need to know what's going on."

Anya pointed toward the armory, where a pair of uniformed soldiers were locking the door for the day. "When they are gone, we are going to have shopping trip, but not like shopping trip in Chicago."

28
Vzlom I Proniknoveniye
(Breaking and Entering)

As the sky darkened with the sun well below the horizon, streetlights came to life, cars filed out toward the gates, and Joint Base Lewis-McChord turned quiet. Apparently, the military worked regular business hours in the Pacific Northwest.

"Is time," Anya said. She flipped the small plastic switch to keep the overhead light inside the Jeep from illuminating when they opened their doors, and Anya and Gwynn stepped from the vehicle with a little breaking and entering on their minds.

Anya picked the first lock on the armory door in seconds, and they were inside the foyer. The security panel was at least a quarter century old, and the Russian made short work of disabling the alarm.

"You're making this look easy," Gwynn said.

"It is easy so far, but we have at least two more locks, and one will be very difficult."

Anya slid her tension arm into the keyhole of the second lock inside the armory and applied gentle pressure to the metal arm. She probed at the pins inside the lock and felt carefully as each pin bound or set. With eight pins to pick individually, the task was tedious and took almost a full minute before the tension arm spun the cylinder and the door swung open.

"Was that the tough one?"

Anya shook her head and peered into the next room. She shone her small flashlight against all four walls, where they met the ceiling. "Good. There is no camera."

They stepped into the larger space, and Anya pointed her light at a steel cage with a massive lock holding the door securely closed. "That is tough one. Do you want to try?"

"No, thanks. I'll let you do it. You obviously need the practice."

Anya slid a small wooden crate to the door of the cage and perched on it. She worked with the lock for several minutes, leaning back and flexing her fingers several times.

"Can you do it?"

Anya said, "Not while you are asking silly questions."

Gwynn shut up, and the Russian went back to work. Finally, the five-pound lock succumbed to her efforts and fell open in her hands. She removed the lug of steel and laid it on the crate beside her. "We are in."

The instant she pulled the heavy metal door from its jamb, a bright white light flooded the space in front of them, and Anya instinctually slammed the door back in place. As soon as it was seated, the light went out, and Anya breathed a sigh of relief. "I was afraid light was maybe second alarm, but is only pressure switch on door."

She opened the door again, this time well prepared for the flood of light, and stepped inside. The walls were lined with rack after rack of M4s, M249s, and M240s. At the back of the cage was a massive safe with explosives placards affixed to the door.

"Are we here for rifles?" Gwynn asked.

Anya pointed to the safe. "No. What we want is inside that."

"It's a combination lock. How are you going to pick that?"

Anya said, "I can open it, but you must be silent while I work. You can do this, yes?"

Gwynn nodded, and Anya pressed her ear to the steel door of the safe, just above the dial. With her eyes tightly closed, she spun the dial quickly at first, but slower with every change of direction. When she believed her work was finished, she leaned back, grabbed the spoked wheel, and gave it a tug. She had expected the wheel to spin and free the door, but it didn't budge. She tried again, but again, the wheel persisted.

"This is not good," Anya said.

"What?"

Anya held up a finger as she studied the door. "I have idea." She pressed her ear back to the cold steel and returned to her task of slowly spinning the dial. Soon, she leaned back again, grabbed the wheel, and it practically turned itself. Anya smiled up at her partner. "Ta-da!"

Gwynn rolled her eyes. "Now that we're in—and we're in deep—are you going to tell me what we're doing?"

"Yes, now you can know." She shone her light against stacks of ammo cans until she lit up a crate marked C4. "That is why we are here."

"Are you serious? Did we just break into a U.S. Army armory to steal explosives?"

"Not only explosives," Anya said. "We need also blasting caps and detonator."

Their shopping cart was soon full, and they retraced their steps out of the layers of the armory to their waiting Jeep.

Anya said, "That is more fun than following rules, no?"

Gwynn giggled. "Yeah, kinda, but if we get caught, we're going to prison for life."

"I have already been to prison inside Russia, and Chase came to rescue me. He would do this again for me."

"You've got to get that man out of your head, girl. He's not yours anymore."

"Don't be silly. Of course he is still mine, but for now, I will let Penny store him for me."

Gwynn held her breath as they approached the guard shack at the main gate. If anyone had detected their robbery, this is where the stop would happen. Her heart stopped when a soldier with an M4 in his hands stepped from the guard shack and into the center of the traffic lane. He held up one hand, signaling them to stop, but Anya kept her foot on the accelerator.

"Anya! You can't run over him. Stop!"

She pressed the brake and came to a stop a few feet in front of the soldier. Gwynn's hand trembled as the soldier approached the Jeep. Against her better judgment, Anya rolled down the window, and the soldier said, "Ma'am, I need you to pull over into that lot and sit tight for me, okay?"

"Is there problem, sir?"

The soldier looked to his right and then pointed toward the small parking area still well inside the base perimeter fence. "Ma'am, pull over there and wait."

Her eyes scanned the scene in front of them. Nothing blocked the road between the Jeep and the main road. She checked the mirrors, weighed her options, and the instant before she would've crushed the accelerator, Gwynn said, "Pull over, Anya. Everything is fine."

Fighting against every instinct inside her, Anya followed the instructions, turned the wheel to the right, and pulled into the parking area. "This is very bad."

"No, it's not," Gwynn said. "Just relax and look behind us."

Anya spun and checked over her shoulder to see a massive truck with "oversized load" signage plastered across the front. As the enormous truck and trailer rolled by, Anya watched the unidentifiable piece of machinery on the trailer pass inch by inch. The rig consumed all four lanes just beyond the gate as it made the southbound turn through the intersection.

With the truck clear of the gate, the armed soldier motioned for Anya to pull back onto the road. As they passed, he said, "Sorry for the delay, ma'am. Have a good night."

Anya winked. "Is okay. I like watching men in uniform."

The soldier almost blushed and offered a sharp salute.

As they turned north on the main road, both women burst into laughter, and when Gwynn finally caught her breath, she said, "That was terrifying."

"No, friend Gwynn. You will only know terrifying when we find Razgromit'."

"Speaking of Razgromit', how do you plan to find him?"

"I am still working on plan for this, but we have much work to do before finding him. First thing is now to find comfortable place to sleep. We have very busy day tomorrow."

They found a small motel in Granite Falls that gladly accepted cash and didn't ask to see a driver's license. The 24-hour pancake house next door fulfilled their only other need for the night, and Gwynn's first night as a vigilante came to an end as soon as her head hit the pillow.

But Anya was in no hurry to sleep. She spent an hour wiring the burner phone into the circuit of the blasting cap and detonator while keeping the C4 well away from the circuit. Blowing up a mom-and-pop hotel in the tiny town of Granite Falls was not how Anya defined mission success.

She slept the required four hours and roused Gwynn just after the sun came up.

Gwynn stretched and wiped the sleep from her eyes. "What time is it?"

"Is time to go."

Cold muffins and coffee from what the motel called a "continental breakfast" started their day.

"Now, we must find boat."

Gwynn slipped her coffee into the cup holder. "Are we stealing or buying?"

Anya said, "Maybe neither of those."

"What other option is there?"

"I will show you."

Gwynn slapped her thigh. "Listen, Anya. This has to stop. I'm your partner, and I'm risking a lot more than you are by going on this . . . whatever this is. You can't leave me in the dark anymore. I need to know what we're doing."

Anya pulled the Jeep into a parking spot and shut off the engine. Ten minutes later, Gwynn knew every detail of Anya's plan.

"Okay, I get it," Gwynn said. "But I don't like any of it."

Anya finished her breakfast. "Is not for us to like. Is only for us to do. Do you have better plan?"

Gwynn shoved her wrapper into the bag. "Any plan is better than that one, but we're so far out on a limb already that I can't imagine how any of this is going to end well."

"Good ending for all of this is two dead bodies of two men who should not be allowed to live. One hurts little girls, and other kills for price."

Gwynn said, "I've got one more serious question. Ever since we heard that Morozov is involved in trafficking young girls, you've been hell-bent on killing him. I get it. Anyone who would intentionally hurt a child is the worst of the worst, but why is that such a raw nerve for you?"

"What does this mean, raw nerve?"

"Why does it bother you so much? It feels personal."

Anya stared through the windshield as if reliving an ancient memory. "When I was child, eleven or maybe twelve years old, Soviet Union tried to make me figure skater and also gymnast. I hated being cold on ice, and I grew too tall to be gymnast. This is when it was decided for me to become weapon for my country. I learned first how cruel men of KGB could be. They did things and gave to me pain no child should feel. Not only pain of body, but also of mind. Is terrible and can never be forgotten. I did not realize yet when I was still child that I would one day become *ubiytsa* . . . a killer. Before I left Russia after your President Ronald Reagan brought down Berlin Wall, I used what KGB and SVR taught to me to find and punish men who hurt me while I was still child. I did to them everything they did to me, and I listened while they begged and cried for me to stop, just like I did when I was their victim. The same pain and fear they gave to me, I gave also to them, but instead of leaving them to live every day with shame and horror, I tore from them their souls and sent them to Hell—first, my Hell, and then to devil himself. I sometimes lie awake and think of those men and wonder how many innocent children they hurt like they hurt me, and I will never have feeling of guilt for what I did."

Gwynn wiped a tear from her face. "I had no idea, and I don't even know what to say, but now I understand. And as if I weren't already committed, I'm one hundred percent on board now. Let's make him pay."

29

TEE-TEE
(TEE-TEE)

Acquisition of the boat turned out to be the easy part. The waiting would prove to be the agonizing element of the plan. Anya turned off her Eastern Bloc accent and rented a twenty-foot runabout from a guy at the dock who couldn't stop staring.

"I think he likes you," Gwynn said as they pulled away from the dock.

Anya waved to the lovesick puppy standing by the fuel pump. "Of course he likes both of us. We are beautiful women."

"Don't get too cocky there, Naughty Natasha. We're getting old."

Anya gasped. "Speak only for self. I am not old, and you are even younger than me, so as you say in America, we've still got it, baby."

Gwynn situated herself on the seat behind the windshield. "Yes, we do, baby."

They obeyed the no-wake signs until reaching open water well beyond the confines of the marina, and Anya pressed the throttle full forward. The bow rose from the water, temporarily blocking her vision forward, but the hydrodynamics of the hull soon overcame the sudden thrust and the boat settled on plane, cruising comfortably at forty knots.

"Not bad," Gwynn said. "Maybe you should've bought the boat instead of just renting it."

"We are on wrong side of country to buy boat. Besides, we have many boats in Caribbean."

"I've been meaning to talk to you about that. What on Earth made you start an adventure travel business in Bonaire?"

"I did not start business. I bought and made it better."

Gwynn persisted. "But why?"

Anya shied away. "Is silly reason you will not understand, but is good investment."

"Try me. I might understand more than you give me credit for."

Anya dodged a buoy and continued across the waters of Puget Sound toward her objective. "When I was little girl, I had *igrushechnaya kukla* named Tee-Tee. I was only child, so Tee-Tee and I would have *priklyucheniya*—uh . . . adventures inside imagination. When my mother was killed when I was maybe four and I became property of Soviet Union, Tee-Tee could not come, and I was never permitted to play. I was only allowed to study, train, eat, and sleep. This is everything. When I met Chasechka, he taught me to play inside ocean and on boat. Sometimes with him, I could be little girl and do things that were taken from me." Anya paused and peered over the windshield. "That is Morozov's island. We will do big circle first."

Gwynn stood and braced against the console. "There's a pair of binoculars in the panel."

"No. We cannot get caught spying on island. He probably has guards who will have also binoculars. If they see us looking back at them, they will be suspicious, and we do not want them to suspect we are coming."

"I get it," Gwynn said, "but I'm not letting you off so easy on the story about Tee-Tee and the dune buggies in Bonaire."

"Okay, I will finish story, but quickly. My life was dark and very cold. My work was terrible, and like most *ubiytsa*, most of my time was for only training, stalking, and killing. This is very sad kind of life. Sometimes, I think about Tee-Tee and I hope she is with another little girl who will love her and also take her on great adventures. This is now what I do for people who come to islands to have fun and have adventures of their own. This is what I give to them. You understand, yes?"

"Yeah, I get it, and that's a pretty cool reason. There's a lot more to you than most people get to see."

"Yes. On surface, I am harmless, pretty girl. Next layer is dangerous and frightening. This is limit of what I let anyone see, but not you, friend Gwynn. You are not afraid of me, so is okay for you to be also inside my heart where I am sometimes still little girl with *kukla*."

"Thank you for letting me in. Forgive me, though . . . I don't know what *kukla* means."

Anya said, "I do not know correct word in English. Is pretend baby person."

Gwynn cocked her head. "A doll?"

"Yes! That is word. Tee-Tee was doll, but not with glass face. She was soft with maybe cloth inside."

Gwynn tried to imagine Anya's stolen childhood, but her life of freedom to be a child and to choose her own path in America was the only frame of reference she could understand. "So, I'm kind of like your Tee-Tee all grown up, huh? You certainly take me on some wild adventures."

Anya smiled at her friend as the rushing wind sent their hair dancing on the air, making both of them resemble disheveled rag dolls. "Perhaps I will call you Tee-Tee."

They cruised around Morozov's small island, desperately trying to remain inconspicuous. At several spots around the perimeter of the island, Gwynn stood on the deck, covering the engine, while Anya appeared to snap pictures of her friend. Instead, she was photographing details of the house, outbuildings, and grounds of Morozov's compound.

After their second circuit of the island, Anya pointed their boat to the north and roared out of sight to a quiet anchorage where they could plan the details of the night to come. Gwynn scrolled through the pictures on the burner phone. "These aren't great, but they'll have to do. I'm pretty sure that's where he keeps the helicopter."

Anya studied the grainy photo. "I agree. This is only place for it."

They studied every angle of ingress and egress and settled on a notch at the southwestern end of the island that was too rocky for any sane person to try to land, but sanity had been missing for over twenty-four hours, and there was no sign of it returning in the coming hours.

As the day wore on, they perfected their plan on paper, and Gwynn said, "This is all going out the window as soon as they start shooting."

"Perhaps this will not happen, and we will get in and out without problem."

Gwynn laughed. "When was the last time that happened for us?"

"Last night at armory inside Army base."

"Okay, I'll give you that one, but we got really lucky. What would you have done if you couldn't pick the lock?"

Anya frowned. "I do not have thoughts like that. I can pick almost any lock with enough time, and we had all night if we needed it."

"I so want to be you when I grow up."

Anya smiled. "Please do not ever grow up. Stay perfect, beautiful girl you are, Tee-Tee, and we will have great adventures together."

They made one final circuit around the island to ensure nothing had changed, and they moved to the ever-lengthening shadows as the sun drooped lower in the western sky.

As darkness consumed the Puget Sound, lights came on, illuminating houses on the shore and other boats on the water. The boat's light switch, somewhere beneath Anya's left arm, would not find itself being used that night. Instead, the two former agents slinked across the water as quietly as possible and approached their landing site on the rocky coast of the small island. Anya double-checked that her knives were in place, and both press-checked their pistols to ensure a round was loaded and begging to be fired.

Anya hovered the boat mere inches from the rocks. "This is final opportunity to change mind. Once we are on island and inside house, we cannot back down."

Gwynn lifted the coiled line resting by the bow, gave Anya a nod, and leapt from the bow. She landed on top of an enormous rock and regained her balance.

Anya cut the engine, and Gwynn pulled the now lifeless boat even closer to the rocks. The Russian pocketed the key, hefted her improvised explosive party favor, and stepped off the bow. Gwynn let the slack play out of the bowline and tied the boat to a vertical rock that appeared to have been made specifically for that purpose. The outgoing tide of the Pacific tugged against the line and pulled the boat away from the rocks.

"I hope boat is still here when we are finished."

Gwynn said, "If it's gone when we get back, we're definitely not taking the helicopter back ashore."

They moved as one, slinking through the trees and staying as low as possible while still making good time toward their target.

The corner of the house came into view, and Anya pressed herself against the base of a tree. "Do you want to pick lock this time?"

Gwynn pulled her kit from a pocket. "Sure, but if I'm taking too long, you have to take over, okay?"

"Of course, but I have faith in you. You have done it many times, and you have very good hands."

"I've done it at home, but never on an actual operation."

"Is first time for everything. I will follow and cover while you work on lock. Ready?"

Gwynn nodded, and they sprinted across the open space to the hangar door. She took a knee and inserted her tools. As she explored the interior of the mechanism with her pick, nothing felt right. She looked at Anya, who stood with her back to the door, scanning the area for threats.

"Something's wrong. I can't feel the pins."

"Did you try turning knob?"

Gwynn palmed her forehead. "Of course not." She gripped the knob and gave it a twist. The mechanism retreated into the door, and she pushed it open, revealing a hangar that resembled an operating room. She reached back and tapped her partner's leg. "We're in."

Anya backed through the door, still searching for aggressors, and found none. Once inside the hangar, she said, "Do not make things harder than necessary. Always check door before assuming it is locked."

"I know, I know. You've told me that a thousand times, but I got excited."

"Stay calm and think."

Gwynn pressed the door closed, keeping it as close to silent as possible, and she turned the deadbolt. The next person through the door would likely have a key. They moved across the spotless floor, and Anya lay on her back beneath the chopper. She squirmed, twisted, and contorted her body to place the explosive charge as far inside the tail boom shroud as possible. A conscientious pilot would find the bomb during a thorough preflight inspection, but if things went as planned, the Sloth and his pilot would make a run as if their hair were on fire when the time came.

After two minutes of work, Anya slid from beneath the flying machine that would soon take its final voyage. "Is pity to destroy such beautiful helicopter."

Gwynn said, "So, disarm your fireworks, and we'll slip inside and cut Morozov's throat."

Anya glared at her partner. "You are turning into animal like me."

Gwynn shrugged. "I told you I wanted to be like you when I grew up."

Anya motioned toward a door at the rear of the hangar. "Let's take a look, but no cutting of throat."

"You're no fun."

The door turned out to be access to the main house directly from the hangar, and the two women took opposite sides of the hallway and eased their way toward lights and the sound of a television. The walls were lined with paintings, but the darkness prevented them from identifying any of them.

Anya drew a fighting knife and gripped it exactly as she'd been taught so many years before. With the blade lying parallel to her forearm and tucked beneath the wrist, she could maintain perfect control and positive possession of the blade.

Gwynn drew her Glock, and although her training hadn't been as intense as Anya's, she gripped the weapon exactly as the instructors at the Academy had pounded into her head time after time. Killing shouldn't be necessary, but if someone wanted to start a fight, she and her vigilante partner were prepared to dispense overwhelming force should anyone push them to that point.

The television sound grew louder with every small step, and the flickering light from the mostly darkened room gave them an enormous tactical advantage. They were approaching from the darkness and into the light. Their target's vision and hearing would be impaired, at least a little, by the television, and they planned to take full advantage of that.

When they reached the opening at the end of the hallway, Anya glanced at Gwynn, and she gave a nod to say she was ready to move. The Russian silently envisioned the dynamic entry into the room and took three long strides, stepping into the room and moving right. Gwynn broke left with her pistol raised and her weapon's light casting a blinding beam of white light directly into Nikita Morozov's face.

The whale of a man threw up a meaty arm to shield his eyes and cursed in growling Russian. Gwynn gave a command Anya blocked out as she gazed into a corner of the room where a thin, dark-eyed man sprang from his chair. The man closed the distance in two strides and struck Anya's wrist with a crushing blow, almost knocking the knife from her grip. She took one step backward and slashed violently across the space in front of her to build some distance between her and the attacker.

With three feet of working space, Anya drew her second knife and lunged for the man, but he was too fast. He sidestepped the attack and shoved her against the chair he'd occupied until seconds before, but the fight was far from over.

Anya repositioned the knife in her right hand and advanced on the man just as Gwynn yelled, "Step away and give me a shot."

Instead of following Gwynn's command, she stepped between her and the man. "Do not kill him. Only keep Morozov still."

The aggressor stepped between Anya's blades and trapped both of her arms under his. As if programmed to do so, the man cast his head backward and threw it forward for a crushing headbutt, but she was too fast. Just as his head came hurling forward, she tilted hers out of the way and threw a devastating knee strike to his groin. The man exhaled sharply with the hint of a whimper near the end of the animal-like cry.

Continuing her aggression, she swept his legs with her right ankle and sent him to the ground, flat on his back. She lunged forward, pinning his arms to the floor with her knees, then pressed one blade into his upper lip and one in his right ear. "I did not come here to fight. I came to bring message."

The man continued to buck and twist his body, even with the threat of her razor-edged blades pressed to his face and head. He wasn't giving up.

"Why do you keep fighting? I told to you I am only here to bring message."

Morozov spoke in a calm, measured tone. "I am afraid you are wasting breath. He does not speak English."

Anya pressed the points of her knives even more forcefully into his flesh and repeated her instructions in Russian. The man took a breath and glared up at her.

She continued in the language he understood. "Be still, and I will not hurt you unless you try to hurt me."

Morozov said, "What is message you bring to my home with violence?"

30

Pogonya
(The Chase)

Anya stared into the soul of the man pinned to the floor beneath her and spoke in angry Russian. "If I let you up, you will sit and stay like good dog, yes?"

He growled. "I will kill you and play in your blood."

She added just enough pressure to the tip of her blade to sink into the soft flesh just below his nose. "I am not one who is bleeding, comrade. Is you, so do not make threats to me. I will turn them on you while you feel my steel inside your chest."

He shook his head like a wolf tearing at a carcass and spat up at her. Without warning, Anya sent a thundering elbow strike to his temple, and the beast he'd been only seconds before became a powerless, unconscious, sleeping child.

She wiped the blood from her blade on his face and stood. "I came here to tell you FBI has warrant for your arrest, and they are bringing Hostage Rescue Team to take you into custody. I bring to you warning of impending danger, and you have your hound attack me. I should kill you where you lie and let FBI clean up mess."

She took a knee in front of Morozov and whispered, "Is one more thing you should know. Painting was counterfeit copy of original I still have, but from inside prison, you will never see it again."

"Anya! Watch out!"

Gwynn's voice parted the air like the crack of approaching thunder, and Anya turned to see the man she'd taken down back on his feet and the glistening tip of a sharpened welding hammer raised above her skull. She rolled to her side and sent a crushing side kick to the man's knee, but he turned away just in time to take the blow on the back of his leg and doing no more harm than bending the knee in its natural direction.

As he stumbled away, regaining his balance, Gwynn raised her Glock and pressed the trigger twice in blindingly rapid succession, but the man had slipped around the corner and out of the room before her bullets could find their mark.

Without a word between them, both women sprinted in the direction Razgromit' had run. Doors slammed in front of them as the assassin made his escape, but they burst through every door only seconds behind him. When they reached the exterior door of the palatial estate, they burst into the darkness of the night only to see the man still running for the water with his lead growing with every stride.

Anya yelled, "Get boat!"

Gwynn obeyed and turned south, running as hard as her legs and lungs would take her. Anya continued down the gentle slope toward the dock and waiting boat that was undoubtedly Razgromit's immediate goal.

His speed was slightly faster than hers, but the time it would take him to cast off the lines and get the engine started should be enough to close the gap. Razgromit' leapt from the dock at a full sprint and landed in the center of the rigid hull inflatable boat. With one swift motion, he lifted both lines from their cleats and tossed them toward the dock.

Anya was closing the distance quickly, but the man had the engine racing in seconds. As he roared away from the dock, Anya drew a knife and took the longest shot she'd ever tried. The blade bounced off the top of the outboard engine and landed harmlessly on the deck of the RHIB.

She spun on a heel, willing Gwynn to show up with their rented boat before Razgromit' put too much distance and darkness between them. As if conjured from the mist, the bow of their boat rounded the point of the island with Gwynn at the wheel and white water spraying from the hull.

Anya timed the running jump perfectly as Gwynn slowed only enough to give her partner a dry spot to land. "He is that way! Go fast as you can!"

Gwynn rammed the throttle full forward, and their vessel answered the call.

Anya yelled, "Give to me pistol," and Gwynn stuck the Glock in her outstretched hand.

Pushing through the opening between the consoles, Gwynn took a position in the bow with her partner's pistol trained in the direction of the RHIB. She followed the wake of the smaller, slower boat and gained a little ground with every passing second. Razgromit' obviously recognized that he was being caught, so he began a series of choppy S-turns, casting a winding, irregular wake behind his boat. As Gwynn plowed through the curving wake, the boat rose and fell like an unpredictable roller coaster. The jarring motion of jumping one wake to only land in the middle of another robbed Anya of any possibility of getting a good shot, and firing blindly into the darkness wasn't a risk she was willing to take.

Gwynn explored the switches at the helm until she found one that brought the spotlight on the bow to life. The brilliant white beam cut a swath through the darkness and gave them an instant of an advantage in locating the RHIB and Razgromit'. Anya grabbed the housing of the light and twisted it in every direction, desperately scanning for her prey. He was out there somewhere, but when her beam suddenly reflected off the stern of the RHIB, their hull struck sand and rocks and brush, bringing the two-thousand-pound speedboat to a nearly instant stop. Gwynn slammed forward, colliding with the top edge of the windshield, and the breath left her lungs. She gasped and pushed herself from the console, begging for her lungs to refill with air, but her immediate concern was Anya's absence.

When they struck the bank, she was thrown over the bow and onto the tiny spit of rocky land holding them hostage. Gwynn continued to convulse, demanding her body to breathe as she crawled over the bow and onto the craggy ground. "Anya! Where are you?"

The Russian struggled to her feet. "Over here. Where is Razgromit'?"

Gwynn staggered toward her voice. "I don't know. I thought I caught a glimpse of the RHIB right before we crashed."

Anya stepped into Gwynn's path. "Are you hurt?"

"No, I just had my breath knocked out of me. I'll be fine in a minute. Are you okay?"

"I think so." Anya tripped and stumbled toward the bow of their wrecked boat, where the spotlight still shone through the night air. She spun the light to the right and saw the RHIB crashed on the shore, just like their boat. "There he is! Find gun. Is somewhere here, but I lost it when we hit."

Gwynn pulled her penlight from her pocket and swept the area in search of her pistol as Anya made her way to the demolished RHIB lying on its side. Still dazed from the crash, she tried to shake the cobwebs from her head, but before she could get her eyes to adjust to the darkness, Razgromit' hit her from the left like a linebacker, and she went down hard, coming to rest in the edge of the water.

She pawed at the rocky shore and dragged herself back to her feet just in time to feel Razgromit's fist land hard on her left jaw. As she went down, she grabbed a rock that fit perfectly in the curve of her palm and slammed the stone into the man's kneecap. He bellowed in agony and went down on his one remaining knee. Disoriented and still shaken from the collision, Anya lashed out with both hands, begging her fists to find their target, and they did.

She felt and heard the familiar crack of her victim's nose breaking and cartilage exploding into his sinuses. The blow should've left the assassin on his back and clawing at his face, but his body and mind were trained and honed to a razor's edge, giving him the acute capacity to swallow the pain and keep fighting. He bounded forward, his eyes full of blood from his destroyed nose, and found Anya's hair. He jerked her head from side to side as he dragged her deeper into the water with every thrash. With only one knee remaining, his balance was terrible, but his strength was superhuman.

She fought like a furious beast, but Razgromit' dodged enough of her attacks to find himself behind her with his arms laced around her neck. He threw himself forward, shoving her face beneath the water and piling his full weight against her shoulders and neck.

Refusing to accept her fate, Anya redoubled her resolve and fought in every direction, pushing against the bottom of the sound and kicking with both feet in an effort to get her mouth above water long enough to refill her convulsing lungs. Her right foot found purchase against the man's thigh, and she kicked with every ounce of strength she had left. Her effort was rewarded with temporary relief from his crushing weight. She arched her back, raising her head from the water just in time to hear the unmistakable sound of stone against bone. She rolled onto her back to see Gwynn standing over Razgromit's demolished skull and holding a bloodstained rock in both hands.

Anya rolled onto her back in the shallow water, her body too battered and her mind too exhausted to register the cold. She lay, catching her breath and staring up into the heavens as Gwynn spun as if twisted by some irresistible cosmic force. The Russian followed her partner's line of sight to see Morozov's helicopter climbing away from the island to the west.

Anya raised her head above the water. "Do you have your phone?"

Gwynn dug into her pocket and produced one of the burner phones they'd bought earlier.

Anya exhaled a raspy sigh. "Speed-dial seven."

An instant later, an orange ball of fire consumed the darkness a few hundred feet above Puget Sound, and Gwynn fell to her knees beside the one person who would change her life more than anyone else.

Epilog
(Epilogue)

In the wealthy neighborhood of Park Tzameret in Tel Aviv, two beautiful women—one American and one distinctly Russian—sipped sweet, aromatic coffee from small glass cups across the table from the former prime minister of Israel and his wife of half a century.

Anya placed her cup on the tray in front of her and spoke in flawless Hebrew. "Thank you for the coffee and your warm hospitality. Let's now get to the reason we are here. Your painting, *Monakh Tsaritsy*, was recently discovered to have been originally painted by Kazimir Malevich. This discovery increases the painting's value exponentially to as much as twenty million dollars U.S."

The prime minister's wife gasped and covered her mouth.

The stoic former Mossad officer and leader of the embattled nation asked, "And how was this discovery made?"

"Is English okay?" Gwynn asked.

"It is."

"Thank you. A brilliant scientist in the employ of the U.S. Department of Justice conducted some nondestructive testing using X-ray technology, among other means, and discovered the beautifully done overpaint of the original signature."

The man finished his coffee and leaned back in his chair. "I hope this man is well-rewarded for his efforts."

Both women lowered their heads, and Gwynn said, "Unfortunately, the operation on which your painting was used didn't end well, and the unorthodox methods we put in play fall outside what the U.S. government considers acceptable, so none of us will be rewarded."

The prime minister furrowed his brow. "Was the culprit apprehended?"

Gwynn shook her head, and the man asked, "Is he still at large?"

Anya and Gwynn shared a knowing glance and smiled. "No, sir. He's no longer at large. I suspect he's having tea with Hitler somewhere in a nice, warm corner of Hell by now."

The man smiled for the first time, perhaps in years. "In that case, regardless of what the American government considers acceptable, I commend you and your man of science."

Anya said in English, "Scientist is Dr. Celeste Mankiller."

"Mankiller, you say?"

"Yes, sir. And her family name is well deserved."

He said, "Perhaps if the Americans don't care for her operational style, and yours, the two of you, and she, might find a home in the dark recesses of Mossad."

Anya bowed her head reverently. "Perhaps."

* * *

Clinique de Genolier, Switzerland

Dr. Stefan Müller inserted a syringe into the IV line leading to Supervisory Special Agent Ray White's left arm and slowly depressed the plunger. "He should slowly awaken soon, but don't expect him to recognize you immediately. His faculties will return in time."

Gwynn and Anya stood beside the hospital bed, practically holding their breath until Ray's eyelids fluttered and slowly opened against the intrusive light overhead. He stared deeply at Gwynn and then Anya before asking, "Mom? Dad? Is that you?"

Gwynn's heart sank, and Anya froze, uncertain of what to say. They shared a terrified look until Ray put on a smile. "I'm just messing with you. What day is it?"

Dr. Müller chuckled and stuck a stethoscope to his patient's chest. "Deep breaths."

Ray obeyed, and the doctor pointed a penlight into his eyes. "How do you feel, Mr. White?"

Ray blinked until his vision was clear. "Did you get the tumor, doc?"

Dr. Müller gave a single nod. "We did, and we expect you to make a full recovery."

Ray rolled his head, searching the room. "Where's Johnny Mac?"

Gwynn told the story, not leaving out a single detail. When she'd finished, Ray asked, "So, Johnny is suspended without pay, you two are on administrative leave with pay, and Tom got yanked?"

Gwynn said, "Yes, sir. That pretty much sums it up."

Ray pressed a button and raised the head of his bed. "And Morozov is dead?"

"Very dead, sir."

He raised both arms over his head, as far as the pain would allow, stretching as if he'd been asleep for a week. "That's about how I expected the op to go, but I thought it would be you two on suspension and not Johnny."

Anya took Ray's hand in hers. "We are happy you are healed. Now, you will come home and clean up mess we made, yes?"

Ray grinned. "I can't think of anything I'd rather do."

Primechaniye Avtora
(Author's Note)

I truly hope you enjoyed reading this story as much as I enjoyed creating it. When I began the research for this novel, I knew slightly less than nothing about great paintings. I knew even less than that about Russian art. Okay, that's not entirely true. I have a strange obsession with Fabergé eggs, so I know a little about that particular Russian art, but I couldn't have named a single Russian painter before diving into this story. The *Monakh Tsaritsy* is entirely the product of my imagination. There is no historical evidence to suggest anyone ever painted a portrait for the Mad Monk, Rasputin, as a gift for the tsarina. If such a painting exists, I'd love to own it, but that twenty-million-dollar price tag is a little steep for me. While we're talking about the fictional painting, I'd be remiss if I didn't make a confession concerning the painting. I have absolutely no idea why I chose to bring a former prime minister of Israel into the story as the owner of the painting. Perhaps my subconscious is setting up something for a future book involving him, but I suppose we'll find out together.

Now, let's talk about Supervisory Special Agent Ray White's tumor. I have a dear friend who was an airline captain who recently endured a malignant glioblastoma. Through countless prayers, God's grace, and a team of remarkable surgeons, my friend not only survived the surgery to remove the tumor from his brain, but he also came out the other side completely cancer-free with no adverse effects of either the tumor or the surgery. He's not been cleared to get back in the cockpit yet, but he's hopeful that news will come soon. I suppose my friend's experience was the inspiration for Ray's ordeal, and the experience gave me an opportunity to explore the softer side of Anya. Dr. Stefan Müller isn't real. Like the painting, he's purely a figment of my imagination. However, the Clinique de Genolier in

Switzerland is quite real, and they have a magnificent reputation as being a world-class treatment facility.

Since I mentioned Anya's softer side, let's talk about that for a moment. I didn't expect Anya to open up and give us a peek inside her psyche the way she did in this story. I've developed her as a powerful, independent, deadly, and sometimes terrifying character with only hints of humanity showing up from time to time. I enjoyed getting to know her a little better, and I have some exciting surprises involving her in future stories. I've tried to show a desire in her to have lived the American life as Gwynn has, but until now, we've never gone any deeper than that when we've talked about her humanity. Anya is one of my favorite characters to write. She's absolutely impossible for me to control. In that sense, I know how Ray White feels. She's such a dynamic and unpredictable element in every story that writing her never gets old. I get a lot of emails about Anya and Penny, and I'm always amused how the two camps are so diametrically opposed. Team Penny wants Anya to go away and let Chase and Penny live happily ever after, while Team Anya wants me to do something terrible to Penny so Anya can rejoin Chase's life. I can't make any promises to either camp at this point, but I'm certainly looking forward to seeing how the drama all works out in the end. Speaking of the end, as far as I know, there isn't one—at least not for Chase. I said when I began writing the Avenging Angel – Seven Deadly Sins Series, that I'd write at least seven novels for Anya and possibly a follow-up series entitled Avenging Angel – Seven Cardinal Virtues. I've still not decided if the second series will happen, but I'll be sure to let you know as soon as I make the decision.

I certainly handed poor old Johnny Mac a wheelbarrow full of trouble in this story, and I suppose I should apologize to him, but that's not going to happen. In all honesty, I've never really liked Johnny. There's something about him that rubs me the wrong way. His bureaucratic ambition may be the thing that bugs me, but I wasn't terribly upset when he was dethroned in this story. I don't know if he'll be back for Book #6, *The Russian's Envy*, but something tells me Ray White will pull a rabbit out of his hat and save Johnny's career. Don't get me wrong... I'm not hoping for that, but that's what my gut is telling me for now.

It's now time to talk about the elephant in the room. When Gwynn and Anya went rogue, I hated everything about the turn the story took, but the more I wrote, the more I enjoyed seeing them work outside the law. Their actions were, of course, criminal and a bit cruel, but there are forces of evil in this world who respond to nothing less, and the Russian mafia may very well be one of those forces.

A sensitive subject came up in the storyline that I intentionally didn't describe in detail. Asimov mentioned Nikita Morozov was involved in human trafficking. This is a despicable crime for which there will never be a justification or defense. There is no limit to the punishment and agony a perpetrator of such an atrocity deserves. Intentionally hurting children is an unforgivable sin against all humanity. My feelings on the subject are mirrored in Anya's expressions of disgust and intolerance for the unthinkable offense. That is why I felt absolutely no regret for killing Morozov in the fiery helicopter explosion.

Finally, I wish to thank you for reading my work and for giving me the greatest job anyone could hope to have. I treasure that wonderful gift from you, and I vow to create the best stories I'm capable of producing for as long as my mind and typing fingers will allow. I love being your personal storyteller, and I'll never take the responsibility of that title lightly.

—Cap

ABOUT THE AUTHOR

CAP DANIELS

Cap Daniels is a former sailing charter captain, scuba and sailing instructor, pilot, Air Force combat veteran, and civil servant of the U.S. Department of Defense. Raised far from the ocean in rural East Tennessee, his early infatuation with salt water was sparked by the fascinating, and sometimes true, sea stories told by his father, a retired Navy Chief Petty Officer. Those stories of adventure on the high seas sent Cap in search of adventure of his own, which eventually landed him on Florida's Gulf Coast where he spends as much time as possible on, in, and under the waters of the Emerald Coast.

With a headful of larger-than-life characters and their thrilling exploits, Cap pours his love of adventure and passion for the ocean onto the pages of his work.

Visit www.CapDaniels.com to join the mailing list to receive newsletter and release updates.

Connect with Cap Daniels

Facebook: www.Facebook.com/WriterCapDaniels
Instagram: https://www.instagram.com/authorcapdaniels/
BookBub: https://www.bookbub.com/profile/cap-daniels

Made in the USA
Middletown, DE
21 December 2023